W9-CLF-278

Sneeze on
SUNDAY

Tor books by Andre Norton

Caroline (with Enid Cushing)
The Crystal Gryphon
Dare To Go A-Hunting
The Elvenbane (with Mercedes Lackey)
Flight in Yiktor
Forerunner
Forerunner: The Second Venture
Gryphon's Eyrie (with A. C. Crispin)
Grand Masters' Choice (editor)
Here Abide Monsters
House of Shadows (with Phyllis Miller)
Imperial Lady (with Susan Shwartz)
The Jekyll Legacy (with Robert Bloch)
Moon Called
Moon Mirror
The Prince Commands
Ralestone Luck
Stand and Deliver
Storms of Victory (with P.M. Griffin)
Wheel of Stars
Wizards' Worlds

THE WITCH WORLD (editor)

Tales of the Witch World 1
Tales of the Witch World 2
Four from the Witch World
Tales of the Witch World 3

MAGIC IN ITHKAR (editor, with Robert Adams)

Magic in Ithkar 1
Magic in Ithkar 2
Magic in Ithkar 3
Magic in Ithkar 4

Sneeze on
SUNDAY

Andre Norton
Grace Allen Hogarth

A Tom Doherty Associates Book
New York

SNEEZE ON SUNDAY

Copyright © 1992 by Andre Norton, Ltd., and Grace Allen Hogarth

A Tor Book
Published by Tom Doherty Associates, Inc.
175 Fifth Avenue
New York, N.Y. 10010

Library of Congress Cataloging-in-Publication Data

Norton, Andre.
    Sneeze on Sunday / Andre Norton and Grace Allen
    Hogarth.
        p.   cm.
    "A Tom Doherty Associates book."
    ISBN 0-312-85222-3
    I. Hogarth, Grace Allen. II. Title.
    PS3527.0632S66   1992
    813'.52—dc20   91-36103
                                                       CIP

Printed in the United States of America

First published in Great Britain under the title *Murders for Sale*. Copyright © 1953 by Allen Weston.

First U.S. edition: January 1992

0 9 8 7 6 5 4 3 2 1

Sneeze on
SUNDAY

1

Fredericka Wing looked at her watch for the second time in ten minutes. If she didn't get to South Sutton before noon she might miss Miss Hartwell and that would be disastrous. The sun burned through the back of her linen dress and her stockings felt sticky behind her knees. July in New England could be hot, as she had reason to know from her own childhood. But the country should be better than New York— She looked a third time at her watch and then, with a frown of annoyance, picked up her suitcase and sought the shelter of the station platform. She walked around to the track side of the one-room building where the words SUTTON JUNCTION were inscribed in Gothic capitals, once gilt, now tarnished and barely decipherable. A large man in shirt sleeves sat on a packing case near the door, chewing noisily and spitting at regular intervals in the general direction of the tracks.

"Train late?" Fredericka asked, trying to keep the note of impatience from her voice.

The man did not answer. He continued to chew steadily and for a moment, she thought he must be deaf. Then he took a plug of tobacco from his pocket and opened his knife with his pudgy right hand and said slowly: "Reckon Cy's doin' his shoppin'. Usually do on Sat'day mornin's. Be long soon now, I wouldn't wonder. Train for Worcester's not due in fer another quarter hour."

Fredericka sat down on the other end of the packing case.

"Cy is the engineer, I suppose," she said.

"Yep. Don't make no difference Sat'day forenoon. Ain't nobody to speak of come from New York till the a'ternoon train."

It was obvious to Fredericka that being a stranger, not the fact that she was the only passenger, made her "nobody to speak of." She was contemplating a suitable answer when, with a hoot of surprise, the midget engine and its single car charged out of the woods as if by magic.

The fat man lumbered to his feet and Cy climbed down from his cab. A moment later a man in a light suit hurried from the train and stopped near Fredericka to bend over and fasten the strap of his brief case. Then he straightened up and, for a moment, looked intently at Fredericka, who returned his appraisal and then dropped her eyes in sudden embarrassment. But she had had time to see that the man's gray eyes really were what novelists describe as "steely," the face set in stern lines and the forehead high. His hair was graying at the temples and his body had lost the leanness of first youth.

Forties, Fredericka thought, and I'm blushing as though I were in my teens instead of a safe thirty-five.

"Hi, Colonel." The low rumbling sound came from Fredericka's friend, the fat baggage man, who now stood behind her to rest from the great effort of drawing a half-filled mail bag across the platform.

"Hi yourself, Willy," the man called Colonel answered. He unfolded a neatly rolled newspaper and sat down on the packing case. Fredericka, having no excuse to linger, now walked purposefully across the track to her waiting train.

A twenty-minute wait for a ten-minute journey, she thought as she settled herself on the dusty plush seat. And now most likely another ten minutes to add to it. But even as she thought this, the engine gave its warning toot and began to push itself backwards out of the station. Except for Fredericka, the car was empty and, in spite of herself, she couldn't resist the temptation to go across the aisle and look out of the window. The man called Colonel had put aside his paper and now seemed to be looking directly at her own peering face. She ducked quickly and returned at once to her seat as, again, she felt her cheeks burn hotly.

"Now whatever possessed me to do that?" she asked aloud, and then: "Behaving like a schoolgirl." But the intent gray eyes followed Fredericka all the short journey to South Sutton and were only forgotten when the excitement of arrival and settling in to her new job put every other thought from her mind.

When Fredericka climbed down from the train at South Sutton Station she felt hotter than ever but, as she looked round her, she was reassured. Here, at last, there was an air of midsummer peace that soothed her tired spirit. Fields dotted with bright black-eyed Susans and white clover rolled up to the track and even struggled through the floor boards of the platform. Beyond the fields there was a line of dark firs and a few low rooftops.

If only Cy would stop the snorting of his dragon, I could probably hear crickets, Fredericka thought. Now I wonder what I do next and where—

"Are you Miss Wing?" a pleasant voice asked.

Fredericka turned, startled, to find a woman standing directly behind her.

"Yes, I'm Fredericka Wing— But wherever did you come from? There wasn't anyone else on the train."

The woman laughed and Fredericka observed that the face which had at first glance seemed plain now became attractive. She was shorter than Fredericka and less angular. She was wearing a sleeveless linen dress which looked clean and cool and her short dark hair had just been combed. She made Fredericka feel travel-worn and dusty.

"I came across the fields, from the other side of the train. But I must introduce myself. I am Philippine Sutton and I have come to meet you because Miss Hartwell, she is so very busy." She spoke slowly with a hint of a foreign accent. Her *th*'s became *z*'s and her *r*'s were rich and throaty.

Fredericka put down her case and shook the proferred hand which felt small and soft in hers. French, Fredericka decided. "You seem to have the right name for anyone living in this town," she remarked, and then: "It was good of you to bother to meet me."

"I wanted to come to the station anyway. I had a shipment coming in—things for my laboratory which I have at the farm. But I forgot—of course you don't know anything about us yet. And I, I don't know anything about you either."

"No. We'll have to explain ourselves, but first I want to see about my baggage." As always Fredericka now became fussed by the tiresome details of life from which she never seemed able to escape. *New England* her friends at college had called it. "I sent my trunk on in advance. Oh, good, I think that's it on the platform."

"I'll wait here," Philippine said. "Then we can walk—my jeep's laid up at the garage for the moment, but it isn't far and I can show you the sights—or some of them. Miss Hartwell's man, Chris, will collect your trunk and that bag too, if it's heavy. There's not much fuss about life in South Sutton," she added, seeing Fredericka's obvious concern.

"No, thanks, I'll manage this case. It's got a change of clothes and all the necessary articles for a badly needed bath."

In a few moments the two women were walking along a wide country road edged with elderly spruce trees. Their feet scuffed up a fine cloud of dust that settled on the grass and clover struggling to grow along the roadside.

"This," announced Philippine, "is rightly named 'Spruce Street'. If we had turned left it would take us out to the farm belonging to my aunt, Mrs. Sutton. Yes—a direct descendant of the Lucius Edward Sutton who founded the town in 1814 and the college six years later. The family place, we call it 'the Farm,' is where Mrs. Sutton and I do a business in herbs, and I have my lab. It's about a mile out of town. It won't take you long to learn the lie of the land since the whole of South Sutton is nothing but a crossroads. Those gates on the left and those impressive buildings you can just see through the trees are Sutton College."

Fredericka looked around her. The air was heavy with the warm scent of hay and the more subtle perfume of the spruce trees.

"I love New England," she said simply, "and this seems exactly as it should be."

"Yes. I love it, too," Philippine said. "I can work here in peace—and forget the other life." She hesitated. "I mean France, in the war . . ." she added.

As she said this her voice became hard and her accent more pronounced. Fredericka looked up quickly. The woman's face was a mask—of hatred, sorrow, fear— Fredericka could not be certain. But in a moment Philippine collected herself and the smile returned to her face.

"I'm sorry. Here all is well and yet—sometimes— the other life comes back. I was put in a concentration camp by the Germans when they invaded France. But we will not talk about it." A look of strain returned to her face and, with an obvious effort, she remembered her rôle as guide. "We come now to Beech Street which crosses Spruce and is really the main street of the town. Along there, on the right are the church—only one, Congregational, and the shops just beyond it. Opposite them are the town hall and the police station, and across the road there on the corner of Beech and Spruce, is the Inn. It's made over from one of South Sutton's earliest buildings—an old coaching inn, 1820, I think it was, and built about the same time as the first college buildings. The food is good. You'll probably want to eat there sometimes."

"Is that all there is to South Sutton?" Fredericka asked.

"Just about." Philippine laughed again. "We turn left here into Spruce Street. The campus is on our left still and here, a stone's throw on the right, is Miss Hartwell's bookstore."

"Oh—but—it's lovely," Fredericka exclaimed. "It's the kind of Victorian I like—the valentine kind—and it has trees—copper beeches and lots of land. It's exactly right."

Philippine who was a little ahead, turned to look back at Fredericka. "I think you'll like it. It is a good house and it's also a good bookstore, which, if all Lucy Hartwell says of you is true, will matter even more to you."

Was there reproof in her voice? Or was it just the foreignness of this stranger? Fredericka cursed herself for being sensitive. It was what happened to well brought up New England women when they got into their thirties and hadn't married. Even New York couldn't do anything about it.

As they walked up the brick walk, the screen door banged open and a large woman hurried out.

"Is that you, Miss Wing? Oh dear—do please forgive me but I've got to leave almost before I see you. But Philippine will tell you everything, won't you, Philippine? Oh dear, I don't know what this town ever did before Philippine came to take charge of us. And Margie, that's my niece, will help too, if you want her. She needs discipline, all the young do these days, but she may be some use. Dear me—"

The torrent of words would have continued forever, Fredericka felt certain, if the speaker had been standing still but all the while she had been hurrying down the path and only when she reached the gate did she stop and turn back to peer at her new employee in a vague, nearsighted way.

"Yes, you're just as I hoped you'd be," she announced unexpectedly. "And we did really cover everything by letter. Just go in. I've left notes around saying what's what."

"It's all right, Lucy," Philippine said gently. "But how are you going to get to the station?"

"Walk—or rather run. I sent Chris on with my bags. He'll probably persuade Cy to wait for me." She waved a large hand vaguely and trotted off toward the station.

"She's a darling," Philippine said, and then laughed as she added, "but a little distraught as you may have observed. Personally I can't see what use she'll be to that niece in California."

"She seems more motherly than businesslike."

"She isn't really. The bookstore is an obsession and you'll see that she's done a fine job with it."

Inside the door a long passage ran straight back to another door which stood open so that one could see the green of trees beyond it. Fredericka could observe the whole ground floor of the house, or most of it, from where she stood just inside the front door—shop rooms to right and left, and back of them two large rooms, also filled with books.

"I'll just whisk you through here and upstairs—and then leave you in peace," Philippine said.

Fredericka saw that the back room on the left side was the office and lending library and that beyond it was an attractive modern kitchen which seemed to have been added to the square box of the house as an afterthought.

"Miss Hartwell always lives in there, and I expect you will, too," Fredericka's guide said, as they looked in through the kitchen door.

Fredericka stopped for a moment to stand in the door at the end of the hall and look out across a narrow porch into the tangled mass of trees and shrubs that crowded, like an invading jungle, toward the small patch of back lawn.

"Very overgrown, is it not?" Philippine asked. "Chris slashes away upon it when he has time. Around the other side"—she waved a vague hand toward the kitchen—"it is more cleared—a few flowers and even a hammock. But you can discover all that for yourself."

Fredericka hurried after her guide and climbed the stairs that went up steeply from a point in the hall midway between the front and back doors.

Philippine finished her explanation hurriedly. "Your room is the yellow guest room at the back, Miss Hartwell's at the front and, on the other side of the hall, an extra shop storeroom at front, bath and a personal storeroom at the back. There's no second floor over the kitchen—so that's all there is. And now I must dash. My jeep should be ready and my lunch—" she stopped abruptly. "But—how stupid of me. What about *your* lunch?"

"I—I don't really want anything at the moment. I'd rather have a bath first and then I'll see if there's a bread crust in the kitchen."

"I'm sure there's *something* there. If not, it's only a step to the stores—you remember—along Spruce Street on the right. If it's really all right I must dash. I am so sorry but we will meet soon again, I hope."

Fredericka heard the clatter of steps on the stairs and then, as the screen door slammed, she sank into the chintz chair and groaned.

Suddenly the door opened again and Philippine's voice, sounding strident and foreign in the quiet house, called: "The bookshop never stays open on Saturday afternoon unless Miss Hartwell happens to want it to. So you'll have the weekend to catch your breath."

"Thanks," Fredericka called.

The door slammed again, this time with finality.

An hour later, Fredericka, feeling greatly refreshed, finished the last of the salad and cold coffee that she had found waiting for her in the kitchen. She had planned to explore the bookshop and the library but a glimpse of the hammock beyond the kitchen window was too much for her resolution. She salved her conscience by taking a block of paper and a pencil from the office desk and when she had stretched herself out in the leafy shade, she wrote the words, *Things to be done*. . . . Then she stopped and chewed the pencil meditatively.

So much had happened since that morning two weeks ago when she had read the ad among the Personals in the *Saturday Review*. She knew it now by heart.

WANTED. Educated woman to run bookshop and lending library, small college town in Massachusetts. Work not arduous. Rest and enjoyment of country possible. Owner-manager called away suddenly. Please reply Box 874

It had sounded like the answer to prayer. Being a branch librarian in New York in July had been bad enough, but short staff, shorter tempers, and hours of overtime had made the thought of escape a rainbow dream. And there was the book started two years ago, the encouraging letter from the publisher—"Work not arduous." There would be time, at last, to write.

At a sound behind her Fredericka sat up suddenly, and the pencil slipped from her hand to the ground.

From the tangle of shrubs and trees a black face peered out at her.

"Beg pardon, Miss. I'm Chris. Miss Hartwell's Chris. Sorry if I scared you. I've been unpackin' books in the stable here and Miss Hartwell, she say I was to ask you if you didn't want somethin' else done afore I went along home."

The tall negro now stood over her and his smile looked too good to be true, but perhaps he was just trying to be friendly.

"Oh. Then you're Christopher Fallon."

"That's right, Miss."

"Well. I do have a trunk at the station. Miss Sutton said you could get it for me."

"Yes, Miss."

"How do you manage? I know there isn't any car."

"No, Miss. I uses the wheelbarrer, fetchin' anythin' from the depot—parcels of books mostly."

"Good."

As the man started to move away, Fredericka felt a sudden impulse to detain him. The silent house and great overgrown garden were all at once oppressive.

"Is it Miss Sutton, or Mrs. Sutton, Chris?"

"Miss, if you means Miss Philippine the lady who met your train. Her aunty is ole Mrs. Sutton that owns the big place out on the turnpike. Her father, that was Mrs. Sutton's brother, he went to the big war, the first one, and married hisself to a French woman. But they both got themselves killed in this war we had just presently. Ole Mrs. Sutton she went and hunted for Miss Philippine until she foun' her at last and brought her back home."

"Hasn't she any children of her own then?" Fredericka couldn't resist asking. Then she was immediately sorry for the question. Was she prying into affairs that were no business of hers? Why must she analyse every word she spoke? Why must she be so sensitive? She looked a little nervously at Chris but he answered her without hesitation.

"Yes, Miss, she's got two children of her own—Miss Catherine—that's Mrs. Clay, that was. She ain't married jes' at present. She lives in New York but she's jus' visitin' heah right now. Then there's the boy—got hisself all smashed up in the war though."

"He isn't called Colonel, is he?" she asked, somewhat to her own surprise.

"Oh no, Miss. He's Roger—Roger Sutton," he added unnecessarily.

He began to move away toward the brick path that ran round the house to the front and Fredericka said quickly, "There was a man I—er—well, there was someone called Colonel at the junction and I just wondered if it could have been this Mr. Sutton."

"No Ma'am." Chris turned back. The smile had gone at last, and he regarded Fredericka solemnly. "Perhaps it could likely have been Colonel Mohun. He teaches in the college and everyone calls him Colonel 'round here."

Fredericka, for the third time that day, felt herself blushing. She wished now that she hadn't spoken. If only Chris would stop looking at her and go away.

"The Colonel's a good man," Chris said slowly, and something in the way he emphasized the word "good" made Fredericka look up quickly. Yes, it was as if he had said, "Those others, those Suttons, are a bad lot."

"Thanks, Chris. I'll be here tonight, probably working in the shop, so you can bring the trunk any time."

"Yes, Miss."

Fredericka watched the retreating back and wished she hadn't talked so much. As the sound of Chris's footsteps died away, the garden seemed unnaturally silent. She shivered. Was it a sudden cool breeze, or was it something else—a coldness and loneliness inside herself— Who was that illustrator who made trees into witches and ogres? Rackham. Beauty was in the eye of the beholder—was that also true of—evil? Why was she suddenly so disenchanted? She shivered again and got up to walk indoors slowly. She must apply her own mental discipline to such ridiculous imaginings.

2

Fredericka woke herself with a loud sneeze and turned over to look at the clock on the table by her bed.

Eight. Later than usual—much. But there had been the thunderstorm in the middle of the night and she had lain awake for a long time afterwards. She opened her eyes wide and stared at the unfamiliar yellow room.

She sneezed again, sat up, and was sure that she had started a cold. Her eyes ached and her throat felt like sandpaper.

As she dressed slowly, stopping at intervals to reach for a paper handkerchief, she was aware of a curious apprehension that had nothing to do with her cold and nothing to do with being alone in a strange house. Suddenly she sneezed again.

"Sneeze on Sunday, sneeze for—" What was the old rhyme? She finished dressing hurriedly and then looked out the window at the back of the room, over the sloping tin roof of the porch to the patch of lawn and the tangle of bushes beyond. She must explore that jungle later if the sun came out. But not now. The dark leaves hung heavy and dank from their night's wetting and even the lawn was steaming after the heat of yesterday.

Why didn't she stop staring out of the window? Why didn't she go down and put on the coffee and make an effort to throw off this unreasonable depression? Why?

Suddenly she stiffened where she stood. Yes, the wet bushes were moving and there was no hint of wind to move them. As she stared a white face appeared, and then, slowly and cautiously, the body attached to it. A young girl in a checked gingham dress. Fredericka relaxed. But why should this girl approach so stealthily through the wet bushes as though she did not want to be seen. Why, for that matter, did she come at all, unasked?

Fredericka stuffed her apron pocket with tissues and hurried downstairs to the back door, which she threw open suddenly as a relief to her annoyance. Her visitor was now standing in full view.

"Yes?" Fredericka said coldly.

"Oh," said the girl, looking up. "You must be Fredericka Wing."

"I am. And who, if I may ask, are you?" In spite of herself, Fredericka was annoyed at the use of her first name by the stranger, and her annoyance was not relieved by the sight of the unprepossessing girl who stared back at her. Young, certainly not more than sixteen, sullen, untidy, her too-full face blotched with patches of crimson acne.

"I'm Margie Hartwell." The girl paused as if this explanation should be enough for anyone, and then she added reluctantly and as if compelled by Fredericka's evident hostility, "I've come for some things Mom wanted from the storeroom."

Fredericka was about to forbid her to enter the

house when she realized that she was behaving stupidly simply because she did not like the girl and her unannounced arrival. After all, Miss Hartwell had spoken of this child as her niece. With an effort, Fredericka managed to say nothing, but she turned away abruptly toward the kitchen and the more cheerful thought of coffee.

Margie banged through the screen door and Fredericka could hear her heavy footsteps go up the stairs and into the room over the office which Philippine had called the personal storeroom and which she had discovered to be full of family possessions.

This kind of behaviour might be all right for South Sutton, but it was not going to be all right for Fredericka Wing.

By the time Margie returned, Fredericka was finishing her breakfast. The girl stood in the doorway, looking hungry, but Fredericka did not ask her in.

"I wish," she said stiffly, "that another time you would let me know when you want to come into the house. I live here now, you know."

"But Auntie said—"

Fredericka cut her short. "It doesn't matter what Miss Hartwell said. I'm in charge here now and I don't like people banging in and out unasked."

The girl stared at her and the blotches on her face turned an angry red, but she said nothing. After a moment, she turned and went out the back door, slamming it deliberately behind her.

And that's that, Fredericka thought. Now, just because I'm tired and have a cold and was startled, I've had to antagonize that miserable child. She got up and went to the sink to wash the dishes. Outside, the hammock looked soggy and bedraggled. Should she have covered it with something? Oh, blast it, blast everything. If this place wasn't so full of lunatics, she'd have started off on the right foot.—As it was . . .

But as the morning wore on, and Fredericka suffered no further disturbance, she began to feel better. Systematically checking stock, she found it very much to her own taste. Miss Hartwell might be scatterbrained but she certainly knew books.

Her find of the morning was in the small second-hand books section in the room opposite the office—a shelf of the long out-of-print novels of Mary J. Holmes and several other Victorian women writers that Fredericka had been trying to track down for months. Now, if only she wasn't too busy getting settled, she could get to work on her own reading and writing almost immediately. This thought cheered her so much that, somewhat to her own surprise, she began to sing through her short repertoire of hymns. The incipient cold did not help them, but Fredericka had forgotten that she had ever thought of a cold, or been depressed. The Hartwell Bookshop had suddenly become paradise on earth.

She worked through the three rooms carefully and ended up in the Lending Library which she found in good order, as were the papers neatly stacked on the office desk. There was also a pile of books with a note in Miss Hartwell's large scrawl that was now all too familiar to the bookshop's new manager.

These are for P. Mohun. Ordered ages ago. He'll want them sooner than at once. Margie can take a note over to the college for him, or he'll be in.

Fredericka looked through the titles with quickened interest. It seemed that Peter Mohun—Colonel Peter

Mohun—bought books on American military history before the Civil War—Indians and frontier fighting. Was that the subject he taught in the college then?

There were two other books, each with a note on top. Kathleen Winsor from the lending library marked with the name "Catherine Clay" and Carl Van Doren's *Life of Franklin,* marked "Roger Sutton."

Well, Fredericka thought, that ought to tell me something about the son and daughter of the first family of South Sutton. And, also, of course, a little more about this interesting man, Colonel Peter Mohun.

A hesitant ray of sunlight flashed across the desk and as quickly retreated. Fredericka got up and went to the window. Yes, patches of blue sky. Perhaps it would be sensible to go out. What had Philippine Sutton said about the inn? Good food. A look at the kitchen clock showed Fredericka that it was already late for lunch and one should certainly feed a cold but not make the effort of cooking for it. She hurried upstairs to change her clothes to the tune of "Abide With Me."

Fredericka found the Coach and Horses as attractive as Philippine had promised. It was certainly early nineteenth century, a colonial white wooden house with brick ends and wide chimneys, and it had been well preserved. The doorway with its fanlight and side windows was unspoilt, or perfectly restored. The grass that edged the curved driveway was neatly cut and the beds bright with flowers.

Fredericka found the door ajar and went in hesitantly. To her surprise, she stepped directly into a comfortable living room with large chintz-covered chairs and an air of being used and homelike. A log fire was burning in the great fireplace directly opposite the door and Sunday papers lay in untidy patches on the scattered tables and chairs.

Fredericka saw at once that the room was empty and that the clock on the mantelpiece said ten minutes past one. She walked across to the fire and stretched out her hands. How odd to be grateful for this warmth after yesterday's midsummer heat. She stared at the flames absently and then became aware that someone had come quietly into the room behind her. She turned quickly and found herself staring into the face of a woman. The eyes that regarded Fredericka were violet-gray and beautiful, but cold as a foggy winter day. And then the woman spoke and the lovely colourless mask of her face was suddenly creased and spoilt by age and petulance.

"You must be Miss Wing. Miss Hartwell said to be on the lookout for you." She extended a white hand which Fredericka took with instinctive reluctance. "I am Mrs. Clay—Catherine Sutton Clay." She pronounced the middle name with obvious pleasure.

"Oh, yes," Fredericka murmured. So this was the Sutton daughter who had been married and divorced, if that was what Chris meant by saying that she was not married just at present! The limp hand in her own had unexpected strength. And then, remembering her manners, Fredericka added: "How do you do?"

"Not too well, thanks," Catherine answered unexpectedly. "I've left New York too long and now the slow decay of South Sutton has set in. I don't suppose you've felt it yet. But you will . . ."

Fredericka could think of nothing to say and the woman shrugged impatiently. "You'd better get lunch if that's what you came for. Chicken on Sunday and the longer you wait, the less there is of it!" Then she muttered under her breath; "If friend James doesn't come soon we'll get cold ham." She sank down into a chair and waved an expressive hand toward the dining room.

I mustn't dislike any of these people, Fredericka thought miserably as she muttered a word of thanks and moved toward the sound of rattling plates and cutlery that she could hear through the door at the far end of the room. But I don't like her, and I have a hunch that I never will, customer or no customer.

The dining room seemed to Fredericka's over-wrought nerves to be crammed with people who all looked up to stare at the newcomer as she stood hesitant in the doorway. But when the hostess had greeted her pleasantly and shown her to a quiet corner of the room, she looked around with some surprise to discover that, in fact, very few of the tables were taken. The first person she saw was Colonel Mohun who, as yesterday, looked directly at her with intent appraising eyes. And then when she stared back, as though hypnotized, he smiled, and the severity vanished from his face. Fredericka also smiled and then looked down at the menu in confusion, as she felt her cheeks flame with sudden telltale colour. The typed card was not worth serious attention since there was no question of choice, but it gave Fredericka a chance to recover and, after a moment, she was able to look around the room, if not in the direction of the distracting Colonel Mohun.

There were several large tables round which sat husbands, wives and children who looked as though they might be professors' families. They had an unmistakable "Sunday treat after church" look about them. Fredericka now realized that the noise which had greeted her entrance came from one of these tables, where a young man of about two in a high chair was producing tom-tom beats of spoon against bowl, and bowl against cup, in a manner that he found most satisfying.

"All he needs is a brass band in support," a deep voice said, and Fredericka looked up to see Colonel Mohun standing over her. "Please forgive me for introducing myself in this informal way but we are informal about introductions around here and, of course, having been primed by dear Lucy Hartwell, I had a good idea who you were when I first saw you yesterday at the Junction. I want to ask about some books I've ordered but perhaps I ought not to trouble you now."

Fredericka mumbled a few words about the books which she hoped sounded adequate, but instead of moving away, this strange man said quietly: "I was just finishing my coffee. Would you mind if I joined you for a few moments? Lucy asked me particularly to give you a welcome."

Fredericka now became acutely aware that the small boy's tom-tom had stopped beating and she could imagine that not only his, but every other pair of eyes was regarding them both with interest. She stared stupidly at her plate and could not bring herself to look up. Then she heard herself say in what seemed a very loud voice: "Of course. Please do."

"We're a small town in every sense," her visitor went on easily, when he had rejoined her with his cup of coffee. "I mean, there aren't enough of us to begin with. We gossip; we regard any new arrival with excitement and—yes, I admit it—suspicion; we're clannish; but on the whole we mean well."

Fredericka felt warmed by the solicitousness of his words and the friendly sound of his quiet ordinary voice and, all at once, she found her shyness gone and heard

herself speak to this stranger as though he were a childhood friend.

"I'm sorry if I've given the impression of unfriendli-
ness to any of you," she said, thinking guiltily of her
morning encounter with Margie. "It's all a little bewildering after New York—or perhaps bewildering isn't the
right word. 'Frightening' is more like it. For some reason
you're all larger than life–size, as though I were seeing
you through a magnifying glass."

"Yes, I know exactly what you mean. Sudden
changes have all the horror of nightmare, but you'll be
all right when you get to feel as though you were one of
us. And you will, much sooner than you think. Let's see
what I can do to help. I'm Peter Mohun . . ."

"Yes, I know."

"Good. I teach in Sutton College—an extra-special
course for these extra-special summer students." He
looked around the room and smiled again. "You know I
can't get used to teaching married men with wives and
kids all over the campus—even if I am twice their age."

"You mean these are *students?* I thought they must
be professors only they looked too young." She paused
for a moment and then asked: "What is so special about
what you teach?" She was relieved to see that her dinner
was arriving without any fuss. The typed menu was,
indeed, only a state of fact.

"Didn't Miss Hartwell tell you about the college?"

"Well, no. We had a brisk exchange of letters and
then she departed at the very moment I got here. Miss
Sutton did tell me a little when I arrived yesterday—but
not much."

"Just like Lucy. Well, I'll be Guide to Ancient Monu-
ments, and fill in the details Philippine may have missed.
Sutton College was founded in 1820 by Lucius Edward

Sutton in memory of his son who was killed in the war of 1812. This son, James Thayer Sutton, had been travelling to a diplomatic post on a blockade runner which was sunk by the British. For this reason the old man, ancestor of the husband of our own Mrs. Sutton who still lives at the Farm, the family place—what was I saying—Oh, yes, the original old man founded Sutton College to train men for the Consular and Diplomatic Service of the U.S.A. The students are sifted carefully and are apt to be older than the usual run of college men, hence the families, and they are apt not to be poor since most men who go into this branch of the service need cash in support of salary."

"And Lucius Sutton founded the town too,?"

"Oh, yes, that was in 1814. As you may have noticed we have some fine specimens of what I believe the experts call Gothic Victorian architecture. Your new home is a good example. And the college is a copy of Magdalen College, Oxford—even to a made-to-order stream. I find it all very soothing."

Colonel Mohun seemed in no hurry to leave, and, after a moment of stirring his empty coffee cup absently, he signalled the waitress to refill it.

Fredericka looked puzzled. "You teach—er—Diplomacy then?"

"I think that would be a tall order. No. I don't really belong in the original scheme of things. In 1941 the college added a new department—unfortunately housed in prefab huts, still it could be worse—this is called, grandly, The Department of Military Government, and is partly financed by the government. In this department we take only college graduates. They're our prize specimens."

"And you teach?" Fredericka persisted.

"I?" The colonel frowned. "Oh, just a vague course in Military Intelligence." He saw that Fredericka was ready with another question and he went on hurriedly, "I'd much rather spend all my time with the Indians— fighting the nice simple wars in the good old days of border strife before the Civil War."

"Oh, yes, those books you wanted . . ." Fredericka said suddenly.

He finished his coffee quickly and stood up. "May I drop by for them later this afternoon? I'm acutely conscious that you've heard all about us—or rather me— and I've heard nothing about you."

"I was eating." Fredericka smiled. "And I'm too New England to talk at the same time. Yes, please do come in. A bookshop is a soulless place without people, especially on a cold, wet Sunday—" She stopped and sneezed suddenly. Searching her pockets for a handkerchief she looked up at him to say: "I don't suppose you know the rest of that silly rhyme. It's been teasing me all morning—You know, 'Sneeze on Sunday. . . .' "

"I'm afraid I do, and we'll just have to face the fact that it's the worst day in the week:

Sneeze on Sunday and safety seek,
The devil will have you the rest of the week?

"Oh dear! And I'm starting a cold. Perhaps I'll put it right by sneezing again tomorrow."

"No hope there: 'Sneeze on Monday, sneeze for danger.' "

He looked at her with what was meant to be an expression of fierce foreboding and then grinned suddenly. "But if you can produce one on Tuesday—ah, then there's relief for you. But perhaps you know that one."

"No. I seem to have forgotten them all."

"Well, perhaps that's just as well for the present." He turned away maddeningly, and walked quickly from the room.

"And that's that," Fredericka decided. Tuesday—it must rhyme with "danger." She felt suddenly depressed and the early morning's anxiety returned. It's just this damn cold, she thought. A cold always aggravates every unpleasant thing.

It was at this moment that she heard again the throaty voice of Catherine Clay who had come in with a thickset, heavy man, and was now sitting two tables away. *"Can't,"* she was saying, "why can't I, James? That miserable upstart. God, I could kill her with my own two hands . . ."

"S-s-h!" Her companion looked around anxiously. Fredericka busied herself with her apple pie and he seemed not to notice her.

"If you weren't jealous, my dear, you'd see her as others do. She's a good woman and I don't know what your mother ever would have done without her." He, too, sounded angry.

Catherine raised her voice again and fairly spat the next words at him. "Don't tell me you've been charmed, too. Good God, and I thought you loved me!" She lowered her voice, and, as she leant across the table to her companion, her body seemed to quiver with the strength of her feeling. She now spoke rapidly and her thin hands gripped the edge of the table. Fredericka strained her ears and lingered to play with her pie, but she could distinguish no further words. As she looked covertly from the man's heavy sensuous face to the woman's, so obviously flushed by anger and passion, she began to tell herself a story worthy of one of her Victorian novelists. She picked up her bill with some impatience and hurried to the door. I wonder who James is, she thought, and then, if I let myself go any more, I'll be writing an irrelevant chapter in my book, headed, "More Here Than Meets the Eye."

The "good woman" was obviously Catherine's cousin, Philippine Sutton who had been found in France by Catherine's mother. Reason enough for jealousy. And James, whoever he was, had piled fuel on the flames. Fredericka wondered how soon she would see Philippine again. Yes, certainly, if Fredericka were given a chance for judgment, she would choose Philippine every time. But James was obviously smitten—or had been; it was hard to say.

Fredericka was aware that her thoughts were rambling, that she was over-exercising her imagination, and that she had a cold. But as she walked back to her bookshop home under the dripping trees, she was not wholly miserable. There was now the comforting thought that the Colonel would drop by for his books— and perhaps she would ask him to stay for supper. Her tidy mind remembered that there were eggs and cheese for a soufflé.

3

The Saturday of South Sutton's great bazaar dawned clear and hot and the anxious eyes scanning the skies for danger signals were relieved at all the weather signs. There might be a thunderstorm later on in the day, but that was to be expected in July, and would only add a little excitement to the festivities.

Fredericka got up early and sorted the collection of rental library culls promised by Miss Hartwell as the shop's donation to the bazaar, and she had no sooner finished her task than there was a light knock at the front door. Fredericka waited a moment but her guest was more polite than most, and did not walk in. Fredericka hurried out and was delighted to discover Philippine Sutton on the doorstep. It had been a week since their first meeting on the day of Fredericka's arrival and she had felt pleased by this first gesture of friendship and then a little hurt to find that she had been welcomed and, it seemed, forgotten.

"I am so sorry I have not been to see you before this.

I have never been so busy at the lab and the orders for herbs have been pouring in. Roger and I have been hard at work every moment since you came—" She waved a hand in the direction of the road where Fredericka could see the jeep and in it a man slumped over the wheel. "Now we have come to see if we could take the books over to the church hall for you—and even now, we can't stay."

"How good of you. But can't you both just come in for a cup of coffee? I haven't met Mr. Sutton," she added hesitantly.

Philippine frowned and then smiled. "Roger," she called, and then louder: *"Roger."* The man turned but made no reply. "Come and have a cup of coffee."

"Really, Phil, we haven't time to stop. You said—"

Philippine, with a gesture of impatience, hurried down the path to the car. She spoke to Roger quietly and, a moment later, the man uncoiled himself and followed Philippine up the walk. But it was obvious in every line of his body that it was the last thing in the world he wanted to do.

As he came nearer and Fredericka saw his scarred and seamed face, she could understand his reluctance. She also realized that the sensitiveness which made him hate to be seen would also make him bitterly resent any move that might be interpreted as sympathy. She shook his hand which was firm but cold in hers and then said: "Come in," abruptly, and hurried ahead of them into the kitchen. As the two women sat down at the table in the window, Roger took his cup and stood leaning against the shelves with his face away from the light.

Conversation was difficult at first and soon the two women were doing most of the talking with Roger standing by nervously. It was obvious that he was anxious to be on his way.

"You can see from our clothes that we are off for the day," Philippine said. "We must collect the wild herbs before they dry up altogether." Roger was wearing a torn and very dirty pair of khaki trousers but his shirt was clean and his hair neatly brushed. He did not seem to be dressed for anything in particular. Philippine was wearing jeans and a plaid shirt, open at the neck. It was true that she looked much less spick-and-span than when she had first met Fredericka, but much less carelessly dressed than Margie and the other village girls were at all times.

"You both look good enough for the party, to me. But aren't you coming then?"

"No," Roger announced suddenly. He walked across the room to put down his empty coffee cup in the sink and then stood over Philippine, nervously clenching and unclenching his hands.

I couldn't stand *that* for long, Fredericka thought. Then, as she looked across the table at Philippine a look of understanding and sympathy passed between them. We could be friends, Fredericka thought, but we're both too occupied with our own affairs so there won't be time.

As if to underline this thought, Philippine got up to go and Fredericka sighed as she returned to her desk. She had wanted Philippine's friendship and, if one could make the effort, there must be something worth finding out about Roger Sutton— Couldn't he be helped? She reached for the pile of publisher's catalogues and tried to forget her visitors. She could hope for a quiet morning in the shop since everyone would be busy getting ready for the bazaar. But she had no sooner managed to concentrate on her morning's work than Margie Hartwell came walking in the back door.

During the week Margie had given up even the formality of knocking, and Fredericka had given up trying to make her change her ways. This morning the girl was excited and looked better than Fredericka had imagined to be possible. Even the bad complexion had been skilfully hidden under a mask of face cream and powder and for once her dress was clean and neat.

"I'm not working today," she announced at once, "except, of course, at the fete. But that's more fun than washing bottles and test tubes which is about all I ever do in the lab lately. I guess they'll shut up shop for the day at the Farm. Mrs. Sutton's coming, of course. She always does, but Roger won't—he hates crowds, and I don't know about Philippine. They say they are going off to hunt wild herbs and heaven alone knows when they'll be back."

Fredericka, for some reason, did not feel it necessary to mention her early callers. "Is Mrs. Clay coming?"

"Oh, *her!* I wouldn't know. I expect she will if dear James gets back in time."

"Are they engaged?" Fredericka couldn't resist asking, and then regretted her question when she saw Margie's look of Pleased Informer that she had often had occasion to observe before.

"Engaged? Everything but, I should think. What he sees in her I can't think but, of course, he's no ball of fire. Lately, though, he's been hanging around the lab a lot. I think, myself, he's sweet on Philippine—and that makes more sense. . . ."

Margie was prepared to go on about this pleasant subject indefinitely but Fredericka felt it would be wise to call a halt. "Well, you needn't help here, either. Why don't you run along and join in the preparations."

But Margie, contrary as always, pouted and said slowly, "I'd just as soon help. Mom said I could so long as it wasn't *dirty* work."

"I really haven't anything for you to do." Fredericka felt suddenly tired. "Unless you'd like to sit down with a book and wait on any customers."

"Oh, there won't be any customers this morning—and I don't like reading much, so I guess I will go along then."

And before Fredericka could attempt a reply, Margie had flounced out the front door and disappeared down the path. Once more Fredericka returned to her desk and this time she was not disturbed. Margie's prediction proved accurate and there were no customers at all. For once, Fredericka was glad of this as she planned to shut up shop early and spend the afternoon as well as the evening at the bazaar.

When Peter Mohun called for her at half past two she was quite ready and waiting outside in her best pink linen and large straw hat.

"You don't half look a picture, you don't," he greeted her. "And if that's too negative for you I'd say, 'ascribed to Gainsborough'; will that do?"

Fredericka laughed and a feeling of holiday took possession of her. "Did he ever paint the oppressed working classes? I feel like Maid's Day Out and more than ready for it," she answered. "Not in the least like gentry keeping their gloves clean."

"Good. So do I, or rather, so don't I. These things must always be approached with the whole heart committed. Otherwise— Hello! There's friend Carey—Thane

Carey and his wife, Connie. I'd like you to meet them. Shall we ask them to sit with us at dinner?"

"Yes, of course. But who is he?"

"Oh, he's our chief of police—swell guy—and shares our passion for murder. And luckily Connie's a fine listener."

"Enter the cop," Fredericka muttered.

"No need to be snooty," Peter said stiffly. "He happens to be my good friend."

Fredericka blushed and then stumbled over her words. "Oh, I didn't mean that. I was only thinking of that murder mystery you and I were talking about last night."

"Did I hear the words 'murder' and 'mystery'?" Thane Carey greeted them. "My bloodhound's ears prick eager forward."

As Peter introduced them, Fredericka decided that she liked this young man and his wife. He had an honest, serious and ugly face in which none of the features seemed to match, but he was tall and well-built and immediately gave the impression of being both capable and businesslike. His wife was equally attractive. Her calm blue eyes gave one a sense of repose and she seemed the perfect foil to his restless energy.

"I'm on 'dooty', Mohun, so don't detain me long. Not murder, I fear. Only after pickpockets and petty thieves." He laughed pleasantly and Connie smiled.

Peter suggested that they should all sit together at the bean feast and talk shop—both book and crime, and the others agreed with alacrity.

"You'll like Thane and Connie," Peter said when the two had disappeared in the crowds.

"I like them both already. Does he do anything besides police the town?"

"Oh yes. He teaches, like me—and writes a little, also like me—"

"And me—"

"You, too, Brutus? Now how did you keep that interesting fact from me all this time?"

"I'm more eager than successful," she said quickly. "I haven't much to talk about yet. But I'm hoping to have time really to produce something now."

"Well, you know my line of country from the books I buy. What's yours?"

"I'm trying to write a joint biography of that band of Victorian novelists, the ones Hawthorne called 'scribbling women'; Susan Warner, Maria Cummins, Mary J. Holmes, etc. It's a far cry from your Indian warfare."

"Do you find you are getting any time to write?"

"So far, not much. That bookshop seems more of a thoroughfare than I'd realized and no amount of planning keeps customers away."

"Which is, perhaps, fortunate. But I think you ought to use Margie more. I couldn't possibly write at all unless I had some quiet mornings."

"Margie doesn't seem to me the perfect answer," Fredericka said a little stiffly.

"Perfect? Of course not. Nothing in this world is perfect. But she's a good kid at heart and will be O.K. when she gets rid of her adolescent complexes and that very bad case of acne which is part and parcel of the same thing."

Fredericka said nothing. Her feelings about Margie were best not expressed to anyone so obviously sympathetic to her as Peter. They walked on in silence until they came to a gaily decorated booth marked "Herbs and Tussie-Mussies."

"Bet you don't know what a tussie-mussie is," Peter

announced. "Here. I'll buy you one and then you'll know." He dragged her to the booth and then stopped in surprise. "Why, Mrs. Sutton, are you tending shop yourself? Where are all your assistants?"

"Hello, Peter. How do you do, Fredericka—I hope I may call you by your first name. As a matter of fact you see me in a state of distress. Catherine promised to take the booth for me—I'm not supposed to stand, the doctor says, because of a wretched sprained ankle. Catherine's just not appeared. However, that's not your worry. What can I sell you? How about a tussie-mussie for the lady, Peter?" She picked up a small bouquet and smiled.

Fredericka had met Mrs. Sutton, who had made several visits to the bookshop. She was tall and must once have been handsome, but now she looked old, and lines of worry had left only a memory of beauty in her face. She's ill, or sick with anxiety, Fredericka felt; but she had no time to dwell on these thoughts because Peter was saying: "I like the look of that one, Margaret, but is the message fitting?"

"Poor Miss Wing looks bewildered. A tussie-mussie is a bouquet with a message in the language of the flowers. I've written them all out and perhaps you'd better read this one first, Peter, and see."

Peter read the scrap of paper and grinned. "Perfect," he said.

"Can't I see it?" Fredericka asked.

"Not yet, but you can have the pretty posy," Peter answered, folding the paper carefully and hiding it away in his pocket. Then he looked across at Mrs. Sutton. "Can't we relieve you for a while?"

"Oh no, dear Peter. It is good of you, but I've sent for Margie. She may sulk but I'm sure she'll come. Oh, here she is now—thank goodness."

Margie pushed her way through the crowds, and as Fredericka and Peter left, they heard her say: "It isn't my job. Catherine needn't think she can get away with this," and Mrs. Sutton's voice low and soothing.

"Poor Margie," Peter said. "I can't blame her. Catherine will always look out for Catherine and get away with it and the plain kids like Margie will have to fill the breach."

"It won't hurt Margie," Fredericka couldn't help saying, and then at once regretted it when she saw Peter's frown.

But soon Margie and everyone else was forgotten in the fun of that hot summer afternoon. Peter and Fredericka went from booth to booth, and then sat under the shade of a nearby tree to drink lemonade and discuss life. The lazy contentment of those hours would never be forgotten by either of them even when, later, they knew them to be an overture to nightmare.

Supper was laid in the Church Hall at six—long trestle tables covered with flowered crêpe paper and dotted with steaming bowls of baked beans, platters of ham, salad and rolls. As they entered the barracklike room now crowding with people, Peter and Fredericka stopped to admire a quilt for which the ladies of the Church Guild had been selling tickets all the week. A carefully printed notice said that over five hundred tickets had been sold and that the lucky number would be drawn after supper.

"Please let it be me," Fredericka breathed. "It's the loveliest thing I've ever seen. I've taken all of five tickets."

"Trousseau?" Thane Carey asked, coming up quietly behind them in time to hear her prayer.

"No, only hope chest," Fredericka said, laughing, as

they found Connie and then joined the scramble to get places together at one of the tables.

When they had settled themselves as comfortably as possible on their hard chairs, they discovered that Margie had landed, either by accident or design, on the other side of Peter, and Fredericka sat between Peter and Thane Carey, who at once began to talk about his interest in crime and in detective fiction. Connie, on his other side, listened quietly and hardly ever spoke.

"I'm not all that knowledgeable," Fredericka said at length. "But I am interested, and one thing that fascinates me is the way you detectives always say that crime in real life is a very different thing from crime in fiction."

"But isn't it? How much crime have you met in real life?"

"I confess—not much. But I do know that often the writer of detective stories can in fact be good at detection himself. I've just been reading John Dickson Carr's *Life of Conan Doyle.* The Oscar Slater case and the Edalji case at Great Wryley were both solved by Doyle himself in order to free innocent men—and, I may add if you'll let me, in spite of the attempts to cover up made by the authorities."

"That was England, of course, not America," Carey said quickly.

Peter turned from Margie who was still grumbling about her wasted afternoon, and the fact that Catherine never had turned up at all.

"You know, Carey," he said, leaning across Fredericka, "Miss Wing is determined that South Sutton is the perfect place for a murder in the grand manner—"

"On the grounds," Carey said easily, "that the country is the place for crime. Of course, Miss Wing, you've sent your arrow to the heart. You were talking of Doyle just now. Remember this—"

"Are they not fresh and beautiful?" I cried with all the enthusiasm of a man fresh from the fogs of Baker Street.

But Holmes shook his head gravely, "Do you know, Watson," said he, "that it is one of the curses of a mind with a turn like mine that I must look at everything with reference to my own special subject. You look at the scattered houses, and you are impressed by their beauty. I look at them, and the only thought that comes to me is a feeling of their isolation and of the impunity with which crime may be committed there . . . But look at these lovely houses, each in its own fields, filled for the most part with poor ignorant folk who know little of the law. Think of the deeds of hellish cruelty, the hidden wickedness which may go on, year in, year out, in such places and no one the wiser?"

"Goodness, do you know Doyle by heart?" Fredericka asked.

"No, but I wish I did. *The Hound of the Baskervilles* used to scare me silly when I was a kid. I read it over and over in a kind of orgy of pure horror and—well—I've loved Doyle ever since."

They all laughed and then Peter said: "Speaking of being scared to death at a tender age, I remember almost every word of a book written by Celia Thaxter which described the murder on the Isle of Shoals. A fisherman who had been considered a family friend for years rowed across the bay in the dead of winter, murdered two defenceless women with an axe in the middle of the night, chased another into the snow, and when

captured at last, tried to put the blame for the murder
onto two completely innocent men who were out fishing
at the time, and were in fact the husband and the
brother of one of the murdered women. It was a wild
melodrama with a Gothic background and it gave me
glorious nightmares."

"I confess to a weakness for crimes committed by
professors and love university settings. Perhaps that's
why I've got my eye on South Sutton," Fredericka put in.

"Oh, you mean those stuffy Oxford dons who get all
mixed up with keys and times," Peter said.

"Yes, those, and true cases like the Webster one,
the classic example of murder in Harvard University."

"That's a beauty," Thane said enthusiastically. "Do
you know it, Mohun? Dr. George Parkman murdered by
Professor Webster who owed him money. No one
dreamt of suspecting such an eminently respectable old
guy but the janitor spied on him, and, oh boy, what did
he see? The old professor dissecting the corpse and
burning it in the college furnace!"

"Yes, I agree, a beauty. And didn't Oliver Wendell
Holmes act as witness?"

"That's right. Good old New England, the perfect
seat of perfect crimes," Carey said, laughing.

Margie, who had been listening with paralysed in-
tentness, now said in a very loud voice: "All right then,
why don't you start searching for the body of Catherine
Clay who disappeared after lunch, no one knows where,
and hasn't been seen since? Not that anyone would care
if she had been done in," she added bitterly, but in an
undertone.

"My dear Margie," Peter turned to her, "has that
woman ever come back from anywhere when she was
expected to?"

"No-o. All the same, if you're wanting to have a murder mystery in South Sutton, it's a good beginning."

"Wrong again," Thane said. "Unless there's some pressing reason we begin with the body, not with the search for it."

"Just like the police," Margie roared. "Perhaps there wouldn't be any dead bodies if you paid attention to signs and portents."

Thane, Fredericka, Peter and Connie all turned to look at the girl's white face, now startlingly blotched with crimson. "Good God, she's *serious*," Thane said, jumping up. "Hey, kid, what are you driving at?" But before anyone could stop her, Margie had jumped to her feet and run off through the open door into the darkness of the summer night.

"Let her go, Carey," Peter said. "It's just what her mother calls her 'theatrics.' Nothing she likes better than to get a good rise out of an unsuspecting audience. And she's got a score to settle with Catherine so she's *wishing* her dead."

After a moment the chief of police sat down and went back to his strawberry shortcake. "She's mad, then," he muttered a little shamefacedly. And then they talked of other things until the great moment when all the paper plates had been cleared away, a hymn sung, and a few words appropriate to the occasion said by the minister, whose name, Peter whispered to Fredericka, was the Reverend Archibald Williams. Then, at last, the long awaited raffle of the quilt.

"Thirty-five," the minister's wife announced in a very loud voice, as she drew the slip from the hat.

"Why—Why—that's one of *mine*," Fredericka gasped, "and I—I asked for it because of my birthday. I mean—Oh dear—what do I do now?"

"Rise and claim your prize, my dear," Peter said gravely.

And that was how Fredericka happened to be carrying a beautiful patchwork quilt when she unlocked her door half an hour later, and how she happened to go into the kitchen before she went up to bed.

When Peter said good night on the front porch, she asked him to come in, but he refused.

"I'm sorry, Fredericka, but tonight I have a report to make out and will be working late in my office. You can see the beacon light from here no doubt."

Fredericka swallowed her disappointment and went into the house with her quilt, which she at once took upstairs and spread out on her bed for further inspection. Then she decided that it might look even better hung on a wall, but the only wall not covered with books was the one in the kitchen.

She went to get the steps under the sink and, in the glare of light from the window, she looked out at the hammock. The steps were never used and the quilt lay forgotten for days in the kitchen rocking-chair.

Someone was lying in the hammock, and lying very still.

"I knew we shouldn't talk about those awful crimes," Fredericka said out loud to reassure herself. "But I'm just as crazy mad as that child, Margie. It's no doubt Margie herself sleeping off her fit of adolescent exhibitionism, and giving me a good fright, to boot."

Her words, spoken to the empty room, sounded strange in the silence and their very primness reminded Fredericka that she was herself and not Harriet Vane. As she opened the back door and stepped out onto the porch, a cricket shrilled beside her and she stopped still in terror. Then, slowly, she walked around the path to the hammock.

For a full moment she stared at the body of Catherine Clay. There was no mistake possible now. One hand dangled helplessly to the ground and the face staring up into the light from the kitchen window was distorted with pain or anger—but rigid and still.

Fredericka put one hand to her mouth to stifle the scream that rose in her throat, and forced herself to put the other down to touch the awful face. Then she drew it away quickly and turned to run blindly, instinctively, in the direction of the campus and the beacon light that Peter had promised her would be there.

4

Fredericka pounded on the thin door of the prefabricated hut. The sound echoed like hollow drum beats in the silent night.

"Good God!" Peter said opening the door quickly. "No need to wake the dead. Who the devil is it?"

"It's me, Peter. Oh, Peter, Peter she *is* dead. Margie must be a witch."

"Fredericka, it's *you*. What are you talking about?" Then, seeing her white face, he grasped her arm and found that she was trembling. "Here, come in and tell me what's the matter. There can't really be anything wrong, Fredericka. You're having a nightmare because we talked too much nonsense."

"No. No. Peter, I can't come in. You must come back with me. It's—it's Catherine Clay. She's dead. There—at the bookshop. In my hammock, in my yard." Fredericka forced herself to say the words slowly and distinctly and, at last, Peter realized their meaning.

"All right, Fredericka, I believe you if I must, but

first, before I make a move to come with you, I'm going to give you a bracer."

He led her into the office and opened a drawer of his desk to take out a small silver flask. Then, from a cupboard, he produced a tumbler and poured out a stiff drink. "Brandy. Do you good. Here, don't drink it too fast."

Fredericka choked, looked up and tried to smile, then gulped the rest like an obedient child taking a dose of medicine.

When the brandy had worked its magic and she felt suddenly better, she stared up at Peter whose face looked owl-like in the light from the green-shaded lamp on his desk. "Thanks," she said, and then: "I'm all right now. Please come. I—I don't like leaving her alone there."

"If she's dead, my dear Fredericka, five minutes can't make much difference," he reminded her gently.

"I know, but—"

Afterwards both Peter and Fredericka were to wonder at her urgent desire to return at once to the bookshop. Even then some instinct must have warned her that death had not been natural. Yes, even then—

"But what?" Peter asked sharply.

"Oh, I don't know. I just feel we ought to be there."

"All right," Peter agreed quietly. He took her arm to steady her as they hurried across the campus, over the road, and around the Hartwell house to the hammock.

To Fredericka's great relief the body of Catherine Clay lay exactly as she had last seen it. She stood back behind Peter so that she could not see the staring eyes.

"I suppose she *is* dead," Peter said. He took out a torch from his pocket and flashed it over the still form. Then he began to mutter to himself, "Yes, the eyes and," he touched her body lightly, "rigor even. I wonder how long she's lain here. Poor miserable creature." He turned suddenly to Fredericka. "We mustn't touch her. I'll call Carey and we'll have to let Mrs. Sutton know at once. Here, you come inside and get busy making us all some coffee."

They went into the house together and in silence. Peter went straight to the telephone in the office and Fredericka to the kitchen where she began to fill the percolator with the careful precision of a sleep walker.

When the coffee had started to bubble and Peter had come back to the kitchen, they sat down stiffly and smoked in a silence which became so oppressive that Fredericka felt she must speak. In a strained voice, she said: "Could you, I mean, would you mind telling me a little more about *her*—"

Peter turned to her quickly. "You mean Catherine—of course. I've just been thinking about her myself because in an odd way I'm not surprised at her death—I might as well think out loud."

"Please do."

"Well, it's mostly gossip but probably fairly accurate. She was married quite young, stayed married two years, got comfortably divorced and then threw all her own and her acquired wealth into starting one of those marble-fronted beauty parlors, or whatever they are, on Park Avenue, and ran through it all in a very short time." He paused and then went on slowly, "It has even been said that, as a last desperate resort, she began peddling dope to her customers and picked up the habit herself. This was a great financial help to the business for a short time but, in the end, a dead loss due to the unexpected intervention of the police. Now she's looking—or was looking—for a rich man and a quiet life."

"That heavy dark man I saw with her at the inn last Sunday—is he—I mean *was* he, the one?"

"James Brewster. Yes. He's the family lawyer, works in Worcester but has an apartment here for his week-ends. Rumour has it—or had it—that she wanted him for husband number two and that, though attracted by her snake-like charm, he was still able to resist. He's sup-posed to be a great one with the ladies and he's been a bachelor long enough to know how to resist. Also he has money and she had none, which aggravated the situa-tion . . ."

"Aren't the Suttons rich, then?"

"They manage now. But the old man died some-where around the time of the depression, leaving Mrs. Sutton with a life insurance policy that paid his debts and very little more. But Margaret Sutton had guts enough to turn to and develop this herb farm which is now famous all over the country. She sold herbs in little packets with recipe books and what-have-you. And then, after Philippine came, she branched out with this so-called laboratory."

"I see. Philippine seems to be her mainstay."

"She is. And old Mrs. Hartwell works for her as bookkeeper and Margie, as you no doubt know, is very energetic in the lab. While all this hard work went on, Catherine played about like a disappointed film star and her brother Roger hid his battle-scarred face from the light of day."

"It must have been grim."

"In a way, yes. People get used to things though. But—considering what has just happened—perhaps I'm wrong—perhaps they don't."

He stopped speaking and stood up at the sound of a car in the road. Then he said quietly, "It's helped to talk. Thanks." A moment later Thane Carey's quick steps could be heard on the walk, the screen door banged, and he was there, hovering over them as if in accusation.

"What is it, Mohun?" he asked.

"Margie's prophesy come true. Catherine Clay dead, and in Fredericka's hammock. Come with me. You stay here," he added brusquely, turning to Fredericka. But his words were wasted. She had no desire to do anything else.

The two men disappeared through the back door and Fredericka sat still on the kitchen stool listening to the very ordinary sound of the bubbling percolater. Before Peter and Thane returned another car roared up in the road outside and braked sharply. Fredericka tried to get up and go to the door but could not bring herself to move. Presently she could hear voices, and then Mrs. Sutton, Mrs. Hartwell and James Brewster walked in the front door without ceremony.

The events of that evening were to remain in Fredericka's memory all the rest of her life, but in odd patches as though a whole series of scenes had been lit with bright lightning flashes and then blotted out with the blackness of deep night.

The two men came in from the garden, looking over-life-sized and awkward in the small house. Mrs. Sutton was helped to a chair in the living room. Fredericka gave them coffee. And through it all could be heard, like an orchestral accompaniment, the thundering imperative demands of James Brewster. He stood with his back to the empty grate holding his coffee cup. Fredericka noticed the heavy dark hairs that covered his large hand and crept like caterpillars down each separate finger. He was like a great disgruntled bear roaring at them all. What did he say? Always the same words, over and over.

"We must keep it quiet until"—until when? "Family name must be protected." In those moments Fredericka found herself hating this blustering animal man and wishing that something—anything—would silence him.

And then at last something did silence him—the voice of authority. Thane Carey said quietly: "I have sent for Doctor Scott and, until he comes and has a look at—at her—we can't have much of any idea of the cause of death. And while we are waiting, I'd like to ask a few routine questions. Do you feel up to this, Mrs. Sutton?"

Margaret Sutton sat forward in the straight chair she had chosen. "It's true then," she said. "Oh, I've been so frightened of this—and then this afternoon when she didn't come I was worried—and I asked James to search for her . . ."

"Really, Carey, this all seems a little unnecessary. We hardly need these police strong-arm methods— My poor Margaret—"

"I'm sorry, Brewster, but I must, as the man in authority, do what seems to me right. I'm afraid you will have to leave my job to me."

"I don't see why you have any job, or indeed why you are here at all. I should think Mohun would have called Dr. Scott at once," James said heavily.

Thane Carey stared at Brewster until the older man turned away with a gesture of disgust.

"You're a lawyer," Carey said at last. "Surely you know that one must take precautions in the case of death so sudden and unexpected as this."

"Precautions?" Brewster flung the word back at him.

"Very well, if you force me to say it. You know as well as I do that there will be an inquest. The police must have the necessary facts."

"Oh dear!" Mrs. Sutton said quietly. It was hardly more than a sigh, but Carey turned to her at once: "I am sorry, terribly sorry about this and, as a matter of fact there's no need for you to stay—I can come and see you tomorrow if necessary . . ."

"Oh no. It's quite all right, Thane. I want to be here with her. She was—she was so *ill* you see. No one, not even I, could help her."

Fredericka, watching Mrs. Sutton's face anxiously, thought for a moment that the woman could not stand the strain. Then with a great effort her thin shoulders straightened, but when she turned to look up at Thane, Fredericka could see that her face was lined with age and ravaged with pain and shock.

The chief of police became businesslike and his questions followed rapidly, one after the other, until they were broken off by the arrival of Doctor Scott.

Fredericka told simply and quietly the exact story of her movements from the moment that she left the house at half past two with Peter until the finding of the body less than an hour ago.

Thane seemed most interested in the fact that she had locked all the doors when she left. "Why?" he asked.

"I don't know exactly. I always do lock my door in New York and it's habit I guess. Also—" she hesitated and then went on slowly—"Well, so many people seem to come and go here and I thought—well—the shop isn't mine and it is my responsibility."

This seemed to satisfy Thane who then turned to Peter. "You saw Fredericka lock up. Didn't that seem odd to you?"

"I didn't see her, as a matter of fact. I called from the gate because I saw that she was ready and waiting for me just by the door. She came straight along when I called. But I wouldn't have thought it odd for a city person with the responsibility of someone else's house, to lock it when she planned to be away for long."

Suddenly Thane turned to James Brewster who, after his rebuke, had gone to stand at the window with his back to the room in an attitude of childish pique. "Margaret says that, this afternoon, she asked you to go and see if you could find Catherine. When was that, and did you?"

Brewster whirled around and a look almost of madness came into his handsome heavy features. "I refuse to answer your questions. I am a lawyer and aware of the law even if these fools are not." He turned back to the window.

"Don't mind him," Mrs. Sutton said gently. "Surely you can understand that this blow has fallen heavily on him—"James Brewster started to break in but stopped when he turned and saw her face. She went on slowly: "I'm sure we all want to be as helpful as we can, and I believe that honest direct answers are the very least we can give you, Thane. James came to the bazaar just before the supper. He was looking for Catherine and we agreed that it would be a good idea for him to make a thorough search 'round the farm and the neighbourhood. You see—" she hesitated "—sometimes when she was unhappy she took some kind of drug that helped her and then she was apt to—to wander off. We both knew this, and that is why we were worried."

At this, James turned around again and glared at Mrs. Sutton. "Really, Margaret, do you want the whole town to know these things? How—how *can* you?"

"I'm sorry, James. I feel sure that Thane knew this already and it wouldn't do for us to conceal anything that might be helpful. The sooner it is all dealt with, the sooner it will be over."

"Thank you, Mrs. Sutton. You have been helpful. Very. Now please forgive me if I ask you one more question. Where were, and are, the other members of your household?"

"Roger and Philippine went off early this morning and must have got back while we were at the supper. I didn't see them and judged they had gone to bed, when I got home. They are usually tired after a day of herb hunting and I didn't speak to either of them. I heard Margie come in. Wasn't that about ten, Martha?"

"I don't know, I'm sure. About then, I expect." Mrs. Hartwell's voice sounded querulous. Fredericka, who had had several occasions during the week to observe Margie's "Mom," thought how much she looked the part. Even now, though obviously agitated, she was also quite unable to disguise her pleasurable excitement. This was, indeed, more than a titbit, for the Village Gossip. Her fat hands moved nervously in her lap and, as she spoke, she thrust her lips forward hungrily.

It was at this point that the doctor's car drew up outside, and, a moment later, he entered the room quietly. He was a middle-aged man, running to fat, and with an untidy family-doctor look about him.

"Evening, folks." He nodded round a little absently as he entered. Then he turned to Thane. "You called me. Where—?"

"Outside," Thane said, and then: "Come—and you, Mohun, if you don't mind."

James Brewster turned once more from his study of the darkness outside the window. "Shouldn't some member of the family go, too?" he asked abruptly.

"No, I think there's no need," Dr. Scott said in his

soft reassuring doctor's voice. "Stay here and we'll come back presently."

After the men had left, Fredericka couldn't think of anything to say to Mrs. Sutton or Mrs. Hartwell, and they sat without speaking. Mrs. Sutton seemed unaware of the presence of the others. Mrs. Hartwell fidgeted nervously and Fredericka felt that the doctor's "presently" had stretched to a very long time when the back screen door banged and the three finally reappeared.

Dr. Scott cleared his throat. Then he looked quickly at Mrs. Sutton and said: "We've had to decide on an autopsy, Margaret. I am sorry—terribly, my dear—but, well, there are certain symptoms that make me unable to determine the exact cause of death."

Mrs. Sutton's hands were clenched tightly in her lap but she said in a low voice: "Of course, Ted, if that's what seems necessary; I'm sure you wouldn't do it otherwise."

And then one of Thane's policemen arrived and moved unobtrusively into the garden. The others stood up to go as if by signal and Mrs. Hartwell said unexpectedly: "Shall I stay with you, Fredericka? I'm sure Margaret can spare me and you won't want to be alone. I'd be glad to."

"It's most kind of you, Mrs. Hartwell," Fredericka said quickly, "but really I'd rather be alone. The policeman's just outside and, well—"

"I quite understand." The usual note of petulance and hurt had returned to Mrs. Hartwell's voice. It would have made a very good story for the next meeting of the Women's Guild—a night of terror. It was obvious to everyone that Mrs. Hartwell did *not* understand, but Fredericka was too exhausted to care.

Fredericka walked to the door and, as she stood for

a moment on the walk outside, she saw that the sky was lightening along the horizon with the first hint of dawn. A bird had wakened to make his announcement to the sleeping world, and Fredericka was grateful to him for his note of cheerfulness. Peter dropped behind the others.

"Sure you're all right?" he asked.

"Quite sure. I'm more than ready for bed."

"Good." He put a firm hand on her shoulder for a moment and then hurried after the others.

But when Fredericka returned to the empty house and the soiled coffee cups, a weight of depression fell on her. And when, with determination, she turned her back on the untidiness and went upstairs to bed, she could not sleep. She turned the pillow and moved from one side of the bed to the other, but she could not forget the cold body of Catherine Clay lying below in the garden and the wretched policeman keeping his silent vigil. Why hadn't they taken her away at once?

Finally, Fredericka switched on the light and got up to put on her bath robe. It was much better, she decided to give up the struggle. She went downstairs, collected the dirty cups and made a fresh pot of coffee. When she called the policeman, he came in and took the coffee gratefully but refused to sit down. He went back to his job, taking his steaming cup with him and Fredericka took hers to the office. Then she opened the middle desk drawer, drew out the notes for her projected book and, with her head in her hands, in a proper attitude of concentration, she began to study them intently. The lives of her three industrious "scribbling women" began to shape themselves in her mind and she reached for a block of paper with eagerness born of her sudden creative impulse and the blessed relief it gave her. It was a long time later that she looked at her watch and saw that it was half past five. Outside, the sky was streaked with crimson and the tentative bird song had now become a mighty chorus. She stood up and stretched. Then, after a moment of indecision, she tiptoed to the kitchen and, with the fascination of horror, stared out at the hammock and the dead body of Catherine Clay. Behind it the figure of the policeman paced slowly up and down like a symbol of grief.

Fredericka had worked away her morbid fears and now, having looked at the body, she felt relieved of the weight of mystery. She could sleep at last and the whole day lay ahead. Sunday. Blessed thought. Unless, of course, the police came to perform their macabre duties and go on with their endless questioning. Surely not that, again. She lifted one weary leg after the other and went up the stairs to bed.

In a few hours dawn brightened into day and the sun streamed in across the carpet, but Fredericka slept on.

5

On a desert island somewhere in the blue Pacific, Fredericka was just reaching up to pick a large grapefruit for her breakfast when she was startled by the sound of tom-toms in the distance. She stood still and listened, tense with fear. The noise increased until it became rolling thunder and then, near at hand, she could hear the clamor of human voices, calling out again and again, as if in distress.

At this moment she woke up. The tom-toms became loud knocks at the front door of Miss Hartwell's bookshop. The voices became one voice, calling, "Miss Wing," and then, more urgently, *"Miss Wing,* are you there?"

With the sound, she returned from the dream to the nightmare of reality—the death of Catherine Clay and the long night. It was Thane Carey who was calling because the police had come as she had feared they must. She looked at her watch—only nine o'clock—and she had planned to sleep the whole day, dreaming away on golden sands under azure skies. But there was no escape.

The thumping became more urgent. She went out onto the landing and called down the stairs, making no effort to keep the fury from her voice.

"Very well, I hear you. For goodness sake can't you even give me time to put on my bathrobe?"

The knocking stopped and Fredericka went back to her room. She took her time but it did not sooth her ruffled spirits. Some moments later she went down the stairs and unlocked the front door.

Thane Carey and a policeman stood outside.

"Well," she said rudely.

"Good morning." Thane took off his hat and looked at her intently. "You locked the door again."

This unwise remark was the spark to set off her smouldering anger. "Yes, and wouldn't you yourself do the same after all that's happened here. And didn't I tell you last night that I have city habits, perfectly good ones that I hang on to, even in the backwoods of Massachusetts," she exploded.

"I'm sorry, Miss Wing, if I've disturbed you." Was there a hint of a smile on his face? Really this was unbearable. "I'm afraid it's all in the line of duty. May we come in?"

"If you must, you must." Fredericka stepped aside for them to enter, and then turned to go back upstairs.

"I'd like to have a few words with you, Miss Wing, if it's possible," the chief of police announced to her retreating back.

She looked down from the landing. "Very well, but, if you don't have any objection, I would like to dress first."

"By all means. There's no rush. I'm going to put my

two men onto a thorough examination of the grounds.
And I will do the house myself, if you don't mind."

Fredericka said nothing in reply. What was there to
say to this officious intrusion? She went into her bed-
room, shut the door and started to dress slowly. The
routine movements had a quieting effect on her and she
began reluctantly to regret her unreasonable anger, and
to remember that Thane Carey even if he was the chief
of police of South Sutton, was also Peter Mohun's friend.

She finished dressing quickly and hurried down the
stairs to find Thane busily reading her sheets of manuscript on the desk. At this sight, her anger boiled up
again, but she managed to keep it in check, and she
made no mention of this unpardonable act of prying.
Instead she said, slowly: "I'm afraid I was rude to you.
You see, you woke me up to all this mess and I've had
more than enough of it already."

"You don't like death in the country as much as you
thought you would, then?"

"I guess I'd rather keep it inside covers," she admitted. Was he implying that this was not a natural death?
What did he mean? She had been talking yesterday
about *murder,* and this— "Will you have some breakfast
with me?" she said quickly. "I think, if you don't mind, I'll
have some anyway. I—I need it!"

"Of course, and I'll join you with pleasure, but just
for coffee. I've eaten already."

Fredericka retreated to the kitchen and tried not to
look out the window. But the impulse was too strong for
her and then she saw with relief that, not only the body,
but the hammock as well, had disappeared. In the near
distance a policeman was beating his way slowly and
systematically through the shrubbery like a bloodhound

on the scent. She turned away from the window and busied herself with breakfast.

Twenty minutes later she sat opposite Thane Carey at the small kitchen table. Sun streamed in through the open window that looked out on the back yard. The sound of bees already busy in the petunias bordering the path outside, emphasized the heavy silence between them. At last Thane spoke, but he looked down at the black coffee in his cup and stirred it unnecessarily.

"I'm sorry about this, Miss Wing," he said quietly. "Yesterday at the bazaar you and Mohun and my wife and I were friends theorizing about murder. Today, mur—" he coughed, "today death has made a sudden change in our relationship. You must forgive me for my intrusion on your privacy. When these things happen we policemen are forced to forget everything but our duty. All the same, I see no reason why we can't both make the best of it and continue to be friends."

"Of course, and I am sorry. I'm not my best in the early morning. Coffee helps, though." They smiled at each other across the table and then, before Thane could speak, Fredericka continued quickly: "You—you don't think it really is *murder,* do you? Mrs. Sutton said she sometimes took dope. Couldn't it be just an overdose by accident as she suggested—or—or at best, suicide—?"

Something in her tone made Carey look up and study her face. "I don't know a thing, and I haven't meant to imply anything, either. We must wait for an autopsy. May I ask why *you* think it to be murder? You don't honestly believe it to be either accident or suicide, do you?"

"I—Why? Oh dear, you're too clever for me. I suppose I have felt it to be so from the start. Perhaps it's just because I had too much to say yesterday. But, well, something in that awful look on her face—and, you'll not forgive me for this—something in the *atmosphere*—has made me imagine things."

"I see. Well, now, my policeman reports that you kept the light on all night. If you wanted company why didn't you let Mrs. Hartwell stay?"

"Oh, I couldn't sleep; so I got up, made coffee, and worked on my book. In this way I succeeded in wearing myself out and finally went to bed."

"I saw your manuscript. Is it to be a novel?"

"No—about some Victorian women novelists, though."

He looked at her with more interest. "I try to write myself but, strange as it may seem in this quiet town, I don't have much spare time. At the moment I'm struggling with crime in its wider aspects, but some day I'm going to take a busman's holiday and write a really good detective story."

Fredericka laughed a little shamefacedly. "Yes," she said quickly. "I gathered as much from what you said at the bazaar yesterday. Perhaps—after this—we can collaborate."

Fredericka saw at once that she had blundered. A mask suddenly hid the pleasant face opposite her and the chief of police said: "Perhaps. Well, I must get on with my work." He stood up and walked toward the door, then he turned to say casually: "You didn't miss anything from the house when you got back last night, did you?"

"I hardly had time to. But I haven't noticed anything wrong this morning. I'll look around if you like."

"Good. I'll be pottering about myself inside and outside, but please don't take any notice of me or of my men. We'll try to disturb you as little as possible, and we should finish and be off within the hour."

Fredericka nodded and then, when he had turned to go, a sudden thought occurred to her. "Oh, heavens—there's that old well at the back of the house. Its cover has rotted away and one of your men may stumble into it. I—I never thought. Chris told me about it and I've been meaning to write to Miss Hartwell but I haven't had time to do anything."

"Thanks for telling me. As a matter of fact, one of my men discovered it without falling in, I'm happy to say, and I think he's put something over it, but it does want looking after."

"Thanks. I'm terribly sorry and I'll get Chris to see what he can do."

Again the chief of police's face became Thane Carey's, the two smiled at each other, and Fredericka got up to wash the dishes with a somewhat lighter heart. By the time she had finished, Thane had completed his round of the downstairs rooms and she could hear him walking about overhead. She decided to go back to her writing and escape all her police visitors until she was free of them.

Some time later, Thane appeared in the doorway, and when she looked up, he said quietly: "We find nothing out of the way in the house and only a few oddments in the grounds and outhouses that can probably be explained away in ten minutes. We haven't touched anything except to take a few fingerprints and I don't intend to bother you with any more questions until I get the doctor's report on the autopsy. Until then, please consider yourself a free woman and"—he looked at her directly—"and, again, my apologies and thanks."

When he had gone, Fredericka tried to get back to

her writing but the interruption had broken the spell, and though she struggled with one sentence for some moments she was forced in the end to give up and throw down her pencil. It was then that she realized how hot the day had become. Even as she sat quietly at her desk she felt sticky and breathless. She lit a cigarette and felt better. Then she got up to go into the kitchen and see if her watch could possibly be right. To her surprise she found that the loudly ticking alarm clock agreed that it was almost one. She made herself a salad and iced coffee and took her lunch on a tray out to a shady corner of the back porch. Then she went back to get a book. Trollope's autobiography ought to give her comfort of a very solid kind.

But in spite of having all the ingredients to spell peace and contentment, Fredericka could not sit still for long. The house and the grounds were too quiet in the heavy summer heat.

Why hadn't Peter come to see how she was? Why did everyone keep away? Surely she had had enough evidence of small town curiosity to know that this lack of it was strange. Perhaps the police had put a cordon outside to protect her. At this thought she laughed outright. A "cordon"—a good word for South Sutton, boasting a chief and two overgrown country boys who were his "force."

She thought over the questions Thane had asked her and the last remarks he had made before leaving. It was all very well for him to accuse her of thinking up things when it was quite evident that he himself suspected that Catherine Clay's death was 'unnatural'. Otherwise why did he suddenly become formal and ask her questions? Why was he so stiff and so obviously relieved when he left her, and was able to say that he had found nothing whatever out of the way in the house? But what had he said about the grounds? "Only a few odd-ments"— Whatever could he mean by that?

On a sudden impulse, Fredericka got up, walked down the steps on to the path and began, systematically, to explore the shrubbery and outbuildings as Thane's policemen must have done.

It was high time that she had a look around anyway. It had been a very busy morning that Chris had inconve-niently chosen to show her the well with its rotting cover and her other visits to the outbuildings had been mainly to the old stable where, as Chris had explained, Miss Lucy stored her "extry books."

Skirting the spot where the hammock had hung, she went from the patch of lawn at that side of the house on through the tangle of bushes and weeds until she came to a tall wire fence that must mark the end of Miss Hartwell's land. She then followed this boundary until she came to the stable storehouse which faced an alley that ran parallel to Beech Street and marked the end of Miss Hartwell's land at the back. The alley must origi-nally have been the carriage entrance to the stable. Fredericka took the key from its nail by the door, un-locked it and went inside. But she did not stay long. A quick look sufficed to show her that all was in order—at least more or less in order. Her survey told her that the stock needed attention, but the empty packing cases were in the old horse stalls and the books that had been unpacked were in orderly piles on shelves in the large central room. Well, she couldn't bother with the stock now. She was glad to escape from the heat inside the stuffy building.

Fredericka next followed the fence as it continued along the alley and was broken by the gate which was the entrance for the back path to the house. About twenty yards beyond the gate she came to an unexpected gap in the fence where the wires had been pressed back and an entrance forced. At this point the shrubbery was especially dense so that the spot was quite hidden. But who would want to force an entrance here when the gate was always open? She looked at the gap carefully and saw that the bent wires were rusted. It was not a recent break then. Some child's prank perhaps.

As she pushed her way on through the shrubbery she came suddenly on another building which she had never seen before. It was evidently an old greenhouse with large leaded panes of broken glass over half the roof and one side. She approached the battered door and was aware of a sudden feeling of apprehension. But when she summoned courage to push it open there was nothing much inside. The room was whitewashed but moss had grown over the stones at the base of the walls and the dirt floor looked damp. The place had, in fact, a thoroughly disused look, except for three or four very odd and surprising things. On the wall facing her at the end of the narrow room hung a mirror. Below it was a small shelf and a chair. Fredericka walked across to examine the objects on the shelf and to her further amazement found them to be a complete makeup kit and various and sundry odd bottles containing pinkish and bluish liquids, and on the shelf nearby a pile of old magazines and comics.

"Exactly like an actress's dressing room," Fredericka said aloud and was relieved at the ordinary sound of her own voice. But perhaps a little damp and chill for a real *prima donna*. More like a playacting child. Yes, certainly, much more like Margie Hartwell. Undoubtedly, these were the oddments discovered by the police. Certainly they were odd, but equally certainly they could be explained away in ten minutes. No doubt Mrs. Hartwell disapproved. She would, of course. Poor Margie. Would any amount of cosmetics ever help that face?

Of course this would explain the gap in the fence, too. Fredericka was able now to laugh at her senseless fears. She closed the door quietly behind her and stood still for a moment. Yes, it seemed obvious that it must have been Margie who had forced the break in the fence in order to get in and out from alley to greenhouse without being seen.

There was little more left to explore except the orchard on the other side of the house but Fredericka felt restless and the thought of going back to the empty house depressed her. It would be better to get right away. She took Margie's quick exit into the alley and turned left to walk in the opposite direction from the town.

Before long the alley road became a narrow track through a thick wood. Ancient trees reached up on either side to make a leafy screen from the hot afternoon sun. It was cooler in the deep shade but Fredericka was aware of a dank smell of decay as in the crypt of an old church. The air was heavy and after walking on for some time, Fredericka grew tired. In spite of herself, she was oppressed by the silence, and when she saw a break in the trees ahead where a granite boulder crouched like a sleeping elephant, she decided to climb its back and sit down to rest. She found a perch on the top that was reasonably comfortable and shaded by a clump of white birches that seemed to be growing out of the rock itself.

Perhaps she could sleep here and make up for her broken night and busy morning. She tried to lie down but the rock which looked so like the soft unresisting back of an animal, proved a most resisting and uncomfortable mattress. She sat up again and hugged her knees. Now she could hear the muted forest sounds—birds chattering quietly in the branches overhead, the faint rustle made by some small animal pushing its way through the undergrowth and the gentle creaking of the trees. Even here, sitting still, the heat weighed down on her. It's as bad as the subway in rush hour, she thought; oppressive—like a physical presence. She put her forehead into the palms of her hands and sighed. There was no escape anywhere.

Then she heard it—the sudden definite sound that could only be a human step. She sat up and listened. Yes. It came again—a heavy crunch, slow and unmistakable.

Fredericka felt an unreasoning panic. Who could be here, walking like this, with stealthy purposeful steps? They seemed to be coming in her direction. If only she could find a place to hide—or bring herself to make a dash for it and run away. But she could not move and she knew herself to be exposed like a statue on her rock. She must already have been seen. In an agony of suspense she heard herself call out weakly: "Who's that?"

Silence.

Again she called out, trying to keep the panic from her voice.

Then someone said: "I'm sorry. I've frightened you."

Fredericka swung around and there, directly below her, through the trees, she saw Roger Sutton. She stared at him without speaking and he looked quickly away. She struggled to find words and finally managed to say: "It's all right" and then, as if some explanation for her presence was needed, she added: "I—just wanted to get away—"

"So did I," he said quietly. Then, almost accusingly, "You found my rock."

"*Your* rock?"

"I'm sorry. It isn't mine, of course, but I've always come here to be by myself ever since I was a kid."

Fredericka, on a sudden impulse, said slowly, "Well, come and sit here now. I'm about to leave anyway."

"No. I'll just go on."

"Please stay for a minute anyway," Fredericka heard herself say, with some surprise. She felt suddenly sorry for this young man who, though he would never be lost in the woods of South Sutton, was so obviously lost in himself.

Roger sat down at a lower level of the rock and turned his back to her. "Forgive me if I seem rude," he said slowly. "It isn't you. It's just—I can't bear being looked at."

"I know," Fredericka answered him quickly. "You don't happen to have a cigarette, do you?"

Roger fished a crumpled packet from his pocket and started to toss it up to her. Then, relenting, he climbed up to hand it to her and stayed to light her cigarette and his own. She did not look at his face and, presently, he sat down near her. They smoked in silence for a moment and then Roger said, "Philippine says my next operation will be successful. Then, perhaps, I won't be the object of pity—or disgust, any longer. Still, I don't believe her."

"I expect Philippine does know though."

"Yes. But she might be trying to kid me. Oh hell, I don't know—or care much any more. At any rate I don't look a fright to Philippine. She's seen plenty worse. She was right through the war in France, you know. Mostly in a concentration camp."

"Yes. I heard that."

"Already?"

"It's a small town. But as a matter of fact, she told me herself." Fredericka laughed a little self-consciously. "And—I guess a bookshop manager can't help soaking up gossip like a sponge."

Roger's answering laugh was pleasant and genuine but he stood up suddenly. "I'm sorry but I must go now. I—I can't sit still for long."

"I'm sorry, too," Fredericka said, and meant it.

"You've been kind," Roger said. "I don't know when I've talked as much as this to—to anyone—except mother and Philippine." He stopped abruptly. Then as he jumped down from the rock he turned to say fiercely, "Everything was just beginning to get right. And then Catherine had to come home—"

The bitterness and hatred in his voice startled Fredericka, but she sensed that if she was to keep him from dashing off into the forest, like the wild creature he was, she must make herself as emotionless as possible. She said quietly, "Please, may I have one more cigarette before you go?"

"Of course," he answered her at once and she noticed with relief that the tension of his body relaxed as he spoke. "You must forgive me," he went on more slowly. "Catherine has made my life a misery from the time we were kids. She was four years older than I and she was a sadist by the time she was ten. She knew all my hidden fears—all my weaknesses—and she hated me because mother loved me in a way she never loved Catherine. It's the old story, I guess—"

He stopped, and Fredericka stared at him. A shadow

fell across his scarred face as a breeze moved the leaves overhead and, in that instant, Fredericka saw the naked hatred in his eyes and in the set of his jaw. Could this man be the killer of his sister—this man, suffering his own private hell and goaded beyond endurance? Why should he talk to her—Fredericka—a complete stranger—like this, unless he wanted to cover up with a show of honesty. Now she wanted him to go. She stood up, as panic seized her, and then she heard herself say in a voice that was hard and unrecognizable: "I'm surprised you admit these things—now."

For a moment Roger stared at Fredericka in his turn and his ugly face became more than ever distorted. He took a step back toward the rock and Fredericka knew that he wanted to strike out at her. But he controlled the mad impulse with an effort that was apparent in every line of his thin body. Then, without a word, he turned away and disappeared as suddenly as he had come.

The breeze moved again through the branches of the trees and its breath was dank and cold. Fredericka climbed down from the rock and then, fighting a childish impulse to dash to safety, made her way back to the path. But the black demon of her own fear pursued her through the Hansel and Gretel wood until at last she reached the haven afforded by the four walls of Miss Hartwell's bookshop.

6

If Fredericka had not been in so compelling a hurry to leave the town for the woods and had turned right instead of left when she crawled through Margie's foxhole she would have run straight into her friend, Peter Mohun, and James Brewster. They were standing, on that hot Sunday afternoon, at the corner of Spruce Street and the alley, and they were in earnest conversation.

"Are you really going to build there, Brewster?" Peter asked. He was a little resentful of the fields he was now indicating with a sweep of his right hand. He had been looking for James all morning only to discover him pacing over the great tract of land fronting on this miserable alley. In the search, Peter had missed his lunch and he was now tired, hot and hungry. Moreover, James was still truculent.

"I can't think what business it is of yours, Mohun." James was also hot and tired but he had eaten a large Sunday dinner at the inn and he was not hungry. On the contrary, he was aware that he had eaten too much. He was troubled by indigestion and by his thoughts which were in a state of turmoil.

"It isn't my business. But all the town is talking about it so it's no secret. Better facts than rumours."

"I'm sorry not to be more helpful," James answered sourly. "This town talks too much anyway. And then you and Carey have to go and create scandal that doesn't exist. You're a fine one to talk about rumours as against facts."

This was better. Peter said quickly: "That's really what I wanted to talk to you about. Let's see if we can get a beer at the inn."

"There's nothing more to say after all your fuss last night."

"I think there is."

Perhaps a beer would help. "Well, anyway, let's not stand here and broil."

They walked along Spruce Street and crossed the road to the Coach and Horses. Peter secured two beers and they went out to sit in the shade of the garden. It was deserted, and a little cooler than inside.

For some moments they were silent and then Peter said, "You know, Brewster, that if you persist in this attitude, you're going to become an object of suspicion in the town."

"Suspicion of what?"

"Murder."

James put his mug down heavily and the beer slopped over the edge and ran down in little rivers on to the table top.

"And who, I would like to know, has said anything about murder?"

"Granted we won't know for certain until we get the result of the autopsy, but Dr. Scott, Carey and I haven't liked the look of this from the moment we saw Catherine's body. There were certain symptoms that looked too much like poisoning—"

"Poison? Nonsense! She took too much dope. We all knew it would get her if she didn't stop."

"Yes. You all knew. It made a wonderful blind, didn't it, Brewster?"

"See here, just what are you driving at?"

"You tried, last night, to hush everything up. You thought Dr. Ted would let it slip by as you wanted him to. But he wouldn't have. Even if Carey and I hadn't been there, he wouldn't have. He's no country bumpkin, James. That's where you miscalculated."

James gripped the edge of the table. The beer tasted sour in his mouth. "You're insinuating things, Mohun. What's more, you have no grounds whatever for these insinuations—"

"All right then. You went to look for Catherine yesterday afternoon. Where did you look? If you have nothing to conceal you should be quite willing to supply this information."

James's face was now green in colour. He put his head in his hands and said nothing.

"You've got to come clean, Brewster. You know it as well as I do, and it might as well be now. After the autopsy it will look worse."

James began to draw pictures with one hairy finger, tracing the beer across the wooden boards of the table. "All right, then," he said slowly, as though choosing his words with great care, "I went first to the Farm. Looked all over the damn place. Not a soul anywhere. Back to the fields out there. I suppose the rumours also had it that Catherine and I were going to get married. She had that in mind, too, and she was obsessed with this idea of my building a palace for her—"

"You weren't obsessed with it?"

"No. Hell, I'm not a marrying man, Mohun. You know that. I'm only just this side of fifty— I've steered clear this long and I intend to stay clear."

"Then what were you doing over in those fields just now?"

"What? Oh, just having a last look around . . ." James said lamely. He took out a handkerchief and wiped his forehead.

"Well—did you find Catherine?"

"Yes. That is, I found her body."

"What?"

"Yes. She wasn't in the fields so I went by the bookshop. She'd said something about taking back that book she'd taken out on Sunday. And there she was—just like you found her—dead in that damned hammock. The book was on the ground. I—I picked it up. And then I panicked. My God, I didn't want to marry the b—the woman—but I didn't want her dead."

"You're quite sure about that?"

"What? See here, Mohun, you're not accusing me, are you? I'm telling you the truth—though God knows why I am." James got up unsteadily. "I'm ill. That's all I have to say. And, what's more, I'll stick to it—autopsy or no autopsy. I left the—body—exactly as it was. I've got the book in my apartment if you want it."

"Yes. I'll just go back with you and collect it— By the way, Brewster," he added as he followed the older man out of the inn, "just why didn't you report this— er—find of yours to the—shall we say since you seemed so insistent on this point last night—to Dr. Scott?"

"Look here, Mohun, I've talked too damn much as it

is. But I'll confess, since I've been such a fool already, that I—well—I just plain didn't want to get involved in this thing. I've got my profession to think of—and my position in this town. She was dead. I couldn't do anything about that. I decided to let someone else find the body—And that is *fact.*"

"I see. It's very clear, Brewster. So you went—where?"

"Back to my apartment. I didn't feel like facing the crowds at that damned church do. I had a few drinks. Later I went out to the Farm—now don't ask me when—I don't know exactly. But I hadn't been there long when you called— And that's every word I'll say."

"Well, thanks then, Brewster. As I said before, it's all quite, quite clear."

As the two men were walking slowly along Beech Street to James's apartment, Fredericka was recovering in the sitting room chair of Miss Hartwell's bookshop. She could still see Roger staring at her, his hands clenching and unclenching at his sides. But she had behaved like a child. Margie Hartwell would have behaved better.

Margie Hartwell. Poor child, with her miserable secret hiding place in the old greenhouse. No wonder she kept making sudden appearances. No wonder she resented the presence of a stranger in her aunt's bookshop. But why was her resentment so deep-seated? All week long she had hindered rather than helped Fredericka. She had even left an ugly caricature between the pages of Fredericka's manuscript. The drawing had been crude but the likeness to herself had been unmistakable. There was no doubt who the artist was, of course, even though Margie had denied all knowledge of it. A tiresome, troublesome teenager but, in the light of today's discoveries, perhaps more to be pitied than despised.

Peter Mohun pitied her but then Margie behaved better to him. Probably he would also pity Roger and have no sympathy with Fredericka's fears. But he would have to agree that Margie and Roger both hated Catherine Clay. Still, there was nothing extraordinary in that. No one had loved Catherine, not even James Brewster, unless his attitude toward her in the inn last Sunday had been merely the result of some lovers' quarrel. But it hadn't seemed so. No, if what Roger had said was true, Catherine had had little love, even from her own mother.

But these thoughts were getting her nowhere. She looked at her watch and discovered, to her amazement, that it was only a few minutes past four. She got up, went to the desk in the office, and pulled her writing things toward her with a gesture of fierce determination. This time she made some progress but the afternoon grew steadily hotter, and presently she began to nod.

After a brief struggle against sleep, she got up, climbed the stairs slowly and threw herself onto her bed. She fell at once into a heavy sleep, from which she did not waken until the church clock was striking six. She turned over and was coming slowly to consciousness when she became instantly wide awake and aware of the frightening silence. To quiet her nerves and restore her common sense, Fredericka got up quickly and went to the bathroom to throw cold water on her hot face. After this she felt better, but no amount of private bustle could dispel the loneliness of the empty house. "Haunted Bookshop" it is, she thought: altogether too haunted. On a sudden impulse, she decided to change her clothes and go to the inn for supper.

As she started down the front path, the sun was

setting behind angry thunderclouds. She scowled up at the sky, and then decided to go back for her raincoat. The house seemed emptier than ever, and she dreaded the thought of returning after dark.

When she walked up the driveway of the Coach and Horses she could hear the hum of voices inside. Goodness, she thought, it's like a swarm of bees. The whole town must be there. And then she heard herself say out loud: "I hope to goodness it isn't a party."

To her amazement, someone behind her answered: "Not a party. It's only that everyone with any sense takes advantage of the inn's Sunday night special. It's a buffet supper, famed far and wide."

The voice with its slight foreign accent and hissing s's was familiar and Fredericka turned quickly to find Philippine Sutton close on her heels.

"Goodness, I didn't hear you come up behind me. I must get over this tiresome habit of talking to myself. It comes from living too much alone."

"I'm sorry if I frightened you. I wear these sandals in the lab and half the time I forget to change them when I take off my white coat. I do apologize. I didn't realize I was creeping up on you like that."

"It's quite all right. And I *am* glad to see you again."

It was true. Of all the people at the farm, Philippine was the most approachable and friendly. Mrs. Sutton had seemed to belong to another world, or to be wrapped in a magic mantle that made her all but invisible to ordinary human beings. Perhaps the wretched woman had made this for herself as a protection from the troubles and anxieties of her life. What a strange and difficult family. Peter had told her that Mr. Sutton had died in 1929 or 1930. There were stories about him, too—that he had hanged himself when his financial losses had overwhelmed him. And then Mrs. Sutton had been left with Catherine who had taken to dope and been consumed with self-interest—even cruel, if what Roger said was true. Roger, himself, a misfit in the post-war world—neurotic and half-crazed by his hatred of his sister. Who else? "Mom" Hartwell who had been taken in to do the accounts. Was she just the stupid conventional gossip she seemed, or was she really a far more sinister character? Her daughter Margie—capable of all the worst manifestations of adolescence. All these ill-assorted people had lived together at the Farm—with Philippine who managed them all. It didn't bear thinking about, she decided, as she followed the neat figure of the French woman into the crowded living room.

Everyone looked up to stare as the two women entered, and Fredericka was once more grateful to Philippine for her sudden appearance and protecting presence. No wonder Roger found her so comforting—perhaps he was in love with her. That would be a further complication to add to the general confusion.

"What do we do now?" Fredericka had suddenly become aware that she had been romancing, and she asked the question with real anxiety.

"The food's laid out in the dining room. We get what we want and then eat it where we like. The maids bring you coffee. You pay in advance—in the dining room."

Fredericka followed Philippine into the dining room and then gasped at the array of food spread out on the tables.

"I know, it is tremendous, is it not?" Philippine asked and Fredericka wondered if she had again been guilty of speaking her thoughts outloud.

"Tremendous doesn't begin to describe it," Fredericka answered at once. She continued to follow Philippine around, heaping her plate with lobster, cold turkey and ham, salad and rolls. Then she saw with dismay that Philippine had taken only a small slice of turkey and a bit of salad. "Oh dear, I've been too greedy," she said, blushing.

"Nonsense. I expect you haven't had a Sunday dinner like ours at the Farm. Come battle, murder or sudden death our meals go on— Oh, Mon Dieu, what do I say . . . ?"

Fredericka put her hand on the woman's arm and felt it to be trembling. "It must have been awful there today," she said simply.

Philippine flashed her a look of gratitude and then, as they moved together to the large screened porch at the other side of the living room, Margie approached them.

"Gosh!" she said to Fredericka and then, again, "Gosh! May I sit with you and *please* will you tell me all about it?" In the excitement of the moment she seemed to have forgotten her former enmity.

Fredericka was completely unprepared for this direct assault, and, to her horror, other townspeople whom she had met at the bazaar and as customers in the bookshop crowded around with anxious questions. Fredericka looked desperately for a protector, but there was no sign of Peter Mohun or Thane Carey; and Philippine had been pushed to the outer rim of the circle that had now closed in around her.

"There really isn't anything to say," Fredericka muttered a little wildly. "It's all been so sudden and so very dreadful. Can't we— Oh, please can't we, just forget about it tonight?" How could they behave like this?

But Margie persisted and several others continued to support her with urgent questions.

Fredericka felt suddenly faint and the pile of food on her plate sickened her. It was at this moment that Dr. Scott's pleasant face appeared directly in front of her.

"Margie, I'm surprised at you," he said, but with more affection than reproof in his voice. "Suppose that you had come home from the bazaar last night to find a dead body in your hammock, would you feel like eating your Sunday night supper if you had to talk about it?"

"Oh!" said Margie, ignoring the subtle reproof. "Oh, so you *did* find Catherine's body in the hammock. Gosh! Oh, I *wish* I'd been there. And do you remember, Fredericka, how I *predicted* it at the bazaar? What I don't understand though, is *how* she ever got there. And *when* do you think?"

By now the press around Fredericka was overpowering. The doctor was forced to put up his plump hand and raise his voice so that it could be heard in every corner of the room.

"I want you to understand that we're not going to hold an inquest here in the inn on a pleasant social Sunday evening. If I hear one more question or remark from any of you, I'll inject a quick silencing shot without a moment's hesitation. My black bag's just outside in the car. Come on, Miss Wing, let's sit down over in that corner. I want to get some reading advice and I understand that, like dear Lucy, you're an authority."

Fredericka longed to put down her laden plate and hug him and, even as it was, she gave him a smile of such heartfelt gratitude that the old man became her friend for life.

At that moment there was a sudden flash of lightning followed immediately by a deep rumble of thunder. It was as though the doctor had been supported by a sign from heaven, and the crowd fell back to let them pass through.

"Sit down here next to me," he remarked as he found two empty chairs. And then, when they were settled comfortably, he fished in his pocket and handed her a small bottle of pills. "Just in case you may find it hard to sleep. Won't hurt you. Good for the nerves, in fact, and I don't know who has a better right to nerves than you do."

"Oh, thank you. You are kind," Fredericka said quickly. "But I expect I'll be all right in a day or two."

"Let's hope we all are." He looked thoughtful and then added, half to himself, "But somehow I can't believe that we'll put all this behind us for some time to come."

"Can't you? Why not?" Fredericka asked at once.

"I was talking to myself, but since, like the old fool I am, I thought out loud, I must explain. We won't know the result of the autopsy before Wednesday or Thursday but something tells me that, when we do, it'll knock the lid right off this town. I may be exaggerating. I may even," he tried to smile, "be wrong, so let's forget it. Instead I want you to tell me what you've got in the library that's new and good escape-reading for a hard-working doctor."

The obvious device worked, and soon Fredericka found herself talking about the latest fiction and nonfiction, then about her job as a librarian and then a great deal about herself—a fact which she was to remember later with some shame.

Philippine came up with a fudge sundae and a large piece of sponge cake which she handed to Fredericka in exchange for her empty plate. Presently she returned with her own, and sat down on the arm of Fredericka's chair.

"I've been listening to you and Doctor Ted, and I've got some reading problems too. But I expect you're too tired tonight."

She stopped and Fredericka said at once, "Oh, no, I'm not in the least tired. As a matter of fact I broke all my rules and had a nap this afternoon." Perhaps, after all, she had been wrong about Philippine. Perhaps they were going to have time to be friends. "Do you like murders, too?"

"We can't seem to get away from them, can we?" Philippine asked quickly. "No—I don't like to read about them. These stories are so stupid and obvious. But I have to confess I like—how do you call it—?"

"Westerns," Doctor Ted put in. "I know your weakness because I share it, and Lucy Hartwell told me about you in order to reassure me and, I suspect, encourage me." He chuckled good-naturedly.

"I've got some new ones in, as a matter of fact," Fredericka said. "Why don't you both walk back with me and get a supply?"

"Good idea," the doctor agreed. "The only trouble is that I'll have to be polite and let Philippine have all the best ones."

"No, Dr. Ted, this time you can have the lot. I want something I can bite into—"

"I've got the new Evelyn Waugh," Fredericka offered.

"Have you read it?"

"No, but I dare to recommend him without a reading."

"Good girl," Dr. Scott said, "and," he added, "a good

business woman, perhaps. Well, the storm seems to have rumbled itself away into the distance. Shall we go along before it decides to come back?" He struggled to his feet from the low chair.

As they walked back together, Fredericka wondered if Philippine and the doctor were aware of her stupid fears and were simply being kind. But she was reassured when they came inside when she suggested it; and sat down in the sitting room.

"I've just remembered that some books came in the other day that must have been ordered for you, Philippine," Fredericka said.

"Yes? What are they, then?"

"All about herbs and things, I think. I'll go and see if you like."

"Oh no, don't bother," Philippine said. "I didn't order them but it may have been Mrs. Sutton. She does most of the professional reading. Anyway, right now I don't believe any of us want anything but our escapes."

"Quite right, too," Dr. Scott agreed. "Well, you get your novel and I'll take my westerns. This young lady ought to get some sleep."

Fredericka went to collect the books and when she returned the other two stood up at once.

"Now one last word of advice, Miss Wing, if you'll forgive me," Dr. Scott said. "Take a warm bath, swallow one of my pink pills, and then straight to bed and not another thought before morning."

After they had gone, Fredericka took Dr. Scott's advice but she did have a few thoughts before she drifted off to sleep. For some reason she hadn't mentioned her afternoon's encounter with Roger. She would have liked to have asked Dr. Scott and Philippine more about him, but some instinct had held her back. Perhaps it was just as well. Too many people already did too much talking in South Sutton, Mass.

7

All Sunday night the thunder rumbled in the distance and lightning flashed along the horizon. In the morning Fredericka woke to find the air still heavy, and the storm clouds black in an angry sky. She dressed slowly feeling the weight of the day pressing against her temples. It might be Dr. Scott's pill, it might be this sultry morning or it might just be herself, she thought, as she moved slowly about the house in an effort to plan the day's work that faced her. Coffee would help, and coffee did help, but Fredericka did not have time to eat breakfast before the customers began to arrive. By eleven o'clock Christopher had not shown up for work and Fredericka felt as though she had been standing upright in a torture chamber all night long. Then, just as she thought that she could count on a free moment, the screen door banged again and the minister and his wife came in.

After a perfunctory greeting, the Reverend Archibald and Mrs. Williams turned to study the shelves in an absorbed manner while Frederick hovered about.

She knew that, like everyone else, they had come to ask questions. She watched their solid backs with resignation, and wondered if she dared to tell them that she hadn't had breakfast, and ask if they would excuse her long enough to make fresh coffee and boil an egg. But just as she had summoned courage to make this suggestion, the minister turned around to ask if she had Bertrand Russell's latest book. She had, but it was in the stable with the batch of books that Chris had brought up on Saturday. She should have unpacked them yesterday . . .

"I'll just have to run down to the stockroom and get it for you," Fredericka said. "Or I can send it around later when Chris comes," she suggested hopefully.

"I'd rather like to see it here if you don't mind," Mr. Williams said. "That is, of course, if it isn't too much trouble."

"No, of course, no trouble at all," Fredericka answered over her shoulder as she hurried away. Best to get it over with and then perhaps they would ask their questions and go.

She found the book without much difficulty but it was obvious that the stockroom needed attention. Would Chris never come? She returned to the Rev. and Mrs. Williams and when the minister had settled down in the comfortable chair in the living room, Mrs. Williams at once opened her barrage of questions. Fredericka felt faint. She had withstood the morning rush and now this avalanche had to fall on her. She did not dare to sit down for fear it would be taken as an invitation to stay. She leant heavily against the solid bookcase behind her.

"The body was in dear Lucy's hammock, you say?"

Fredericka had not said, but she mumbled something that might be taken for "yes."

"Oh, dear Miss Wing, may I just take a tiny peek at it? We have a meeting of the Women's Guild this afternoon and I'm sure they will want to know just how things were."

"I'm sorry, Mrs. Williams, but, you see the police have taken the hammock away." Then seeing the unmistakable expression of cat-after-swallowing-canary on Mrs. Williams's face she realized, too late, that she had made a serious slip.

"The *police,* you say. What does *that* mean?"

Oh, if only I had had sense enough to say "Dr. Scott," she thought. "I believe the police always deal with these things," she said lamely.

"Oh." Mrs. Williams's face fell and then brightened. She had another thought. "Was there any blood? I mean on the hammock, or the ground, or—or—or"—she waved a vague hand—"or on the body?" She lowered her voice to a conspiratorial whisper as she mouthed the last lovely word.

"I—I don't really know."

"Don't *know.* Surely it was you who discovered the body. Well, I'm certain there has been bloodshed. She was a wicked woman and she deserved to die—Have they asked James Brewster anything about this, I wonder. The wages of sin—" she added darkly.

The minister looked up from his book, and Mrs. Williams stopped her flow of words for a moment.

This was Fredericka's chance and she said quickly, "I wonder if you would mind very much if I excused myself for a moment. The customers came earlier than I expected and I haven't yet had any breakfast. I—I feel rather faint with the heat."

"Of course, Miss Wing." Mrs. Williams's saccharine voice had suddenly turned sour.

Fredericka was too exhausted to care. But as she started for the kitchen the back door banged, and a moment later Margie almost knocked her down in the hall.

"Do you want something, Margie? Or have you come to help? I could do with some."

"Oh no, sorry, I can't stay but Mom wanted me to get something from our storeroom so I just ran in."

Fredericka noticed that the girl's face was very white behind the red blotches of acne, and that she also trembled with excitement—or fear, it was impossible to say which. But Fredericka was now completely exhausted. She said abruptly, "Yes, Margie, if you must, but it really would help if you'd come after hours for your personal belongings. I'm busy and it is annoying to have you banging in and out."

"Aunt Lucy said—" Margie began, but Fredericka cut her short.

"I'm sorry, Margie, but I'm in charge now." Then seeing the look of desperation in the girl's face she forced herself to postpone the thought of breakfast, and added, "All right, but I'll just come up with you, I think." What could the child have on her mind now? What fresh deviltry was she up to?

Margie agreed to this suggestion with obvious reluctance and Fredericka followed her up the stairs. By the time she reached the top she had decided to make her bed and tidy her room and not stand over the wretched girl. Margie seemed to take a very long time and when Fredericka looked in she found the girl rummaging through a trunk full of old letters. This seemed harmless enough and Fredericka decided, since her upstairs work was finished, not to wait any longer. She returned to her customers downstairs and found that

they had left. Bertrand Russell lay open and face down-
ward on the chair. Of course Mr. Williams *wouldn't* buy
it nor ever intended to, she thought, furiously. She
picked up the book and put it on her desk, and then sank
wearily into the chair. It must be well past noon and she
was now almost too exhausted to bother with food.

It was at this moment that the skies opened and the
rain that had been threatening all morning pounded
down in a sudden loud tit-tat-too on the tin roof over the
back porch. A cool wet breeze lifted the curtain near the
desk and, with relief, Fredericka got to her feet and went
slowly into the kitchen. The arrival of the storm should
mean the end of the customers—for the moment, anyway.

She saw that the kitchen clock said ten minutes
after three and decided to change eggs and coffee to a
sandwich and iced tea. She put on the kettle and called
upstairs to Margie. When there was no answer, she
called again. Then with a muttered curse, she climbed
the stairs, only to discover that the Hartwell's storeroom was empty. The jumble of boxes, trunks and oddments seemed untidier than ever but there was no sign
of Margie. Fredericka looked into the other rooms and
then realized that the girl must have slipped out without
a word. Infuriating child. The whistle of the kettle blew
with a sudden shrill note and Fredericka went back to
the kitchen and her long delayed meal. There was, at any
rate, the consolation of being alone.

The rain continued to beat down on the tin roof as
Fredericka made her tea and sandwich. She listened to
the sound and, to her delight, it seemed to be saying in
a most definite and reassuring manner, "No customers.
No customers." But she had just sat down at the table in

the window when there was an imperious knock at the front door.

"Dear God," she muttered weakly as she struggled to her feet.

In the hall she met her visitors who had not waited for the door to be opened to them.

"Hi!" Peter greeted her and, from behind him the chief of police said: "Good afternoon." They stood still and expectant, dripping water from their raincoats.

Fredericka, who had been hoping all day yesterday that Peter would appear, now felt annoyed at sight of him. "Come in," she said grudgingly. "Better dump your raincoats here. I'm having lunch, or rather, breakfast and lunch together."

"Why no breakfast? And why so late?"

"Why? Why?" Fredericka said irritably. "I've been answering questions the whole morning long from the moment I started to get my breakfast until the storm gave me my first break." Seeing his look of genuine concern she relented a little. "If you want to ask me more questions, and I can see from your faces that you do, please do it in the kitchen and let me eat my lunch. I can give you iced tea but I'm unequal to more."

"Thanks, Fredericka," Peter answered, and the voice behind him was an echo, as they moved together into the kitchen.

"I haven't much to bother you with," Thane Carey began apologetically. He fished in his pocket awkwardly and produced a small antique silver snuff box. "Is this yours?" he asked quietly, holding it out to her in the palm of his hand.

"Never seen it before, I'm afraid," Fredericka said, "but I wish I could claim it. What a lovely thing it is." She took the box from him and opened it cautiously. Inside were several orange-colored capsules.

"Vitamins?" she asked.

"I expect so. Not yours then?"

"No. Where did it come from?"

"My man found it in the long grass by your back porch."

"Perhaps it's Margie's. She comes in and out that way at all hours, day and night. But," she hesitated, "well, it doesn't look like Margie, does it?"

Thane Carey smiled. "It does not, but we can't rule out anyone, as you are well aware."

"Is it so important then?" It *looks* like a clue, and you handle it as though it was. But a clue to what? Catherine Clay was murdered then—?" Fredericka suddenly felt cold. The two men regarded her intently.

"We can't jump to conclusions. On the other hand— But we must wait for the result of the autopsy before we take any active steps. We ought to have that by Wednesday or Thursday at the latest. It's maddening that there's this delay—but there it is." He reached for the box and started to put it back in his pocket. Then he seemed suddenly to change his mind. He removed the capsules and handed Fredericka the empty box. "Would you be willing to keep this for me and ask your customers if any of them have lost it or known who might have?" he asked.

"Good idea," Peter put in. "Fredericka gets a real cross-section of the town."

"But I don't know when I'll see any of the likely ones again. I'm sure every able-bodied regular customer has crossed my threshold this morning. This afternoon I am expecting only the lame, the halt, and the blind."

Both men laughed a little self-consciously and then Peter said: "Oh, they'll be back again. Never fear."

The chief of police stood up. For a moment he seemed to tower menacingly over Fredericka's head. Then he said mildly enough. "I've got to dash, Mohun. Thanks for the iced tea, Miss Wing. It saved my life."

When he had gone, Fredericka and Peter lit cigarettes and moved into the living room.

"Do *you* believe that it was murder?" Fredericka asked.

"Yes, Fredericka, I do. And it is obvious that you do, too."

"But I don't want to. And I can't understand why or how it happened in my back yard and in my hammock."

"I have the answer to that." He got up, went into the hall, and fished in the large pocket of his raincoat. Then he returned to Fredericka and handed her a book. "That's your answer, I think."

Fredericka stared down at the lurid jacket of Kathleen Winsor's latest novel and frowned. Then she looked up suddenly, "Of course, Catherine came to bring this back. I suppose she didn't like it—or maybe she'd finished it—and then she just collapsed on to the hammock. But—where did you find the book?"

"James Brewster had it."

"James— But how did *he* get it?"

Peter then told her of his talk with James, adding at the end, "The only finger prints on the book were Catherine's and James's and some old ones, presumably yours."

"No wonder James behaved so strangely night before last. And, from what you say it does look as though he wanted to get rid of her, doesn't it?"

"Yes. But if he did, he couldn't have done it at the moment he found her here."

"Why?"

"Because I'm convinced that she was dead already when he got here."

"Yes—I suppose that is one of those unanswerable facts. But James Brewster could have been the murderer. Mrs. Williams supports me in this belief," she added, with an attempt at laughter.

"Well, I haven't ruled him out either. He had motive, as you say, but he wasn't alone in wanting to be rid of Catherine."

"No—I've been thinking of that, too. Everyone hated her it seems—" She thought of Margie and Roger. "—Oh, Peter, I haven't told you about Margie's secret cache in the old greenhouse, but I suppose Thane Carey has. And I haven't told you about meeting Roger in the woods."

"Carey did tell me about the junk in the greenhouse—we decided that it must be a private beauty parlour of Margie's and that it had no bearing on the case. But what about Roger?"

Fredericka told him the story of her Sunday afternoon's adventure but without mentioning her accusation of which she was now a little ashamed. When she finished, Peter said thoughtfully: "I hope Philippine is right and that the next operation is successful. He needs a break and its high time he had one."

"But, Peter, what about his hating Catherine—I mean—?"

"Oh, we can't exclude him, of course." He sighed heavily and got to his feet as though shaking off a great weight.

"Well, I must be off. Storm's let up."

"Oh dear, has it? That means more customers." As she spoke the front door slammed again. "Curses," she said.

"And more of them," Peter agreed. "I too have work—and have had all day yesterday, far into the night and practically nothing to show for it—" He broke off abruptly as James Brewster put his head around the door.

"Am I intruding?" he asked.

"Of course not," Fredericka snapped. She found it difficult at all times to like this man, and now, after what Peter had just told her, and after a hard day and a hot one, he had to be the one to appear. Moreover he looked damnably clean and affable and quite unlike his usual bigger-than-thou bullying self.

"Don't forget the snuff box," Peter muttered under cover of his departure. He nodded toward James and grinned. Fredericka frowned. It seemed a poor joke, and how could he go off so cheerfully and leave her alone with this great beast.

James lowered his heavy body into the armchair that had earlier been warmed by the minister.

"My dear Fredericka—if I may, please, call you by your Christian name"—he paused a little ponderously to await her answer.

"Of course," Fredericka answered without enthusiasm.

"My dear Fredericka," he repeated, "this all seems hard on you who have come so recently into our midst. Catherine was always careless, but I do confess I think she was particularly so to choose such a *public* place to die."

"Public?" Fredericka asked.

"Well, dear Lucy always made her bookshop a sort

of open house to all of us. I'm afraid we imposed on her more than we should have done. But she was tireless— *tireless.*"

"So I've always heard," Fredericka answered coldly, and then went on: "I'm afraid I've got to rearrange some stock. Was there anything special you wanted? I've got some good new fiction in the library."

"No. No. I keep up with the law journals which is about the extent of my reading except for an occasional thriller to give my brain a rest."

"Well, I have two or three new ones."

"No, Fredericka, not today." Then, as she stood up, he said hurriedly: "Well, perhaps I will take one along before I go. You're not trying to speed the parting guest, are you?"

"I'm sorry if I was rude," Fredericka answered wearily. She sat down again, but with such obvious reluctance that James got slowly to his feet. He pulled out a large gold watch from a hidden pocket.

"Good gracious, it's after closing time and I expect you're more sensible about hours than dear Lucy was."

"No. Not at all. It's quite all right, really," Fredericka answered, wondering what he could possibly want. Surely he had, at first hand, all the news that the rest of South Sutton was after.

And then, to her surprise, he said suddenly: "You get along with your last chores, 'stock' as you call it, or what-have-you, and I'll just look through the murders."

"All right, then," Fredericka agreed after a moment's hesitation. What could the man want? "I expect you know where they are."

"I do indeed." He coughed. "You must have had a tiring day. Wouldn't you like to come out with me to the inn for supper? I've had a hard day, too. I couldn't even get in to Worcester. And all this business on top of it."

Fredericka turned around to look at the heavy handsome face. Is that all? she thought. Does he only want to pump me like all the others? I suppose he wants to know what Peter's told me and how much I know. It must be valuable if it's worth a meal to him. Thank Heaven I put that telltale book under the others on the desk. "No," she said quickly—too quickly, she realized at once when she saw that she had made him angry. He frowned and a sudden flush coloured his neck and the sides of his face. His hands gripped the chairback where they had rested softly a moment before.

"It's only"—Fredericka managed to say, in sudden panic—"that I really am too tired even to go out. I'll just get myself something light and go to bed early—if—if you don't mind." In her anxiety, she seemed not to be able to stop talking.

"I quite understand, Fredericka," he said gently. "I'll not stop for that book tonight, then. I'm in no hurry really."

She dared to look up now and saw, with amazement, that his sudden anger had passed like the storm outside. But I'd hate to cross him in anything that really mattered to him, she thought, as she walked with him to the door.

"I believe it has cleared at last," he remarked from the path. "Air's fresher."

"Thank goodness for that," Fredericka answered him and turned back into the house. "And thank goodness you've gone," she mumbled as she found her way through the empty house to the kitchen.

After a quiet uninterrupted meal, Fredericka felt better. The soft night air that came in through the window was cool and soothing. When she had washed her dishes and taken off her apron she put her hand in the pocket of her dress and discovered the little silver snuff box. She took it to the light on the office table and studied its delicate pattern of cupids and love knots.

"Not for snuff at all, really—rather for a lady's beauty patches. No," she said aloud, "somehow I don't think Mr. James Brewster could claim this." She grinned cheerfully as she dropped the box into the top desk drawer. How like Peter that was. She wondered when he would be back. Perhaps tomorrow to see if anyone had claimed the prize.

Bed? Somehow Fredericka wasn't tired any more. Perhaps it would help to tell Miss Hartwell all that had happened since her new manager had taken over the bookshop. And there was that business about the well. She pulled out a large piece of airmail paper and began to write.

Some time later, rested and comforted by this act of confession, Fredericka sealed the envelope and put it in the centre of the blotter where she would see it in the morning. She was singing as she went out into the kitchen to get a drink before going to bed, but she stopped in sudden alarm and stared out of the window. Yes, there was no mistaking the fact that a light was visible through the tangle of shrubs at the back. It flashed and then glowed steadily for a moment before it went out. Fredericka felt herself trembling. She stood still staring out into the darkness and then, suddenly, another light flashed on and shone steadily through the leaves.

"Of course," she said out loud, making for the chair by the kitchen table. "How stupid of me. It's that child— Margie"—But could it be at this hour?—nearly midnight? She got up and went back to the window. Yes, certainly, the light was coming from the direction of the old greenhouse. Well, she would go and put a stop to this nonsense.

But when Fredericka reached the back porch, her resolution failed her, and as she hesitated the light went out and only darkness lay before her, velvety black and impenetrable. One knew, of course, that murderers returned to the scenes of their crime. She backed toward the door and then she heard the sound of stealthy footsteps. They seemed to be coming toward her up the garden path!

Summoning all her courage she called out: "Who's there? Is that you, Margie?" Her voice sounded thin and frightened. There was no answer and the sound of footsteps ceased. She called again, louder and with a show of courage she did not feel.

Silence.

Could she have dreamt it all? Could this be her own wild imagining? She took one step forward, then another; the next took her off the porch. She felt the softness of grass under her feet and then there was a sudden brilliant flash of light directly in her face. She reeled backward, blinded. Then the light was gone and there was only black night and the sound of running footsteps.

8

Fredericka never remembered how she got back into the house after her midnight adventure. She knew only that she locked and bolted the door and went at once to the telephone.

A sleepy voice answered when she finally got through to the police station and asked for the chief of police. The sergeant on duty explained that the chief had not been there all evening. Was it urgent?

Fredericka was about to say that it was urgent—very—and then thought better of it. In the warm circle of lamplight by the office desk, she felt her fears recede. It couldn't possibly have been anyone but Margie—the mad prank of a mad child. Moreover, Margie or anyone else would certainly by now have put considerable distance between herself, or himself, and the bookshop.

"No. No, it isn't important," she said. "I—I had forgotten how late it is. Could I perhaps have Mr. Carey's telephone number at home?"

The voice now had a note of suspicion. "Who is that calling, please—?"

"It's—it's Miss Wing at the Hartwell bookshop."

"Oh yes, Miss Wing." He hesitated. Suspicion had now become solicitude. "Are you quite sure nothing's wrong?—Well then—"

In the end he gave her Thane Carey's number and she put it beside the telephone. Then, feeling both virtuous and courageous, she went upstairs, took one of Dr. Scott's pills and went immediately to sleep.

When Fredericka woke the morning was fresh and cooler after the rain of the day before. The sun sparkled brightly on the wet green grass when she slipped out on to her back porch to look for signs of her marauder and to sniff the air. The path was trampled with footsteps of all sizes and shapes—yesterday's rain and yesterday's visitors had churned the brown earth and flattened the grass. No, there was no evidence. But even in the bright light of day, Fredericka knew that she had not been dreaming. And she was more than ever convinced that her visitor had been Margie. She thought of this as she was cooking and eating her breakfast, and then her mind travelled backwards to the problems that had become crystal clear by the simple process of writing down, as she had in her last night's letter to Miss Hartwell, the significant events since her arrival in South Sutton.

As she poured out her coffee and made her toast she thought of this letter and what she had said, and then, inevitably, that she must get it off. She hadn't bothered with a stamp last night. She'd have to find one and then get Christopher to take it to the post office. If only he would put in his appearance. Why hadn't he come yesterday? During the first week, she had put him on to full time. Surely he understood this. She had expected him all morning and then, when the afternoon's visitors had started to appear, she had forgotten him com-

pletely. Now, thinking of him, she remembered his perspiring black face as it emerged from the bushes that
first afternoon when she had been lying in the hammock.
Had there been something sinister about that face? Certainly the events of these last few days were enough to
make anyone uneasy and suspicious without cause.
Could it have been Chris last night? Of course not. But
why hadn't he come yesterday?

As if in answer to her question, there was a loud
knock on the back door. Startled, and annoyed with
herself for being startled, Fredericka got up quickly and
went out. Christopher stood on the porch, turning his
battered straw hat in his workworn brown hands. He
smiled disarmingly and Fredericka's nightmare vanished.

"Fixin' to come yist'dy, but found it advisable to
help out at the depot with a parcel o' freight for Miss
Philippine."

"But that didn't take all day, did it?"

"No ma'am, Miss Wing. But I then went out to the
Farm where I busy myself with one business and then
another business. Did reckon to come along here afterwards, but they wasn't no time lef', time I got done."

"But Christopher, I thought you were going to be
regularly employed by me now. Wasn't that what we
agreed? I mean, I thought you were my man."

"Yes, ma'am—but the good Lord He say we is
to help one anothers and as they done have all this trouble. . . ." He stopped and then added significantly, "Mis'
Hartwell, she never used to mind much."

"I see." Fredericka bit her lip in annoyance, but she
knew it would be both unwise and quite useless to say
more. "I have some coffee for you," she said quickly.

Christopher's grin returned and he nodded vigorously. "I'll jes' set myself down on the porch here for the time bein'. Mis' Hartwell she don't like my boots for outside to go inside on her floors." He exhibited a pair of muddy shoes heavily studded with nails. As Fredericka turned to go in to the kitchen, she looked back and saw with surprise that Christopher had glanced furtively over his shoulder and then walked to the far end of the porch.

Was everyone queer, or was there something wrong with herself? Fredericka poured out the coffee quickly and took two doughnuts from Miss Hartwell's large crock. When she got back to the porch she found Christopher sitting on the far edge with his feet stretched out before him. He seemed to have shrunk down into his bright plaid shirt, and to be regarding his outdoor boots with deep concentration.

"What's the matter, Chris?" she asked, feeling sudden anxiety for the man.

He took the coffee with obvious gratitude, but did not reply. And all at once, Fredericka knew the answer. Christopher was frightened—plain frightened. That was why he had to get himself as far away from the hammock side of the house as possible. No doubt *that* was why he hadn't appeared yesterday.

"It's all right, Chris," she said quickly. "They've taken the—er—I mean they've taken Mrs. Clay—and the hammock away."

"Yes, ma'am," was all Christopher said, but his look of relief was obvious. He began to dunk his doughnut in his coffee with every appearance of complete satisfaction.

Was it simply superstitious fear or was it a sense of guilt? How much did he know about Margie Hartwell's secret hiding place?

"Chris," she said suddenly, "I was looking about the place on Sunday and I discovered a break in the fence. Did you know about that?"

"Jes' an ole foxhole, I reckon. I told Miss Lucy and she say she ain't worried about no foxes round here." He laughed and the sound grated unpleasantly on Fredericka's oversensitive nerves.

"Well, what about that collection of things in the old greenhouse back there?"

"Those belongs to Miss Margie. Miss Lucy, she say they is not to be removed." He frowned down at his empty coffee cup.

It's a conspiracy against me, Fredericka thought unreasonably. Well, it was no use trying to get anything more out of Chris. She took the coffee cup and went to get the letter to Miss Hartwell.

In searching for a stamp in the desk drawer, Fredericka saw the little silver patch box, and her mind strayed for a moment from her immediate purpose. She could have asked James Brewster if he had observed anyone using it. Perhaps Peter had been serious after all. But surely the box must belong to Margie. It had been found near the porch and it was Margie who used the back way more than anyone else—But it was true that the box didn't look in the least like Margie. It looked more like—yes, of course, like Catherine Clay herself. Catherine probably did come around to try the back door when she found the front locked on that fateful Saturday afternoon. And it was a fact that she *had* come part way around since she would have had to in order to get into the hammock. If only she had asked James, he would have known whether or not it was Catherine's and his reactions would have been interesting—very. Well, she wasn't much of a sleuth.

Fredericka put the box back into the drawer with a gesture of impatience. What would happen to her work if she spent all her time in idle speculations that came to nothing? She found a stamp, stuck it on the letter with unnecessary force, and went back to Christopher.

"I don't know when the mail goes, Chris, but will you please take this for me? Don't make a special trip but I would like it to go out today."

"Yes ma'am. I was fixin' to cut this here grass, and straighten out the contents of the stockroom. Mail don't go nohow this forenoon. Reckon I can take it when I go for the mail round about twelve o'clock."

"Good." Fredericka turned to go back into the house when Chris spoke again.

"I've been thinking further about that ole well. It do make me worry some, all open like it am. I put an ole box cover over it like but it's not much use. Sam Lewis is doin' a job down the road. I could jes' ax him to come by and have a look at it."

"I've written to Miss Hartwell, Chris. We ought to have an answer in a few days. Don't you think we can get along until we hear? I don't really like to involve Miss Hartwell in expense unless I'm sure she wants me to."

"Yes, ma'am, O.K. then." Chris now put his dilapidated hat on his head with an age-old gesture of resignation and loped off through the jungle path. Fredericka returned to her dishes and then to her desk, and, after a few moments, was relieved to hear the clanking whir of the lawn mower. He seems to be doing the side lawn, she thought. So he must have recovered from his panic. That was one good thing.

She continued to work steadily but some impulse made her get up and go to the window when the lawn mower stopped suddenly. Between the two trees where the hammock had hung, Chris was down on his hands and knees. Praying? Fredericka asked herself. Surely not. She was about to go to the door and investigate when Chris got to his feet and returned to the lawn mower. I must pull myself together, Fredericka decided. There is no doubt whatever that he was trimming the grass around the trees—

After this interruption, the morning passed uneventfully except for a telephone call from Thane Carey who had received the sergeant's report. She told him briefly of her adventure and he questioned her closely. Then he said that he was on his way out to the Farm and would, himself, question Margie. He sounded abrupt and hurried and after a few brief pleasantries, he hung up. Well, he doesn't seem to be much alarmed, Fredericka decided as she returned to her desk. Thank heaven I didn't get him out of bed in the middle of the night.

Two or three customers came to return books to the lending library and lingered to ask the inevitable questions. But Fredericka despatched them quickly, having now learned a satisfactory technique for dealing with them. Each time she remembered the little silver box, but none of her visitors had ever seen it before. They looked at it with undisguised interest, however. "Better put up a notice in the post office," one of them suggested.

"I will if all else fails," Fredericka said, slipping the box back into its drawer.

She was still working at the pile of bills and orders on her desk when she was aware that someone had come in behind her. She turned quickly to see Chris standing in the doorway.

"What is it?" she asked, trying to keep the fright and annoyance from her voice. Why did he have to creep so?

"I thought Miss Hartwell didn't like you coming in the house with your boots on," she added severely.

"I took them off, Ma'am, Miss Wing." He handed her a pile of letters. Fredericka looked down at his stockinged feet and one large protruding toe, and was ashamed of her outburst.

"Thanks, Chris."

When he did not at once depart, she looked up at him.

"I saw you had a stamp there from foreign parts—" He coughed. 'France.' Then, in a rush, he added, "Miss Hartwell very kindly give me such stamps for my collection."

"Of course, Chris." She tore open the letter carefully and cut out the stamp.

Chris took it and stared at it for a moment. "Miss Catherine she got one jes' the same as this here one. But she won't be there. No ma'am. Bein' as how she am dead," he added lugubriously.

"No. You take the Farm mail too?" Why all this service to the Farm? And why am I so unnaturally curious? she asked herself.

"Yes, ma'am. I am, as yo'all might say, the postman hereabouts and the freight man and the general handyman, as it were."

"I see. Then I don't wonder you collect stamps," Fredericka said a little absently. She wished now that he would go and let her get on with her work.

At this moment, the back door banged and Margie burst into the room.

"Have you got the Farm mail, Chris?" she asked without so much as a glance at Fredericka. "I'm just going back—"

Chris handed her the letters with a look of disappointment. It was obvious that he would have liked to have personally delivered the letter addressed to Mrs. Clay. His departure was slow and dignified.

Margie flopped down into the big chair and thumbed through the letters. Fredericka, who had had more than enough of Margie, started to express her feelings when she was saved by the appearance of an old lady with a book for the lending library. Fredericka went across the hall with her and soon learned that her customer was Mrs. Pike, and that she had made the quilt which Fredericka had won at the bazaar. Fredericka would normally have been interested in this fact and in the long and detailed story of how the pattern had evolved but she had Margie very much on her mind. Should she ask her about last night or leave that to Thane Carey? The girl had seemed so preoccupied and tense.

Then, in the middle of pink against blue or red against green, Fredericka suddenly remembered that she must ask Margie about the silver box. She made some excuse and the old lady turned rather huffily to the shelves. Fredericka hurried back to the office to find Margie gone, and the desk drawer half-open. She looked inside quickly and was relieved to find the box there, just as she had left it. Perhaps she had, herself, forgotten to shut the drawer properly. She took out the box and, without bothering to make further excuses to her customer, dashed out the back way. She ran all the way to the gate into the alley which she found standing open. But there was no sign of Margie.

"Plague take her," Fredericka muttered as she hurried back to the shop and her fretting client.

For the rest of the day Fredericka was too busy with customers to think of anything else. She ate only a sandwich for lunch and a chocolate milk shake that Chris brought back to her when he took his wheelbarrow to the station to collect freight parcels in the afternoon. He trundled the barrow in by the front gate and around the side path to the back porch where Fredericka stepped out to meet him. The paper carton of milk shake was poised precariously on top of the bundles of books like a lookout on a craggy mountain. Chris handed it to her solemnly.

"Everyone in this town is talkin' like they was murder crimated in this place," he said heavily.

"Nonsense," she said a little sharply, and then felt sorry as she took the drink from the large brown hand and looked into the anxious face.

By night, Fredericka was determined to escape from the bookshop and, though she did not admit it, even to herself, wanted to see Peter Mohun again. Neither he nor Thane Carey had appeared all day and this fact in itself now seemed, to her overwrought mind, to be full of portent. That afternoon a customer had reminded her that there was to be a lecture at the college at eight-thirty. Something about Korea. She hadn't had a thought of going to it until, after supper, she found herself changing into her best linen dress. Half an hour later, she shut and locked both doors, and departed, hurrying across the campus as though escaping from demons. When she reached the hall she discovered that she was a little late and slipped quietly into a back seat.

The large room was crowded with people, but Fredericka could not see any familiar faces near her. She sat back on her hard chair and looked around at the panelled walls and the row of impressive portraits that circled the room. Certainly the college hall was a far pleasanter place than the church one. Fredericka reflected briefly on the rapid decline of American architecture in the fifty or sixty years from the time this hall had been built around 1825 or 1830 to the church hall, a memorial to the worst that 1880 could do. The lecture was given by a correspondent, recently back from the Korean front and he was introduced by Peter Mohun who seemed abstracted and tired, Fredericka thought. She found it difficult to concentrate—a blue bottle fly buzzed around the light above her and the room grew close and hot. At intervals she dozed but, in spite of this, the time dragged until the sudden stir in the room announced her release. She got up at once and followed the crowd out to the lighted porch where everyone was stopping to gossip and enjoy the soft summer night.

Fredericka stood for a moment, feeling alone in a crowd of strangers. She looked anxiously for Peter but he was nowhere to be seen. Perhaps he had to entertain the speaker. Well, there was nothing for it but to leave. She started slowly across the campus, feeling abandoned, and frightened at the prospect of returning alone to the book-shop, when a hand fell heavily on her shoulder. Startled, she turned to look up into the large red face of James Brewster. Her disappointment was acute.

"The thing to do now," he announced easily, "is to adjourn to the drug-store for an ice-cream soda. Personally I would prefer something a little stronger but we are in Rome, my dear Fredericka, and so we must be Romans."

"Must we?" Fredericka asked, and meant it.

He took her arm. "We must, at any rate, make a *pretence* of doing so."

Fredericka decided that anything would be better than to return alone to her empty house. For this reason, she did not withdraw her arm as she longed to do, and they walked together down the dark street.

"It's no joke being the Sutton family lawyer," Brewster said suddenly, but he spoke low and confidingly.

Fredericka who had been avid for news all day was suddenly annoyed. She didn't want to hear about the Suttons from James Brewster. She didn't even want to think about them. But James went on without encouragement. "Shouldn't speak ill of the dead, but really Catherine's affairs were in a shocking state. Wouldn't wonder if she had decided to take a quick way out—"

"Whatever do you mean?" Fredericka was now roused to sudden attention.

"Nothing. Oh nothing really, of course. Philippine's got the family in a much better state with her herb farm. Most remarkable woman. Forget what I said, my dear." He squeezed her arm affectionately but Fredericka did not even notice. She was thinking of the conversation she had overheard in the inn on her first Sunday and of what Peter had told her of James's admissions. James Brewster was suggesting that Catherine Clay had committed suicide. How convenient for him if he had indeed switched his affections from the glamorous Catherine to Philippine whom on Sunday he had called "good" and now thought "remarkable."

"I thought Mrs. Sutton had started the herb business before Philippine came," Fredericka said quickly.

"Yes, *started,* but she is old and really quite worn out. It certainly needed someone like Philippine—" He stopped in midsentence and turned toward Fredericka suddenly. She had walked on without noticing that the crowd had thinned: the white dresses had flashed away into the darkness and the chatter of voices and the sound of laughter had become spasmodic and remote. At the moment that James Brewster turned toward her and she felt his hot breath against her face, she knew that they were alone.

Fredericka summoned all her strength and tried to push him away from her.

"Come, Fredericka, you can't mind a little affection—" He held her arms now and tried to pull her towards him. His voice was sensuous and persuasive.

Fredericka felt trapped and desperately frightened. "Will you please let me go—at once"—Was he trying to make love to her—this lecherous beast—or was he—? Oh dear God, was he going to kill her—? His grip tightened—"I shall scream." She spat the words out in an agony of desperation.

A step sounded behind them and James dropped his arms suddenly. "You must forgive me, Fredericka," he said softly. "You are a most attractive woman—Perhaps—when you know me better—"

The footsteps grew louder and a group of people came up from behind and passed them. Fredericka hurried to keep up with them. She could not speak. She wanted only to escape this great beast who was so near and so terrifying.

They turned into the main street and, a moment later, stepped together into the glare of the neon-lighted drug store.

"As I was saying," James remarked calmly, "that business badly needed someone like Philippine—Oh, there she is now!"

They had walked past the crowded tables and the rows of neat booths along the walls to the back of the large room where the soda fountain gleamed—a Victorian prop, resplendent in pink marble. Philippine, looking cool and fresh in a blue linen suit, was standing at the counter. She saw them and smiled. "Hi!" she greeted them and then, looking up at James, added; "You see how I improve in my American, 'Hi,' I say, instead of 'Ello,' and 'O.K.' instead of 'all right.' Did I not learn fast?"

"James Brewster will be the first to sign your diploma, Phil, and yes, I'll add a golden seal to it, too. Nothing like being in the business." James beamed at Philippine as he answered her.

Fredericka was glad to be forgotten. As she recovered her composure, she watched the two covertly. What kind of a man was this who would force himself on one woman, and a second later, make up to another? She looked at Philippine and admitted to herself that one couldn't blame James for being attracted to her. She looked efficient and capable and yet she had not suffered as a woman—she was better described by James's word "remarkable," perhaps, than his earlier adjective "good."

Feeling Fredericka's eyes on her, Philippine turned away from James and said: "My treat. What would you like? I am having a shake of chocolate milk."

The boy behind the counter guffawed loudly. Philippine, sensing that he was laughing at her, frowned, and for a moment it was as though a dark cloud had shaded her pleasant face. But she recovered quickly and laughed herself. "What do I say now, Jo?" she asked, and then with a look of despair: "And I have just been boasting that I speak such good American!"

The boy looked embarrassed and Fredericka said quickly: "Just limeade for me." It didn't matter what she had. She only wanted to stay in the lighted room and not move again into the darkness.

Jo tossed the paper cup into its silver sconce, filled

it with a flick of his hand, and put two straws expertly into the arsenic-green liquid.

Philippine pretended a shudder of distaste. "How can you drink that bottled poison?" she asked.

"Come Philippine, don't run everyone's life," James said amiably, lowering his large body on to one of the counter seats. "We all know you run yours perfectly but you'll never get a husband if you're too managing."

Philippine pouted like a child and looked up at him disingenuously. Fredericka did not miss the look of understanding that passed between them. She had no desire to talk and it seemed best to stay out of the conversation. Turning away from the counter she held her drink in her hand and looked around her over the tops of the straws. She was aware that her hand was trembling and she made an effort to steady it.

She saw that the room was filled with young people, high school age for the most part, and a scattering of older men and women. They sat crowded into the booths or around the marble-topped tables in the centre. Fredericka recognized a few of the bookshop's customers and then, in the distance, she saw Margie. The girl was standing by herself at the far end of the room reading a comic. She seemed conspicuously alone and forlorn in the noisy room where everyone else of her own age was apparently having such a good time.

In spite of her own discomfort and her antagonism to Margie, Fredericka could not help feeling sorry for the girl. She was about to go and ask her to join them in a drink when Philippine, who had been watching the direction of her gaze, said: "I've asked her already but she says 'No.' Margie is always having—how do you say it?—the sulks. She is a nice child really but she thinks everyone doesn't like her—and so they don't because she thinks it."

"Can't anything be done about her face?" James asked.

"It's a nervous thing, I think, really," Philippine said with obvious concern. "We've tried everything."

"All your fancy herbs?"

"Yes. I guess we'll just have to wait and see if she doesn't grow out of it. Poor kid."

As though aware that she was being observed and discussed, Margie looked several times in their direction and then put the comic back on its pile and banged out of the door.

"Bother the child," Fredericka said under her breath. She had failed again to ask Margie about that wretched box. Well, too much had happened too suddenly. She couldn't think of everything at once. Even Peter would understand that—But she couldn't tell him about James. He would think—What would he think—?

She was still standing, deep in thought and sucking absently at her straws when a familiar voice said: "Aren't you making a rather childish noise, Fredericka? Your drink happens to be finished!"

She looked up into Peter's friendly gray eyes and tried to hide the joy and relief she felt at sight of him.

"Have another on me, and stop that racket," he persisted. "And then I'll 'see you home,' as they say in this town."

"Thanks to both," Fredericka said. She turned quickly to include Philippine and James, and to her amazement found that they had disappeared.

Seeing her look of surprise, Peter said: "They left as I came in. You were in such a trance, you saw nothing.

I expect they both kissed you goodbye and you were quite unaware of it. Now tell me what's on your mind. That may help us to bear up under the burden of our loneliness, don't you think so?"

9

As Fredericka and Peter Mohun walked back to the bookshop together, she found it a blessed relief to forget her anxieties, to talk of ordinary things and to pretend to herself that Margie and even James were figures of her imagination and that the dead body in her hammock had been nothing more than the climax of a bad dream from which she had now awakened.

Sensing something of this, Peter did not press her to tell him what she had been worrying about when he had found her in the drug-store, and the bad news he had for her could wait, too. He slid his arm through hers and said easily: "I'm very glad it happened to be Fredericka Wing who came to South Sutton, and not the kind of librarian I had pictured when Lucy Hartwell announced that she had found a manager *pro tem.*"

"I am glad it was, too," Fredericka answered, ignoring the implied compliment but enjoying it all the same.

"I don't know very much about you though—even now. You were a librarian. You are writing a book. I know that. How goes it? And what else have you written? Come clean, girl, please, and tell all."

"I've played at writing all the years of my life without success. I once actually finished a murder-mystery—" Fredericka stopped abruptly. Her words had sounded too loud in the darkness and silence of the night. They hung in the air like an evil omen. She hurried on, trying to bury them, to put them back into the nightmare from which she knew herself to have wakened. "That—that wasn't any good, though. I couldn't be bothered with *clues*. They all seemed so obvious. Now, at last, I really have hope for my present undertaking—the Victorian women one I told you about. A publisher has even written me an encouraging letter."

"Good," Peter said quietly. He had observed with some anxiety the note of hysteria in her voice. This thing was getting her down—as well it might. "But you haven't told me much about it or where you've got to."

"Don't urge me. I'll go on all night if you do. I'm absolutely steeped in the works of these incredible Victorians. I find Miss Hartwell has a whole shelf of the novels I've been looking for—some of Susan Warner, Maria Cummins and Mary J. Holmes and I'd searched every library in New York. They really are an extraordinary group of women—all bestsellers 'round about 1850–60— But I expect I've told you all this before or am being enlightening about something you know more about than I do."

"I have just heard of *The Wide, Wide World*—but beyond that I confess total ignorance."

"That is, of course, a beautiful example of the teary school but it's interesting all the same." She stopped and was silent for a moment. Then she went on slowly. "You know, just before I came here I spent hours copy-

ing out the quilting party scene from Susan Warner's
Queechy. It was a frightful job because the print was so
fine, I couldn't type directly from the book but had to do
it longhand. It was worth the effort though, pure Ameri-
cana—"

"No doubt that's why you won Mrs. Pike's quilt."

"I know. It's certainly one reason why I *wanted* it so
much. But it just shows what a state I've got into when
I confess to you that the beautiful thing is still on the
rocker in my kitchen where I dumped it when I came in
that—that night. What's more, Mrs. Pike, herself, came
into the shop today for no other reason, I'm sure, than
to tell me that she had made that quilt, and to talk about
it. But I was so fussed about catching Margie and asking
her about that miserable box that I couldn't even talk to
her—and there was really so much I wanted to say."

"It's understandable, though. This business isn't exactly what you bargained for and you're too intelligent
to be able to shut your mind against it."

"I ought to be too intelligent to panic, though. If only
it wasn't quite so *evident* that I'm not as brave as I'd like
to be." She hesitated for a moment and then said
quickly, "Did Thane Carey tell you about my last night's
adventure?"

"No." Peter tightened his hold on her arm. "What
happened?"

"I don't suppose it was anything except a mad prank
of Margie's but—well—I didn't like it much." She then
told him briefly what had happened, and, when she finished, she thought again of telling him about her more
recent adventure with James, but, again, she thought
better of it.

For a full moment Peter was silent. They had now
reached the gateway to the college campus and were

about to cross over to go up Miss Hartwell's walk, when he stopped abruptly and said: "This settles it."

Fredericka was startled and a little annoyed. Was he going to leave her here? Had she given him some mysterious clue? She had been dreading the moment when she would have to lose Peter's comforting presence, but even if he came in, the night would be all the blacker and lonelier when he left.

"Settles what?" she asked.

"I'll tell you in a minute. The fact is that I have some news for you, too. It isn't really for you but I think I must tell you, though it isn't my business to at all, and I happen to know that Thane's calling on you early tomorrow— No, don't start to run like a hare— He's not going to arrest you!"

"Arrest me?"

"Oh damn, you've got hold of the wrong end of the stick somehow. Now just listen to me quietly for a moment, and don't faint until I come to the end of my sad story."

"I don't faint."

"That's a good thing. Where was I? Oh yes. We were able to put on some pressure and the result of the autopsy has come in early. As we all suspected—yes, you, too, and don't deny it—Catherine Clay was poisoned. It is unlikely—I might as well say impossible, that she took her own life because those capsules in the little silver box—"

"Then it was hers—that's what I had about decided—"

"Yes, but don't interrupt for a minute. As I started to say, those capsules were solid full of yellow jessamine— perhaps I should say Gelsemin $C_{24}H_{28}N_2O_4$. Our theory is that, immediately after lunch on Saturday she took what she thought to be one of her vitamin pills and it was, instead, a large dose of poison. She then visited the bookshop, probably very soon after you and I left, to return that book and, perhaps, to collect you to go to the bazaar with her since it would have been about the right time. But by the time she got to the shop she was feeling ill. The symptoms are nausea, pain in the brows and eyeballs, dilation of the pupils (this was noticeable, of course, but we put it down to the fact, admitted by her mother, that she sometimes took dope), paralysis and dimness of vision—more than enough to make anyone want to lie down—"

"Good heavens, Peter, she must have suffered agonies there all by herself in that miserable hammock." Fredericka spoke calmly, but one hand clutched Peter's sleeve tightly.

"It may not have been too bad, actually. There was no evidence that she was actually sick and it was a good-sized dose. No, the chances are that she felt odd, lay down, passed out and knew no more."

"But that—that awful look on her face?"

"It may have been purely muscular," Peter said, but without conviction.

Fredericka tried to forget the face which had haunted her all the long week, and, with an effort, shifted her thoughts from Catherine to her murderer. "Oh, Peter, who could have done it? Who hated her that much?"

"Ah—that's the crux of the whole matter. If we'd only listened to Margie at the supper. We come back to Margie every time. She knows something, I'm sure, but she's frightened to tell, so she just hints and runs away. I wonder what in thunder she was doing last night. If only . . ." his voice trailed off. Then he said slowly: "The murder looks more like hatred than expediency, doesn't it?" Then, suddenly aware of the hand that was clutching his arm so fiercely, he went on quietly: "You mustn't take this too hard, Fredericka. I tell you all this because I am convinced that the best thing in the world for you now is to put your very good mind onto helping me. Even your Victorian women will have to wait. We'll put crime detection first for a little while."

In spite of herself, Fredericka was interested. "But why *you?* I wondered about it yesterday when you said you'd been giving James the third degree. I mean I thought Thane Carey was the one—" She stopped and then said apologetically: "I don't mean to be rude, only—well, you're not Scotland Yard in disguise or anything, are you?"

"Do you know that we have been standing in front of the campus gate for five full minutes and that we could be much more comfortable in your living room, if only you would ask me in? No, don't interrupt, I haven't finished. I have a further suggestion to offer. If you don't mind, I will just run in to my room and collect my toothbrush. Then if you'll let me sleep on the couch in the office I'll play watchdog for tonight. I'd been afraid to suggest it but after what you have just told me I must. By tomorrow I expect Thane'll put a man on to the job. Of course you're not in any danger. The fact that you weren't touched last night is proof of that. It's just that I think you'll rest more comfortable like."

"Oh, Peter," Fredericka said, and the relief made her words trip over each other, "Will you? I mean, won't it be grim?"

"Not in the least. As a matter of fact, I know that couch well. There was a burglary scare once and I played guard for Miss Hartwell until the thief was appre-

hended. Of course, you'll have to give me breakfast and
the town will hear about it from the alley cats and *talk,*
but I'm banking on the fact that they'll have something
so much more interesting to talk about that they'll over-
look us."

"But you haven't told me *why* you know so much
about all this—and—" But Peter had left her standing
alone by the gate.

"Back in two minutes," he called cheerfully.

As the sound of his footsteps died away, the silence
closed in around Fredericka. She moved toward the gate
and leant against its cold iron face—conscious of her
need for support and more than ever ashamed of her
own terror.

"Scared, weren't you?" Peter laughed as he rejoined
her.

"Well, yes, I confess it."

"Understandable, but no need to be. Otherwise
Carey would have sent a man around at once after he
talked to you on the phone this morning. Look at it
reasonably and let your mind, not your emotions, run
the show. Catherine Clay's death *here* was accidental.
There's nothing to connect the murder and the bookshop. She could have taken that pill at any time and died
anywhere. What's more, you're the least likely of anyone
to be victim number two. You're new to the place, and
though you found the—er—*corpus delicti,* you don't
know anything more about what happened than twenty
or more others do. You were at the bazaar along with me
and nearly everyone else in the place. I'm just staying
here tonight in order to help your beauty sleep, as I've
already pointed out."

They had entered the house and as Fredericka
switched on the light she could see the broad grin on his

face. "And how badly I need it, my dear Holmes," she said, and was able to smile back at him. "Of course you and I alibi each other for the afternoon, but from what you say, those poisoned pills could have been put in— well—almost any time, but I suppose in the morning. Vitamins are usually taken after meals."

"I like both your smile and your talent for deduction. Now I happen to know that dear mad Lucy keeps a small supply of nightcaps in a cupboard on the right-hand side by the kitchen sink—of all places. Shall we indulge, or was that revolting limeade strong enough for you?"

"I didn't like it much," Fredericka confessed. "Well, since you know so much about it, perhaps you'll do the honours. And, I just *might* join you."

Later, sitting in the living room with their drinks, Peter said quietly: "You asked, quite reasonably, why I'm in on this show. And just so that you will know I'm not the murderer in disguise, I'll try to explain myself— though it isn't easy." He hesitated for a moment and then went on slowly as though choosing his words with care. "You know that I teach at the college and that I am trying to train bright young and not-so-young men to be better diplomats, or, shall we say, servants of their country in foreign parts. My actual subject is called "Military Intelligence." What you don't know, and neither do very many other people, is that, during the war, I was an O.S.S. officer, and, well, I've kept up my interests in crime detection on a peacetime level, ever since. Perhaps, since for some reason I feel I can trust you (and I trust I've learned to be a good judge of character, too), I can go as far as to tell you that I still am an army officer on the administrative side. I am technically on leave for this job which is considered by the government to be of considerable importance. And while I don't somehow feel that our Catherine was an oh-so-beautiful spy, there is always the chance that murder so close to Sutton College could have serious implications. And even if this turns out to be a village affair, as well it might, Thane Carey doesn't seem to mind my being in on it under the circumstances."

Fredericka looked at him directly. "I appreciate your confidence in me, Peter," she said simply. "I—well, I do realize that I've not been much help to date, but I think I can honestly say that I'm far more afraid of uncertainty and black magic than I am of facts, no matter how horrible they are. I'm grateful to you for giving them to me and—well—for offering me the job of Watson to your Holmes. I'll try to be of some use. And now I'm going to sleep on this—thanks again to you."

"Good girl." Peter smiled and as she stood up, he did too. "Not scared of bears chasing you up the stairs, are you?" he asked.

"Not when the army is within hail," she answered, and then said: "What time do you want breakfast?"

"Six-thirty."

"Good grief. Well, I'm not quite so sure now that I like being a female Watson, and you may have to thump on the ceiling at six."

"O.K. I want to get away from here before your Chris or friend Carey arrive. I'd never hear the last of this." He fished in his pocket awkwardly. "I picked this up when I got my toothbrush." He handed her a small book. "You can borrow it for a very limited time. It's my bible but it—well, it sort of explains things."

Fredericka took the book from him, and sensing that he did not want to say more, muttered a quick "Thanks" and "Good night," and started up the stairs.

But, once more, Peter called her back. "What was worrying you so much when I found you and your pals in the drugstore?"

"Oh that—I tried to tell you before—I had just decided that the box must belong to Catherine, but that's ancient history now."

"Yes, but you score again for deduction— Good night."

"Good night," Fredericka said once more and, this time, succeeded in leaving him.

As she undressed slowly, the memory of her evening's encounter with James faded. It was good to know that Peter was in the house and within call. So it was *Murder*. It was true that she had known it all along. She had felt it in the very atmosphere, even before she had seen Catherine's face as she lay dead in the hammock.

Fredericka got into bed determined not to take another pill—to think of nothing—to let her mind slip easily into unconsciousness—to feel secure and at peace for this blessed protected night. But when she had put out the light, her thoughts raced madly around the problems and strange happenings of this new life. How different it had proved from what she had expected and how different, too, from the apartment-to-library and library-back-to-apartment routine that had been her whole existence for the last ten years of her life. She tossed and turned, felt hot, then cold. And inevitably, she began to think about Peter Mohun—and to wish that it had been he who had wanted to kiss her. The thought embarrassed her and she blushed hotly in the darkness: Until this moment she had deliberately avoided all thought of him as a man. He had been her kind friend, he was now her Sherlock Holmes and, for the time being, her watch dog. She must not, must not, *must not*, think of him in any other way. . . .

There had been no one in her life since Stephen Good who had married someone else. She had always persuaded herself that Stephen had been the only love of her life—that there would never, could never, be anyone else. But she had been a child then, barely twenty. For fifteen long years since then, she had lived on this belief. But was that only because the men she had met afterwards had failed to "capture her imagination" as he had done? Somewhere she had read that it was this, more than anything else that turned friendship to love. And Peter Mohun—there was no doubt about it—Peter Mohun was a man to capture the imagination, and stir the sleeping heart. But how did Peter Mohun feel? Was he a man of steel and flint like the heroes created by her Victorian novelists? He had been married, she knew, and divorced, if one could count on town gossip. But she must not think of love. She must not allow herself to spoil a friendship that promised so much.

This firm resolution taken, Fredericka turned over so that she could look out to the luminous night sky and its pinpricks of light, like the lovely star pattern of her quilt. She must do something about that quilt tomorrow. She turned her back on the night. But still sleep would not come.

And then she remembered the book. She had carried it upstairs after Peter had given it to her and had put it on the bed table. But from that moment to this, she had forgotten it. She sat up, turned on the light, and opened the book to the title page. *Spycatcher* by Oreste Pinto. She turned the leaves slowly and presently came to a pencilled passage.

The potential spy-catcher needs at least ten qualities, seven of which he must be born with and three of which can be acquired by his own efforts.

1. *Phenomenal memory.*
2. *Great patience and regard for detail.*
3. *Gift for languages.*
4. *Knowledge of practical psychology.*
5. *Courage.*
6. *Baedeker-like knowledge of the capitals and important towns in Europe.*

Beside this item Peter had scribbled, "or the U.S.A. for that matter."

7. *Thorough knowledge of international law.*
8. *Must be born actor.*
9. *Gift of detection (in many ways this is a highly developed sense of logic).*
10. *A practical experience of previous dodges.*

Fredericka studied this list with interest. Obviously to track down the murderer of Catherine Clay was well within the province of the spy-catcher and indeed could be considered essential training under several of these heads. As if to underline this, Fredericka came on another marked passage.

The task of counter-intelligence in peace or war is similar to that of the police. It is, first of all, to prevent spying and acts of treachery against the well-being of the state, and, secondly, if such acts are committed, to trace and arrest the person responsible.

Well, Fredericka thought, that seems to make every-thing crystal clear. No wonder Thane Carey lets him in on his local excitement. No wonder. She picked up the book again and went on through it carefully, giving espe-cial attention to the marked passages. By the time she was ready for sleep, it was well after two A.M., and, as she reached to turn out the light one thought emerged from her reading. It was evident—more than evident, since this book was his bible, that Colonel Peter Mohun, U.S.A., was a dedicated man. It would be wise, therefore, for Fredericka Wing to remember this, and to stop ro-mancing. From this sound, if somewhat sad, reflection, she was at last released by sleep.

Fredericka was awakened by a curious thumping noise that for some moments set her heart beating wildly and made her sit bolt upright in the half darkness. Then she heard a muffled voice:

"Fredericka, FREDERICKA WING—are you dead, too?"

Peter. Of course. She reached over the side of the bed and banged on the floor with the heel of her bedslip-per.

Silence.

Fredericka got up quickly and went to the head of the stairs to call down the advice that she would appear in ten minutes.

She did it, too, and won a smile of approval from her self-appointed boss whom she found busy in the kitchen.

"I didn't read in your book that spy-catchers had to be cooks."

"Oh, but that goes without saying. Scratch meals under difficulties. And," he hesitated, and then went on quickly, "as you may have gathered they have to do without wives."

Fredericka said nothing in reply to this. Since she had gathered as much from her reading, she didn't think it necessary or even very polite to have it announced with a megaphone, and at such an early hour in the morning.

She managed to say nothing, however, and, after a few moments, Peter went on cheerfully: "So you've read my bible? What did you think of it?"

"I think, as the author himself suggests, that your job is: one, inhuman, and two, thankless."

"How right you are. Clever Fredericka. I'll graduate you *cum laude* before I finish with you."

"Thanks. Am I allowed to fry the bacon?" Fredericka asked a little stiffly.

"Granted." Peter answered, darting her a quick sideways glance.

A moment later she said: "I've learned lesson number one—the one contained in your bible—so you can take your book home now. If it's so desperately important, you may miss it."

Peter began to whistle tunelessly and Fredericka's annoyance evaporated. By the time they sat down at the table by the kitchen window, she was able to laugh happily, and to enjoy their early morning meal during which they did not once mention murder, marriage or allied subjects. For that hour they talked only of unimportant and pleasant things, and for that hour, they were both content.

10

Promptly at nine o'clock on that Wednesday morning of the week following the death of Catherine Clay, Chief Carey put in his appearance at the bookshop. He was very official and businesslike and it was obvious that he had expected to have to rouse Fredericka as he had on his first visit. He was therefore somewhat taken aback to find her hard at work. And, for Fredericka, his arrival was a distinct anticlimax.

It had been seven-thirty, or shortly after, when Peter had left, and the hour and a half since then had dragged away slowly. She had given Chris his coffee when he appeared at eight and had tried to talk to him but he had been quiet and uncommunicative. After several abortive attempts to find out what people were saying in the village, Fredericka decided that it would be best to give up this early morning attempt to be Dr. Watson and put Chris on to the attack on the shrubbery as a way to work off his obvious anxieties.

Fredericka had then gone back into the house and

wondered what to do next. Hours ago it seemed, she had washed the breakfast dishes and straightened the office so that all evidence of her night's visitor had been removed. Now, with Chris at work in the yard, the long day lay ahead and the kitchen clock said definitely that it was only a few minutes past eight. Work had been the answer for Chris, very well then, she would take the medicine she had so readily prescribed. She would forget the whirling merry-go-round of evil happenings in which she had been caught, she would even forget Peter Mohun. Yes. She would tackle the last issue of the *Publisher's Weekly* and check through it for orders.

But though she managed to look busy, the medicine wasn't working. The pages blurred before her eyes, a fly buzzed angrily against the window screen, and she was acutely aware that she was very short of sleep. If ever this wretched business was over— But she must get to work at something. Thane Carey would be coming. She couldn't go back to bed at this hour. And then, scarcely aware what she was doing, she reached for a large pad of clean yellow paper. Her pencil hung over it for a moment and then wrote the word Suspects. After that the list of names followed easily. It began, inevitably with Catherine's immediate family. *Mrs. Sutton?* Could anyone be less likely? And yet might she not have killed Catherine to save her from herself? *Roger?* Possible, and by his own evidence he had hated his sister and for good reason. *Philippine?* Equally possible, but why? She might have wanted to marry James and it had certainly looked that way. Yes, and James obviously had the same idea in mind, but Philippine would never have needed to *murder* Catherine to achieve this when James was as good as hooked already. *James?* As she wrote his name, she saw again his sensuous face. A very likely suspect but she mustn't be prejudiced by her own personal feelings about him. In the bright light of day she was able to persuade herself that James Brewster had probably wanted nothing more than a little evening's entertainment. Well, perhaps he got it with Philippine. Yes, he certainly had preferred Philippine to Catherine but surely a man like James could slip out of any entanglement—unless, of course, he was secretly *married* to Catherine. That was an interesting idea for Dr. Watson to suggest to Sherlock Holmes. Yes. And James had seen Catherine dead and had not told anyone. *Mrs. Hartwell?* Very unlikely— A gossip and a busybody—possibly as a cover-up, though, for the real Mrs. Hartwell. She could be spiteful and scheming. It showed in her face. But what motive except the universal hate? *Margie?—*

Fredericka put down her pencil and stared at the backs of the books on the shelf over the desk. Margie had hated Catherine. This was an undeniable fact. Margie had been distraught and difficult all week. And, it was Margie who had given the warning on the night the body had been found. No one had paid much attention when she had fairly screamed it out during the bazaar supper but it was worth remembering now. Margie was emotionally unstable—the kind of girl who, when she was younger, must have run away from home; and who now in adolescence might do anything spectacular and theatrical in order to draw attention to herself. It was most likely Margie who had come snooping about the night before last. But *murder.* No. It wasn't possible.

Fredericka now shifted her gaze to the yellow pad and the list of names that she had written down. She could go on adding to it forever, of course, since anyone in the village had opportunity and Catherine Clay was not loved. No, it would not be difficult to find motives.

She picked up the pencil and wrote *Chris?* It could be guilt or some secret knowledge or just plain fear, that had so changed him in these last few days. What motive could he have had unless Catherine had something on him? Something to do with her dope supply perhaps? But how in tunket could he get poison into vitamin capsules? No, it was more likely that Chris knew something that he was afraid to tell. She stared down at the block of paper before her. *Yellow.* "Yellow jessamine," Peter had said. Surely that was a flower of some sort. And wasn't that the kind of thing that one would find in the Farm laboratory? That meant—but did it? She'd have to ask Peter about this. Anyone could have gone into the lab when the place was deserted as it often was with Margie gallivanting about town and Philippine and Roger more often than not off after wild herbs. And it probably would take less skill than practice to get the poison into the capsules. Peter hadn't said anything about yellow jessamine being a likely product of the Farm lab. But perhaps it had been too obvious to mention. Perhaps he had wanted her to think this bright thought for herself.

It was at this moment that Thane Carey arrived. He walked in the front door quietly and without knocking. Fredericka tried to slip the telltale yellow pad under the open copy of the *Publisher's Weekly* without being too obvious about it. Peter had given her specific instructions. She was not to let Thane Carey know that she had had advance information. Peter had said, moreover, that he wanted her position as Watson to be a secret one for the time being. Understandable. But Fredericka knew herself to lack one of the spy-catcher's most essential qualities. She was not a born actor. Fortunately, on this occasion, Chief Carey did not give her a severe test. His suspicions and thoughts were elsewhere.

"Good morning," Fredericka greeted him. She swung around to turn her back on the desk.

"Good morning," he said quickly. "I'm sorry to barge in on you like this but we all got the habit with Lucy Hartwell who, for some reason, didn't like knocking."

"It's quite all right. I'm getting used to it now," Fredericka answered, trying not to show the relief she felt at his lack of interest in what she had been doing.

"I won't keep you long. May I call you Fredericka, since everyone else does? It—well, it makes me feel less like the chief of police, and I'm afraid I've got to be just that, at any rate for the time being." He coughed a little self-consciously.

"Of course, do, Thane. But—but what do you mean?"

"Catherine Clay was murdered," he announced quietly.

And, as he spoke, it was not difficult for Fredericka to look startled. Foreknowledge had not erased the grim fact. The fear and horror remained. She said nothing, but there was no need, and, after a moment, Thane went on to tell her about the poisoned capsules, the manner of death and all the other details which she had already learned from Peter. When he had summarized the facts, he stopped for a moment and then said a little sharply; "You've still got that box?"

"Yes. It's right here." Fredericka opened the drawer a little apprehensively and, to her relief, found the box. She handed it to Thane.

"This object itself isn't much use to me. But there

are so many puzzling things about it," he said as if to himself.

"Did you find any fingerprints before you gave it to me?" Fredericka asked.

"Only Catherine Clay's. My man picked it up with a handkerchief most carefully but there wasn't even another smudge."

"Then you must have known it was Catherine's when you gave it to me to find out—I don't quite understand."

"We thought it must be hers but we were really looking for people's reactions to the sight of the box," Thane explained.

"I see," Fredericka said, "and you didn't want to tell me too much just then . . ."

"Well, no—not then"— he went on hurriedly, "the odd thing to me is that the murderer should have made the manner of death so apparent. I mean, why so few pills—the one she took presumably, and only the two or three that remained?"

Fredericka was interested. This was the kind of deduction she liked. "But surely," she said quickly, "the murderer intended her death to look like an overdose of dope. Everyone seemed to know that Catherine took it. It never occurred to him—or her—that there would be an autopsy—and a few pills made it so much easier on the manufacturing end. Besides Catherine probably had only two or three left in the box just then. No, I think the murderer would have expected you to be looking for the dope syringe. Vitamin capsules are innocent enough." She stopped for a moment and then another thought occurred to her. "If it got to the point of an autopsy, of course, then the fact that the poison was yellow jessamine would be known and the way it had been taken of less importance."

"I see your reasoning but I must say it sounds very female, to me," Thane said slowly. "And I still think the murderer would want us to be in the dark about how the poison got inside Catherine and would have made some attempt to recover that box afterwards, with or without finger prints."

Fredericka started to say: "Maybe that's what James Brewster was looking for—" and caught herself in time. After all she wasn't supposed to know about James. Instead she said quickly; "Yes, but no one knew where the death would happen. Short of trailing the victim, the murderer wouldn't know either, and by the time the news got around, you had a police guard on the body, and the whole place combed for clues."

"It's an odd thing about murderers. They always seem so ready to believe that death will be assumed to be natural but, in a case like this, it almost never is."

"No, I guess not. And yet South Sutton is a sleepy little town. If Dr. Scott had been as easygoing as village doctors are supposed to be—and there hadn't happened to be an intelligent chief of police, then—"

"Yes, but that presupposes someone who didn't know either Dr. Scott or me and I must say that seems unlikely. Incidentally, Fredericka, if you continue to pay me compliments, I shall begin to suspect *you,* and I confess that I would very much dislike that—not because I wish to spare you anything, of course, but just because it is such a relief to be able to rule out two people in this place— It gives me someone to talk to."

"Two people?"

"Yes, you and Peter Mohun."

"I don't quite see how we're in the clear but if you do, I'm certainly not going to argue with you."

"Well, I work it out this way, though perhaps I shouldn't enlighten you. Catherine was in the habit of taking the vitamin pills after meals. This has been agreed by every member of the household, and everyone who knew her. That means that it was the after-lunch dose that did it and that, since the morning dose didn't, the switch over in the box happened between, say, ten A.M. and two P.M., and most likely in the morning as soon as the after-breakfast pill had been taken. Catherine was at the farm all morning. Several people saw her. At some time during the morning the box was on the sideboard in the dining room. Margie acts as though she knows more than she has told but she does say that she saw the silver case there after breakfast and so did someone else—a maid, I think. Fredericka Wing couldn't have got out to the Farm to make the exchange—well, you *could* have, I suppose. But you were keeping the shop open and Chris says you didn't leave the place."

"I see— But Peter—"

"We'll leave him out of this. I don't know why I'm talking so much as it is."

Fredericka couldn't resist asking one more question. "But doesn't the fact of the box being there at the Farm and—and a sort of flower or herb kind of poisoning—point to someone out there? I mean, can't you narrow it down?" She stopped abruptly, seeing his frown.

"No. Look at it this way. Suppose the murderer wanted to make it look like someone out there. It would be a beautiful blind, wouldn't it? All those herbs, poison and plain, are labelled and easily accessible. Nothing whatever is under lock and key and the whole town runs in and out of the place all the time. And now I really have talked too much, and I am unworthy of my—I was going to say *stripes*—but perhaps *badge* is the right word." He smiled pleasantly, however, and then added: "Perhaps I should just confess that Peter says you can be trusted. How he knows I can't think. But there it is, and like a lot of other people in this town for me what Colonel Peter Mohun says—GOES."

Fredericka said nothing and after a moment Thane got up. "I haven't mentioned that business about Margie paying you a midnight visit but I can assure you that it has been very much on my mind."

"It was Margie then?"

"I'm quite certain it was but she won't admit it. Scared stiff to, I suppose. I even told her we knew about her beauty parlor in the greenhouse but that was a mistake. She only became more clam-like than ever. If she wasn't such a kid, I'd resort to third degree—"

"Someone ought to be able to win her confidence and trust. That would make more sense." Fredericka thought guiltily of her own failure but then Margie had made her an enemy from the moment of their first meeting.

"Well, we can but try."

Fredericka followed Thane to the door and watched him put on his hat. Then he grinned back at her from the path. "Scorcher, isn't it? Just my luck with a thousand and one people to see and they'll all be bears, I wouldn't wonder."

"You seem to have covered a lot of ground already," Fredericka couldn't resist saying.

"I work late and early. But so far, only the obvious suspects and that's about one fiftieth of the job. A policeman's lot—and all that!"

He doesn't look in the least like a policeman, Fredericka decided as she returned to her desk and the comparative comfort of the office. He doesn't even wear a uniform and his disreputable hat is only a concession to the sun. But perhaps chiefs are like plainclothes men. Perhaps they graduate out of a uniform or keep it pressed for state occasions.

It was only ten-thirty. And already the day had been hours long. Well, the bookshop must come first, and Fredericka Wing must get back to work. With a great effort of will, she tore her list of suspects off the pad and began to jot down titles and publishers. But after a few moments she remembered that it was early closing day in the village. Miss Hartwell had said she could shut up the shop or not as she wanted. Perhaps she would lock the doors and retire to her sanctuary in the apple orchard where she had escaped often in that other life— that blessed week before the murder. There she could read in peace even if her mind was in too much of a turmoil to write. Chris would be knocking off at noon, she felt sure . . . and she didn't really want to be alone in the shop . . . . On such a hot day customers would be few and far between. . . .

This serious matter decided, Fredericka returned to her list but she had added only one title when Mrs. Williams appeared. Her visit was ostensibly to "borrow" Bertrand Russell which her husband wanted to quote in his sermon but it was obvious that, in fact, she wanted to discuss the latest developments in South Sutton's first murder case. Fredericka had no sooner got rid of her than Margie made one of her sudden back door entrances, came straight to the office, and sank limply into the big chair.

Fredericka's annoyance faded at sight of the girl's flushed face and distraught manner. "What's the matter,

Margie?" she asked kindly. Perhaps now, at last, she could talk to the child. Confront her with facts and force her to an admission of whatever it was that she was hiding.

"Nothing." Margie's voice was sullen.

For a moment Fredericka said no more, and made a pretence of returning to work.

"Mother wants that cookery book I told you about last week."

"I don't think it's come yet."

"Chris has just brought up a parcel from the post office. I saw him taking it back to the stockroom when I came in." She hesitated, then said: "Shall I go down and see if the book's in it?"

The thought of Margie undoing a parcel that hadn't been checked and mussing up the stock was too much for Fredericka.

"No, I'll go," she said, without enthusiasm. But perhaps if she humoured the child, she would divulge what was on her mind.

Fredericka had gone halfway down the back path when a sudden thought occurred to her. That cook book couldn't possibly have come in so soon. Margie was up to some mischief, and Margie was on the suspect list— more than that, Margie's mischief could be serious. She turned in her tracks and hurried back to the house. She slipped off her shoes at the back door and returned quietly to the office.

Margie, with her back to the door was searching frantically through the desk drawer.

"What are you doing, Margie?" Fredericka asked sharply.

The girl stopped her search as though she had been struck, slammed the drawer and swung round. Her eyes were frantic and staring and her cheeks crimson. She looked not only frightened, but ill.

"I—I left a notebook here when I was in the other day," she said quickly.

"Surely not in my desk drawer."

"Well. You might have put it in. I didn't know."

"You could have asked."

Margie made no reply. She seemed to crumple suddenly and slumped into the chair.

"Are you ill?" Fredericka asked. She was now torn between anxiety and anger.

"No I'm not. But if you think I'm going to say anything more to you, I'm not. What business have you to keep someone else's silver box in your drawer anyway?"

"So that's what you were after." Fredericka sat down, and put her hand on Margie's knee. "Come Margie," she said quietly, "tell me what it's all about." But Margie's face had set in a mask of hatred—or fear, Fredericka couldn't be sure which. After a few fruitless attempts to make the girl speak, Fredericka lost her temper.

"Margie, I must say to you now and for all time, that, if you can't behave yourself, you needn't come here at all. Miss Hartwell said you would help me. *Help* indeed. You barge in and out without knocking. You rummage in the storeroom. You play insufferable childish pranks. And now you rummage in my desk—"

"*Aunt Lucy's* desk." Margie's face was now blotched with deep purple stains—and her words sounded strangled.

"You'd better go then, Margie, before I lose my temper altogether. I'm in charge here now, as it happens. And for the time being this is *my* desk." Fredericka felt suddenly ashamed. Why did this child enrage her so?

She struggled with herself but before she could speak again, Margie had got to her feet quickly and had slammed her way out of the house.

What a fine detective she had turned out to be. Whatever would Peter think of her? Oh well, it was too hot to care—too hot to chase after the wretched girl. Fredericka looked at her watch and saw with relief that it was after twelve. She would just get some cold coffee for lunch and then lock up and escape. The orchard would be hot, perhaps, but less so than the house and no one could find her there. Blessed thought.

When Fredericka looked out the back door and saw that Chris was still working away at the shrubs with his pruning knife, she called to him and he dropped his tool as though he had been attacked. Then he stooped to pick it up and turned to come toward her. It was like a slowmotion film.

"Sure am hot," he volunteered when he had come close enough to be heard.

"Yes. I thought you might like some iced coffee," she added. Suddenly she didn't want him to go. She didn't want to be left alone. Peter had spoken of a police guard but Thane Carey had said nothing about it.

"Sure thing." Chris answered her with a tired smile and, as Frederick turned to go in, he sank down on to the porch and pulled out a red and white spotted handkerchief to mop his face and neck.

Fredericka carried his drink and a plate of sandwiches out on to the porch and after she had had her own lunch she went back to find him still sitting as she had left him. He looked up at her and she could see the panic on his face.

"I reckon I ought to give you-all the benefit of my perteckshun this afternoon," he said slowly.

"Oh no, Chris. I—I'm all right. I don't think anyone wants to do me any harm," she said with a thin show of courage.

"No, Ma'am, Miss Wing, that ain't the trouble. It's jes' these kids around here. I been chasin' them off'n the place all the morning. Comin' in every which ways to see where the—the murder been done at."

This was an unexpected development. Annoying.

"There's one of 'em now." A tousled dark head appeared through the shrubbery and, finding itself observed, as quickly withdrew.

"Up to mischief all the hours of the day and night—Don't mean no harm though."

"No—unless they start collecting souvenirs." Fredericka had no great love for children and a few weeks filling in for a children's librarian in a branch on the lower east side of New York had given her a wholesome respect for their capacity for devilry. But country kids should be more manageable. Still . . . She was thoughtful for a moment. This could be used as a reasonable excuse to telephone the Police Station and ask for a man to guard the place. She couldn't expect Peter to come another night—and she mustn't admit to being afraid— No, if this worked it would be wonderful. She got up quickly and, after mumbling something to Chris about waiting a few minutes longer, she went in to the office to telephone.

The sergeant on duty was polite but not very helpful. Once more, she asked to speak to the chief, and this request was followed by a long pause. Then, at last, she heard Thane Carey's voice.

"Sorry, Fredericka," he said, before she could speak, "Sergeant Brown tells me you've had to call up and ask for a man and I had intended to send one around long ago. I might have known the kids wouldn't miss this swell chance to play up. The trouble is I've got to get help from Worcester and the two men I asked for haven't come in yet. But I'll send Brown down anyway. I'll be here until the others come in. They're due any minute now."

"That's all right, Thane, I'm afraid I'm being a nuisance. I wouldn't mind so much except that it's Miss Hartwell's place, not mine." She was pleased that her voice sounded casual and concerned, but not too concerned.

"I know, and both Peter and I think you ought to have someone around anyway. In fact we'd like to strew men around all over the map. That's why I have to have help."

"But there's no hurry, Thane," Fredericka said quickly, "I've got Chris here. It's his afternoon off but I'm sure he'll stay until your extra men arrive."

"O.K. then. Thanks." The receiver clicked abruptly and Fredericka was aware of her disappointment. She had been longing to ask where the other men would be placed and whether or not there was any fresh news. But perhaps it was just as well for him to be businesslike, especially on the telephone. She got up and went back to the porch to collect the soiled dishes. Chris appeared to be half-asleep in the midday heat and when Frederick roused him, he seemed a little reluctant to stay on alone. For this reason, she decided to postpone her retreat to the orchard and returned without enthusiasm to her cluttered desk.

As Fredericka worked, her mind kept returning to Margie. What had she been doing in the greenhouse in the middle of the night? Why had she been so upset today? Why did she want that miserable box? A sense of guilt overwhelmed Fredericka. If only she could bring herself to like the girl or even feel sorry for her, then she might have persuaded her to stay and have gotten a confession from her. *Notebook.* What absolute nonsense. The more she thought of Margie, the more her own sense of failure increased. Peter had always been so much kinder to the girl than she had been. He would have quieted her overwrought nerves and drawn her out slowly. What a fine Watson Fredericka was turning out to be, she thought, and what a fine compassionate motherly female, too.

Fredericka was relieved to be released from these uncomfortable thoughts by the arrival of the policeman. It proved to be Sergeant Brown whom she knew, because it was he who had been on duty outside on the night of Catherine Clay's death. He was a pleasant open-faced young man and much nicer, Fredericka decided, in the flesh than on the telephone. Perhaps it was the effect of the police station and the shadow of Thane Carey. She offered him iced coffee which he accepted with alacrity, and then said he'd tell Chris to go along and that he himself would "just hang about" outside. Fredericka told him of her plan to escape to the orchard to rest and work in peace and he nodded his approval.

"I should think you'd be dead, Miss Wing," he said. "This isn't what we usually provide for newcomers to South Sutton, Mass."

"I'm quite aware of that. It's a lovely place."

Sergeant Brown started to enlarge on its beauties but Fredericka cut him short with, "Yes— Well, now I must get my things together."

The young man moved off toward the back door smoothing his beautifully brilliantined hair with a large sunburnt hand before replacing his cap. But just as he opened the screen, he turned back to call loudly: "Now don't you worry, Miss Wing. When I'm on duty, I'm on duty, if you know what I mean. I'm O.K. as a watchdog."

"Watchdog." Good. It made her think of Peter, and that was good, too.

As Fredericka went out by the back door she called goodbye to Chris, who answered her cheerfully. Ten minutes later she had made herself a nest in the long grass under an ancient pear tree and had opened her book. In another ten minutes she was fast asleep.

11

After her nap in the orchard, Fredericka felt much better. She got slowly to her feet and picked up her clean pad of paper, her unused pencil and her unread book. Then she looked at her watch and was amazed to discover that she had slept for three hours. When she got back to the house, Sergeant Brown was nowhere to be seen and, feeling the silence and the loneliness, she managed to bang the screen door as she went indoors. The noise reassured her and it occurred to her that it might also summon her protector. And she was right. In a few moments Sergeant Brown put his head inside the kitchen door where Fredericka was making some fresh iced tea. He took a glass when she offered it to him and lingered a moment to gossip, with his broad back leaning against the door frame and his giant's feet crossed before him.

"Have the children kept you busy?" Fredericka asked, sipping her own tea with pleasure.

"No." He laughed, and then added: "It's like having

a cat in the house just to keep away mice. Policeman's the same thing as regards kids."

"I'm afraid it's been pretty boring for you then. I'm sorry."

"To tell you the truth I can do with a quiet spell. We've had all the fireworks we want in South Sutton for some time to come. Amen."

"I would have thought you were young enough to like fireworks." Fredericka felt that she was being stupid. But even a dull and pointless conversation was better than no conversation at all. The broadness of Sergeant Brown's back and the sight of the revolver in its holster were very reassuring. She offered him some more tea quickly and filled his glass before he could refuse.

But she had slept too long. She couldn't concentrate and, after a time, she couldn't think of anything more to say herself. Sergeant Brown refused a third glass of tea and muttered something about getting back on the job. As he left, he said over his shoulder: "Nothing to worry about, Miss Wing. You can count on Jim Brown. I'll stay within call, but if this afternoon's a fair sample, I'm not going to be wanted much longer—worse luck!"

As it turned out, the peace of Sergeant Brown's first afternoon held for two days and two nights, but Thane Carey did not take him off the job of guarding Fredericka and the bookshop. This was a great relief to the new manager, who could not shake her conviction that the peace was a false one, a lull before the final storm. Even at the post office the cheerful voices of the gossips were subdued and heavy with foreboding. In the bookshop, people no longer stopped to talk. Fredericka, who had become unnaturally sensitive, felt that, by having the corpse lie in her hammock, and, even worse, by discovering it herself in the first place, she had assumed the position of chief suspect in the eyes of the town. She thought it unfair to divulge, even to Philippine and those most frequent customers who were becoming friends that she had been freed of suspicion by the chief of police himself. But the loneliness, caused by the unfortunate circumstances of her position, increased. Sergeant Brown's comforting presence released her from fear but not from worry. The worst of it was that, since the night that Peter Mohun had slept on the office couch, she had seen nothing of him. She thought over the events of that evening and tried to remember every word that they had spoken to each other. But it all added up to the message he had given her in his hateful book. Perhaps that was why he found it necessary to leave her so severely alone.

On Friday evening as she was washing her dishes and thinking dark thoughts, she suddenly flicked her towel furiously. Why did she have to care whether or not Peter Mohun was dedicated heart and soul to his spy-catching? Why did it matter if he didn't come to see her?

"As if I wanted him to . . ." she heard herself say out loud to the tall glass that she had been absently polishing for all of ten minutes.

"Wanted *who* to do *what?*" A voice directly behind her spoke suddenly.

The glass crashed to the floor and broke into tiny fragments as Fredericka swung round.

"Oh, Fredericka, my dear, I *am* sorry." This time Peter Mohun's voice was wholly solicitous. He reached out his hand as if to give her reassurance, but she shrank away from him and leant back against the sink. "I am an unregenerate fool, a demon, a beast—whatever you like to call me, I shall accept with bowed and penitent head."

When Fredericka still made no reply, he blundered on helplessly: "It's these crêpe soles. It's useful sometimes to silence one's approach, I confess it. But I should have knocked. That's another thing. Lucy objected to the racket, so I and all the rest of the town, I expect, have developed the habit of walking straight in."

"It's, it's quite all right. Silly of me to be such a fool." She felt an urgent need to make some move. "I'll just get the dustpan and sweep up this mess and then—"

"Then I hope you can spare me a little while to talk, to gossip, and maybe even to laugh." He watched her intently as she walked across the room to the cupboard and fumbled nervously with the catch. When she came back he took the brush and dustpan from her and said: "My job. You go and set yourself down. It's so hot, I suggest the porch. O.K.?"

"O.K." Frederick agreed gratefully. Anyway he seemed to have forgotten what she had been muttering when he came in. She must get over this trick of talking to herself. It came from living too much alone.

"And now," Peter said at once when he joined her, *"who* has failed to do *what* that he should do?"

"Oh, Peter, I was just muttering away to myself about nothing."

"Oh no, you weren't. You were making a solemn and serious pronouncement and I have a hunch, though perhaps it's a little conceited of me, that the guy referred to was Peter Mohun."

"Well, I did think you'd have looked in to see how I was before now." Fredericka was grateful for the half-darkness that hid her hot and flaming face.

"I meant to, as a matter of fact, but I've been on the go every moment since I left this place so early of a morning—" He hesitated and then said slowly, "I tried to warn you that I'm an unreliable guy—"

Suddenly Fredericka's pent up anxiety and annoyance poured out in a quick rush of words: "Oh, you don't need to tell me all that again. I read your bible, and I'm not stupid—"

"Of course you aren't stupid. But I am," Peter said quietly. He reached across the space between them and took her thin hand in his large one.

For a moment neither of them spoke and then Peter said slowly, "I'm a mug, and I've behaved like one. The trouble is that my marriage was a mess—my fault probably, but anyway it was; and when at last I got free of it, I took a deep breath and decided to stay free. The dedication to work is what I've put in place of love and marriage and I just wanted you to know that—I suppose because I—well—I like you so much, Fredericka, and I was scared something would happen to our friendship."

Fredericka sat up a little more stiffly but she did not take away her hand. "If I'm to be honest, I might as well confess that I—I like you, too, Peter, and perhaps I might have, well, come to like you too much. So really I'm glad you've been honest with me. It's been a tough two days and I was peeved because I thought you'd abandoned me. So let's call it quits and—and—well, carry on as Holmes and Watson, both dedicated to the case in hand."

She laughed shyly and Peter joined her. Then he said: "Yes, the case in hand. That's the trouble. That's why I've left you so severely alone. I knew Thane's bodyguard was watching over you and I simply had to get to work. Frankly, Fredericka, I'm scared stiff. Even the air in this town is unhealthy, and on all sides I don't like what I see."

"Could you be a little more explicit?"

"I'll try, and perhaps you can help me to think out loud. The obvious suspects start with the family—or rather with those who live at the Farm, but they don't finish there."

"Yes, I know. After you left on Wednesday I made a list and tried to think of motives and opportunities. I've been thinking of them ever since."

"Good. Any results?"

"Only that there are plenty of people who hated Catherine, that Philippine and Brewster seem thick as thieves, and Margie has something on her mind."

"Well I have two new clues for you and we'll see if you can put them into their right places in the puzzle. One: A large supply of dope was found in that immense carryall bag that Mrs. Hartwell always carries everywhere with her."

"No! Not 'Mom' Hartwell!"

"Oh, yes. When questioned she denied all knowledge of it, of course—goes around muttering darkly about being 'framed.' She puts the blame on Philippine and says she has considered all along that Philippine is a bad influence on Margie."

"That's something quite new. First hint of criticism of Philippine."

"Not quite. Mrs. Williams has thrown out a lot of hints about her goings-on with our James. And that reminds me of item number two. James *has* bought that land behind the alley. What's more, hidden away under some old prints in his desk, we found a whole set of architects' drawings for the sweetest little house you ever saw. It was a Boston architect—our James is a cautious bird."

"And what does he say about that?"

"I haven't confronted him with it. I'm keeping it up my sleeve."

"Well, you have been busy."

"Yes, very." He was silent for a moment and then he went on: "James is behaving strangely, I must say. I think the fact that he's made his little half-confession has gone to his head. But he's still trying to hush everything up. I suppose if it had been ordinary scandal and not murder, his behaviour would seem quite natural. He's certainly doing his damnedest to keep the news out of the papers—to put the damper on and to make it into suicide for the benefit of the public."

"Yes, he tried that one on me." She was going to say more about what James had tried on her. Instead she went on quickly: "But he can't get away with it now, can he?"

"Well, Thane's backing him up. Oh, I know South Sutton is full of murder talk and burnt up with excitement on top of the heat, but it's still a private affair and hasn't got into the national headlines. None of us want that to happen—it would be bad for the college, for one thing."

"And I suppose the less fever and fuss, the less chance of another murder."

"Don't say it, Fredericka. That thought's never been out of my mind for one moment. Frankly, I'm worried sick about that kid, Margie."

"Margie?" Fredericka's voice was sharp with anxiety.

"Yes. You said a minute ago that she had something on her mind. What makes you think so?"

"She came dashing in on Wednesday morning, not long after Thane left. She was looking for that box. Oh dear, I think I could have got something out of her if only

I'd been patient and kind, but the fact is, Peter, it isn't in me to be patient and kind with a girl like that who manages to be so maddening—"

"I know."

"I don't think you do. She doesn't irritate you the way she does me. She took against me from the start and whenever she appears I can't wait for her to go. She just has a gift for rubbing me the wrong way." Fredericka paused, and when Peter said nothing, she added hurriedly: "I'm terribly sorry. In my better moments I really wish I could help the child."

"Well, I haven't had any more luck with her than you have. She shut up like a clam every time I tried to question her, and the worst of it is that what we took for fright is, in fact, illness. She's in a very bad way."

"Oh, Peter, I thought she looked sick on Wednesday. I could kick myself for the way I behaved. Would it do any good if I went to see her now?"

"No, I don't think so. I'm afraid she's too bad—Doctor Scott's keeping her pretty well doped."

"Good heavens, Peter, can't you *do* something. Is *she* being poisoned?"

"The devil of it is, I don't think she is. She doesn't seem to have the symptoms of a poison case. It's, well—it's much more like 'flu—or some kind of an infection."

"Peter—we've *got* to get her to talk. She may *die* if we don't."

Fredericka's distress was so great that Peter again reached out for her hand in the darkness. "Look here, Fredericka, what do you think I've been doing these two days? I've been at the Farm damn near every minute. If she has been poisoned, she's not getting any more now. We've got special nurses night and day who watch the liquids and medicines like hawks and she isn't eating anything, of course."

"It's—it's *that* bad?"

"Yes. I promise you that we're doing all we can. I wanted to take her at once to hospital but her mother wouldn't hear of it. Mrs. Hartwell was nearly frantic when we found the dope. Now, of course, she's as near insane as makes no matter. Of course neither she nor anyone else at the Farm dreams of poison, or lets on, if they do. It's only Thane and I and Dr. Scott and we think it quite possible that we're madly imaginative on account of Catherine's death."

"Is it wholly like an infection—or 'flu? What does Doctor Scott call it?"

"Virus. But there are one or two odd things about her. She rolls her eyeballs wildly. I thought it was fear or panic at first but now the pupils are dilated all the time. Well, if she isn't better this afternoon, Dr. Scott is going to insist that she go into hospital for tests."

Fredericka withdrew her hand and put her palm against her hot forehead. She couldn't talk about Margie any more. "What about the others?" she said quickly. "Do they behave in a normal way?"

"Oh yes. Perfectly. And they're all angelic to Margie. Mrs. Sutton has moved her into the spare room and is paying all the bills—the Hartwells are terribly hard up. Margaret practically supports them. Of course we have an eye on the lot of them, but they're *perfectly* normal in every respect. I suspect it's the relief of not having Catherine around the place."

"Roger?"

"Well, of course, he isn't quite normal at the best of times. But do you know before Margie got so bad he spent a whole afternoon reading to her. He's about to go back into hospital himself."

"Yes. He told me. It's for another face operation, isn't it?"

"Yes. It's been planned for weeks. There's no question of doing a bunk or anything." He stopped suddenly. "Look here, Fredericka, it's time you went to bed. But before you do, just think over your list of suspects and try to remember anything—even the least important nothing—that might give us a glimmer."

Fredericka pressed both hands against her closed eyelids and made a great effort to think. Mrs. Sutton, Roger, Philippine, James, Mom Hartwell, Margie—Chris— Suddenly she sat up. "Have you and Thane questioned Chris?" she asked.

"Yes. Both of us. But no results of any importance. Why?"

"Oh, it may be my imagination, but I think he has something on his mind—or, at any rate, I think he's scared. You see he knows them all at the Farm so well. He's always doing odd jobs for them and he has a kind of dog-like devotion to them all—even Margie. He goes out there every day with the mail, you know."

"The mail—Now *there's* something to look into. I wonder . . ."

"Oh, Peter, I do remember something now. When was it? Yes, I know. It wasn't the Monday after the murder because Chris didn't come that day. He was terrified, I think. No, it was on the Tuesday. He brought me the mail and asked for a French stamp on one of my letters. It seems he's a collector. Then he told me with a certain lugubrious pleasure that he had a letter for Catherine Clay with a stamp just like mine—it was an airmail one,

I think—and remarked with painful obviousness that she wouldn't be able to get it because she was dead."

"I see. Interesting. A letter from France two days after her death. Very interesting."

"Yes. I was surprised. Could it be anything to do with her dope supply, do you think?"

"Possibly. Anyway, it's worth investigating. We're on to the dope business—that is, we're making efforts to trace it. I may have to go to Washington, but I hope not."

"I hope not, too," Fredericka said, and then could have bitten her tongue out.

"Well, it may not be necessary." Peter stood up. "I must be off now, I'm afraid, but I can't thank you enough for your help tonight. Just talking to you has been a comfort, and now Miss Doctor Watson has really given me a clue—bless her!"

"There was another thing I thought of. Catherine and James couldn't have been secretly married, could they? It would give him such a beautiful motive."

"I think you have designs on James. All the same it's an interesting idea, but I think we'd have discovered it by now. Anyway, why hide it? And now, I'm off—"

"Can't you just stay for some coffee or—or—something stronger from Miss Hartwell's cupboard?"

"No, I'd like to, but I mustn't. It isn't too late to look in on Margie and have a word with Mrs. Sutton about that letter for Catherine."

"I've just remembered that it was Margie, not Chris, who took the letters out to the Farm that day. She came in and asked for them."

"Did she now?"

When he said nothing more Fredericka waited for him to go on. But he seemed to have fallen into a deep study. At last she said: "Well, I'll just walk around to the front with you, if you must go. I'd rather like to see where my protector is and whether he'd like an innocent police-like nightcap since you turn me down."

As they skirted the house, they saw that the reading lamp was on in the office, and that Sergeant Brown was sitting in the big chair with a pile of comics on the floor beside him.

"It's almost insulting in a bookshop, isn't it?" Fredericka laughed.

"Yes, with all those lovely volumes so handy," Peter agreed. "Nevertheless it makes me feel good to see him there, comics or no comics."

"Me, too," Fredericka agreed quietly.

They walked to the gate in silence and then Peter said hurriedly: "Good night, Watson—and, again, my thanks and blessings."

"Good night, Sherlock," Fredericka answered, and then: "Try to let me know about Margie tomorrow, if you can."

"I will. But I can't promise. You do understand, don't you?" When Fredericka muttered a half-hearted, "Yes," he added quickly, "And now DON'T WORRY." As he spoke, he disappeared into the darkness before she could answer.

"Don't worry, indeed," Fredericka spluttered to herself, as she went inside to brew coffee for Sergeant Brown. But, in spite of herself, Fredericka was comforted by the fact that she had been able to help Peter. And, if Peter, then certainly Margie, too.

That night she slept well.

Saturday proved a busy day in the shop and Fredericka decided to keep open all day, mainly because she didn't want to miss Peter's half-promised call. But by late afternoon he had not appeared and she was contemplating escape to the inn for supper when there was a dismal shriek like a note of warning from the main road. Fredericka rushed down the front path and looked along Beech Street in the direction of the shops. As she did so a great white ambulance turned the corner and disappeared in a cloud of dust.

Fredericka's heart beat furiously and she felt choked with fear. It must be Margie. There couldn't be any doubt. The ambulance had been coming down Spruce Street from the direction of the Farm, and it had turned into Beech which was the direct route to the County Hospital. She walked back to the house slowly and found Sergeant Brown standing by the door.

"Ambulance?" he asked.

"Yes."

"They say Margie Hartwell's sick."

"Yes. Colonel Mohun told me last night that they might have to send her to hospital for tests."

All at once the thought of the inn and the gossiping people sickened her. She turned impulsively to Sergeant Brown and said that she was about to get her supper and wouldn't he like to share it with her? He agreed with such alacrity that she was aware how much she had neglected him.

"I'm afraid I've been too busy to pay attention to you until this moment," she said apologetically, "and you are good to keep out of sight when the customers are around."

"They'd only talk their faces off," he said cheerfully. "Besides, I take my time off during the day when Chris is here."

Fredericka realized suddenly how little thought she had given to his time off. He was now her guardian and she had come to take his presence for granted.

He followed her into the kitchen and offered his assistance. "My wife says I'm not too bad at this," he announced as he took off his coat and rolled up his sleeves. He had just started to make some ham sandwiches when the front door banged.

Fredericka untied her apron and hurried out into the hall, hoping to find Peter. But it was Philippine and James Brewster who stood in the doorway.

Philippine began to speak at once and without greeting.

"Margie's terribly ill, Fredericka. We're worried sick, and now they've taken her off to hospital."

"Yes," Fredericka said, and then added quickly, "but won't you come in. Sergeant Brown and I were just getting ourselves some supper. We'd be glad to have you join us—both of you."

"Sergeant Brown?" James said.

"Yes. He's a sort of bodyguard," Fredericka explained. She was sorry now that she had mentioned his presence. Perhaps they weren't planning to stay, and she wouldn't have needed to. It did seem silly.

Philippine laughed good-naturedly. "Good thing. I should think you'd hate staying here all alone."

"I do. But, please won't you come in?"

"No," Philippine went on quickly. "I really just came by to pick up some things of Margie's. Mrs. Hartwell's too upset to—poor woman."

James now came forward from behind Philippine. "Don't include me in that refusal, Phil. If there's some coffee going, I'll have some while you do your rummaging."

Philippine frowned. "You know we promised to get out to the hospital at once," she said.

"I know, but you've got to collect the junk, haven't you?"

Fredericka said with more enthusiasm than she felt, "I suppose the things you want are in the storeroom, Philippine. I'll just go up there with you, and Sergeant Brown can give James his coffee." She raised her voice to call, "Sergeant Brown," and when the young man put an embarrassed head around the door, she added, "are you handy enough to give Mr. Brewster some coffee? I've just got to go upstairs for a few minutes."

When the sergeant agreed to "have a try," James moved heavily into the kitchen and Fredericka was glad enough to get away from him as she followed Philippine up the stairs. At the top, Fredericka hesitated. She was now a little ashamed of her officiousness. Philippine could find the things herself. She knew where the storeroom was.

"It's just some papers Mrs. Hartwell wants—hospital insurance or something, and some of Margie's things," Philippine explained.

"They're probably in here, then," Fredericka said. She was unable to resist the temptation to go with her visitor to the storeroom.

Philippine opened a trunk and looked through a box of papers hurriedly, removing one or two. Then she stared around the room a little vaguely and picked up a few oddments that looked to Fredericka more like toys than anything else. "I don't know what she does want, except for these papers," she confessed.

"I should think some extra nightgowns, if there are any," Fredericka suggested practically. "There are clothes in that chest of drawers under the window, I think."

Philippine kept looking around the room at the collection of objects strewn on the floor, window sills and tops of tables and chairs. But in a moment she went to the chest and, after looking through several drawers, did, in fact, find some pyjamas that looked more like Margie than Mrs. Hartwell. "I'll just take these, then— and fly," she announced, slamming the drawer with an air of finality.

Fredericka closed the door and followed Philippine down the stairs. They found James and the sergeant in earnest conversation. The subject seemed to be taxation. The air in the kitchen was thick with cigar smoke and Fredericka was very glad to see James get up at once when Philippine called to him.

At the door Fredericka put her arm in Philippine's. "Give my love to Margie," she said quietly, "and try not to worry too much. I'm sure things will all come right," she added with more cheerfulness than she felt.

Philippine turned and kissed her impulsively. "You are good, Fredericka," she said. "It's all so grim at the Farm that it's been wonderful to see you, even for a moment."

"Come back soon," Fredericka called, as they disappeared down the path.

"I will." Philippine's voice came from the distance— "and thanks," she added as the car door slammed.

I suppose she does love that beast, Fredericka thought as she turned back into the house. She returned to the kitchen to find that Sergeant Brown had discovered, and turned on, a ventilating fan that she had never noticed before; and that supper was laid out on the table. She sat down gratefully and was able to enjoy not only Sergeant Brown's sandwiches and coffee but, somewhat to her surprise, his pleasant, untaxing conversation.

12

Sunday morning meant no alarm clock but Fredericka was so used to being roused at seven that she woke as usual and hated herself for having become such a tiresome creature of habit. And then, to make matters worse, she couldn't even enjoy lying in bed once she had awakened. Her mind leapt on to the day ahead and the work undone, even on a Sunday.

Moreover, this morning there was Sergeant Brown to think of. He was probably pottering around in the kitchen by now and longing for his breakfast. She was troubled that Thane had given him so little relief from the job. It was all very well for him to say that it was a soft one and that Jim Brown had probably had more sleep in the past week than in any other week in his life. But it wasn't exactly a picnic to spend one's nights on the narrow couch in the study and to keep getting up at all hours to do a night-watchman's round. It was true that he had had time off—a good deal of it—during the days. But he had told her last night at supper about his wife and their small baby. It couldn't be much fun to do a job like this, especially when there wasn't so much as a compensating flicker of excitement beyond scaring away a handful of mischievous kids.

As Fredericka dressed she kept stopping to look out at the back yard and her jungle, but her thoughts were still centered on young Brown and then on younger Margie. They both made her feel old and selfish. How easy it was to fall into a neat narrow path when one lived only for oneself. She sighed heavily as she stood for a moment looking out at the brilliant green of the grass against the darkness of the shrubs and trees. She tried to escape her self-criticism by opening her eyes and allowing them to absorb the beauty of this morning. A faint mist lay in patches on the ground, like great spiders' webs, and above the trees the sky was intensely blue and cloudless. The window was open and the air that touched Fredericka's face and arms was soft, and laden with the warm sweet scent of full summer. As she stood, the quietness soothed her troubled mind and she was aware of a happiness that she had never known before.

What had happened to her in these three weeks of horror and fear and strain? It was as though, until now, she had walked safely and quietly along her private pathway, living more and more within herself and for herself. Now suddenly she had become aware of the fullness of life because she had touched death, sensitive to goodness because she had known evil, and, yes, capable of love and of unselfishness, because her eyes had been opened to see. . . .

Sergeant Brown had the coffee percolating noisily on the stove and he was just lifting eggs and bacon from the frying pan as Fredericka entered the kitchen.

"Oh, you are good," she said by way of greeting and then, "Did you get any sleep?"

"Good morning," said Sergeant Brown politely. "As a matter of fact, I slept too well and I'm feeling I ought to earn my keep somehow. So—I got breakfast. I hope you don't mind."

"Mind? Never has breakfast looked so good to me. The only trouble is the awful fear I have of losing you. If only something would happen so that it would be essential to keep you here for the length of my stay. But I guess I'd have to be the guilty party if that were to happen. You wouldn't consider leaving the police force, would you?"

"No, Ma'am," Sergeant Brown answered her seriously, and without a moment's hesitation.

Fredericka laughed and was aware suddenly that before she came to South Sutton she would have minded—very much—if anyone had gone into her kitchen to help themselves to her food and cook a meal without her permission. And now it was true that she didn't mind—that she was, in fact, delighted.

Their meal finished, Sergeant Brown dried the dishes and then Fredericka asked him whether or not his chief had given him the day off.

"He didn't say, Miss Wing. And I thought, seeing as how you're alone on a Sunday without Chris or any customers, you'd rather I stayed."

"Nonsense," Fredericka said at once. "I'm going to church this morning." Until that moment the idea of church had not occurred to her and she was a little startled at her sudden decision, but she hurried on: "Then, well then, I'll probably go to the inn for lunch and I'll spend the afternoon in the orchard where I can't be found. So, for heaven's sake, let me enjoy myself with a clear conscience. You go home to your wife and infant for the day." She hadn't quite the courage to offer him the night as well.

His face brightened. "Gee, swell," he said and then, "you're sure it's O.K.? Hadn't I better make it all official though?" he added, after a moment's hesitation.

"No, I'm sure if Thane Carey didn't say anything to you, he was leaving it up to me, and there are no two ways about it—I want you to go home and have a good time." Fredericka was now enjoying her own generosity.

Sergeant Brown needed no further urging. In one moment he had put on his coat and, in another, he had started for the door. But as Fredericka followed him into the hall, he turned back to say: "Gee—Thanks. I'll be back before dark."

"Will you get supper for us?" Fredericka asked, laughing.

"You bet," he called as he disappeared down the path.

At any rate he hasn't had to live on those awful sandwiches this last week, Fredericka thought, as she went to find a duster and run it systematically along the bookshelves. Wonderful how once a week was enough in the country.

Then, the house in order, she went to get ready for church and her early morning's happiness persisted. But, later, sitting upright on the hard wooden pew of the South Sutton Congregational Church and listening to the flat tones of the Reverend Williams's voice, her old doubts and anxieties returned.

She was, in fact, alone and a stranger. No one else sat in her pew. She looked around her and it seemed that the whole village was packed solidly into all the other pews— Was it her imagination, or was it not true, that by being in the bookshop's hammock the murdered body of Catherine Clay had made Fredericka an outcast? What were these people thinking? What were they saying, some of them, with their heads together while their minister droned on in the sleepy midsummer heat? Suddenly a dreadful thought occurred to her. Suppose she was seriously suspected. Suppose Sergeant Brown had been set as watchdog not *for* her but *over* her? But then he wouldn't have taken the day off. Or would he? Did Thane and Peter really suspect her? It couldn't be so.

The service over, Fredericka looked around for a familiar face and could not see one. She now regretted the impulse that had made her want to go to church. She hung back as the others crowded past her to the door. There seemed, to her distorted eye, to be hundreds of them, but there weren't of course. The church was small and the aisles narrow.

As she emerged into the full glare of the sun she blinked blindly and stopped for a moment at the bottom of the steps to get her bearings. A group of young girls and boys were deep in whispered conversation near her. Catching the word 'Margie', she listened without shame.

"She's been taken to the hospital," one of them was saying.

"My mother says she's going to die—that nothing will save her now," another contributed.

"And my father says we'll do well to get rid of the stranger in our midst," an older boy put in.

One of them looked around apprehensively and, seeing Fredericka said "Sh-sh" very loudly, at which they all looked at her and then looked quickly away.

They fell silent, and Fredericka decided that it would be wise to move off and leave them to it. As she did so, she heard a very audible stage whisper. "It's true," the voice said, "nothing like this ever happened in South Sutton before *she* came. I remember Margie saying—"

Fredericka could not catch the final words and did not want to. The morning's glory had faded and she felt old and tired. The worst of it was that she probably deserved this attack. She was faced with the bitter truth that she hadn't been kind to Margie—she hadn't even been decent. As she walked back to the bookshop, she was so troubled by her own thoughts that she forgot her plan to go to the inn. But, once inside her own quiet kitchen, the vision of more people, gossiping and unfriendly people, sickened her. She looked blankly into the refrigerator to find something for lunch and then decided not to eat anything. The sound of the door slamming in the empty house seemed to announce her loneliness and isolation, not only from South Sutton but from all human beings. She stood up quickly and made an effort to fight back a sudden rush of self-pitying tears.

Taking herself firmly in hand, she was able to remember that she had been happy before she went to Church. She reminded herself of the comforting friendliness of Sergeant Brown, of Philippine, of Thane Carey and, above all, of Peter. And then she wished that she hadn't thought of Peter because to think of him increased her loneliness. Why had he stayed away so long? That night on the porch—was it only Friday?—now seemed an eternity of time away. Of course he hadn't promised to come in and, of course, he and Thane must be frantic with Margie's illness and the dead-end feeling he'd confessed to. He couldn't really suspect Fredericka, herself. That was madness. Why, he had said that she had helped him. Could that be true or was she now reaching for any little straw that she could cling to?

She returned with determination to the refrigerator but the salad concocted from leftovers was tasteless and she was conscious of the heat and the smell of frying that must have clung to the room since Sergeant Brown's breakfast. Then she remembered that he had discovered a ventilator and went to turn it on. The loud whirring noise was, at first, irritating, and then comforting, because it forbade all thought. She finished her lunch and decided to retreat to the orchard as she had promised Sergeant Brown. Perhaps this afternoon she would be able to substitute writing for sleeping. She looked up at the clock and saw Peter Mohun standing in the doorway.

She stared at him blankly as he came in and snapped off the ventilator fan.

"Good God!" he said. "Anyone could shoot you and no one hear a sound above that damn thing. I was determined this time to announce my arrival and I've been banging on the front door for a good ten minutes. You scared the wits out of me—you and your blasted fan."

He sounded really annoyed, a fact which gave Fredericka some unexpected pleasure, but before she could think of anything to say he asked, "Where's Jim?"

"Jim? Oh, you mean Sergeant Brown—He's—he's—"

"Come clean, Fredericka." He paused, then went on rapidly, "Never mind, I can guess. You let him off for the day, didn't you?"

"Well, yes, I did. As a matter of fact, I've been suffering from a guilty conscience, having given the wretched young man precious little thought all week."

"You're not supposed to think about him. He's Thane's business, not yours."

"But I've discovered that he's a very nice young man, with human feelings just like yours and mine— Oh, Peter, don't scold me. I've been sick about how I treated Margie. I've got to make up for it *somehow.*"

Peter smiled at her. Then he pulled out the other chair from the table and sat down.

"Wouldn't you rather go outside?" Fredericka asked.

"No. I'm afraid I can't stay. As a matter of fact, Carey's dropping by any minute to drive me to the airport."

"The airport?" Fredericka found it hard to hide her distress.

"Yes. I am going to Washington, there's no getting out of it. I can't tell you more now because, for one thing, there isn't time, and for another, it isn't wise. But you must listen to me. You are *not* to do any more New England conscience acts of kindness to Jim Brown or anyone else. If all goes as I think it's going to, then he and the rest of us can return to our normal lives very soon. Until then we're not going to take any chances." He reached across the table and took her thin shoulder in his large hand. "Look at me," he said severely.

With some difficulty Fredericka managed to do as he ordered.

"Now," he continued, "I can tell you this much. Your news about Chris's possible information and about that letter have proved to be pure gold. You are the best Dr. Watson any man could want."

"Did you find the letter then?"

"No. It had disappeared. And it was too late to ask Margie—poor kid. But Chris, bless him, had some old envelopes Catherine had given him before. He hadn't got around to taking the stamps off and so I found the address I wanted. That's why I'm going to Washington—"

"But—Peter—" There were a thousand questions Fredericka wanted to ask but he held up his hand.

"I'll tell you all when I know all, Fredericka. Right now you mustn't know anything, not even what you've told me and what I've told you. Keep it absolutely to yourself. *You understand?"*

"Yes. But—"

"No 'buts' about it."

The sound of a car outside and steps on the path interrupted him and Fredericka's mind leapt suddenly to another quite different subject. "Please, Peter, don't tell Thane I let Sergeant Brown off. You can see how all right it is," she said urgently.

"Well, then, if you insist on deception, you'd better come to the airport with us and keep Carey amused until Jim gets back. When will that be?"

"Before dark, he said."

Peter looked at his watch. "Three-twenty. I guess you can string Carey along that long. But you're not to come back here until your protector returns. Go to the inn, if necessary. I don't want you to be here alone. Understand?"

"Yes," Fredericka answered. She was torn between joy at his concern and anger at his officiousness. Surely she could look after herself. Everything had been quiet for days now.

Thane Carey was now banging at the front door.

When Fredericka and Peter joined him, he said at once: "Where's Jim?"

"Gone for a coke," Peter said quickly. "It's O.K. I did duty for him and now Fredericka's coming along to wave me goodbye."

Thane grinned. "O.K.," he said, "but I'm not sure I like your interfering with the law like this."

They piled into Thane's small car and it was not long before Fredericka realized that its size was deceptive. She watched the speedometer creep up to seventy with some anxiety.

"Come, Carey," Peter said, "we're not all that late, are we?"

Thane grinned again; "Police privilege."

"Showing off," Peter remarked and then added with more firmness, "Come on, Carey, if you could see Fredericka's face you'd know she doesn't like it any more than your wife does."

"O.K. O.K." Thane answered amiably and the car slowed imperceptibly. "Good car though, isn't it?" he asked Fredericka.

"Wonderful," Fredericka managed.

"You women are all the same," Thane said. He was now driving at a steady fifty. "You'd rather creep along like this, than fly and be free and, incidentally, just as safe with a good man at the wheel. But you'd never hesitate to dash across the road in front of a bus or hop on a moving train."

"Well, if they do those things and I say *if*, then they're in a good position to realize the hazards of fast driving," Peter contributed. "Now if a female jumped out from the roadside when you were doing eighty plus, you'd save her life, no doubt, by smashing up the car and killing yourself."

"Not a chance of it. But I see your reasoning." Thane laughed.

"I guess it's as well for me to keep quiet," Fredericka said, "since I'm so outnumbered, and just a female."

"How wise you are, Fredericka. Now if only my

wife—you know Connie, don't you." He broke off abruptly: "Do you know, friends, we're here. In spite of having to *crawl*, I believe it's a record, even for me."

There was no sign of the plane on the field so they all climbed out of the car and went into the barracklike wooden building where they found a counter and hot coffee. As they sat on their stools and, by mutual consent, talked quietly about unimportant matters, the door banged open suddenly and Roger Sutton came charging into the room. He went first to the ticket window and they could hear him asking in a loud voice if the plane was late. He then turned as if to come over to the counter but, seeing the others, he swerved quickly and hurried off toward the door.

Peter got down from his stool and called to the retreating back.

If Roger heard, he took no notice, but Peter followed him outside.

"He acts frightened," Fredericka observed.

"I think it's just his usual shyness," Thane said slowly. "I've got to know him better since the—well, since I've been spending so much of my time at the Farm, and I like him. In fact, I would say that the hope for that family lies there."

"But hundreds of men must have had worse face injuries than his—in fact I've seen plenty of them in the library in New York. If he has stuff in him why can't he rise above it?" For some reason she did not want to confess to Thane that she had talked to Roger in the woods and seen his naked hatred for his sister.

"I'm no psychiatrist, Fredericka, but I would say that some of the best men are the most sensitive. If this last operation is successful, he'll look a lot better and then if only he could marry and feel like a normal human being . . ."

"When I first heard about the family I imagined he and Philippine might have more than a cousinly feeling toward each other but now James Brewster seems to have cut him out."

"It's more complicated than that, I think. He likes Philippine and gets on with her because she is—well, almost professional, in her attitude toward his injury. It makes him feel at ease with her. But I don't think it's more than that, or ever was—"

He stopped speaking as Peter came back with Roger who lagged behind him and was obviously reluctant to join them. Could anyone *look* more guilty then he does, Fredericka thought. I wonder if Thane and Peter are right to be so sure of his innocence. Perhaps they weren't. Perhaps Peter was taking the same plane on purpose.

Knowing that it would be best to turn away, Fredericka swung around to face the coffee urns and tried to catch the eye of the waitress who was having a heart-to-heart talk with a mechanic at the other end of the counter.

Peter sat down beside Fredericka, and Roger next to him. There was a moment of awkward silence and then Thane leant across Fredericka and Peter to say: "Everything all right at the Farm, Sutton?"

"As right as it can be," Roger muttered.

"Is Mrs. Hartwell at the hospital?"

"Yes. She was there all night." Then with surprising force, he added: "It's a good thing, too. Mother's had just about all she can stand."

"I know," Peter said quietly. Then he interrupted

himself to say; "Coffee?" as the waitress came up to them.

"Yes, large and black. Nothing to eat."

Fredericka now stole a look at Roger under cover of the general discussion. One hand was tightly clenched, the other, which shielded his face, was trembling and held stiffly open to show the long bony fingers. Fredericka had never seen Roger dressed in anything but faded blue jeans and an old shirt and she was surprised to observe that he now wore immaculate town clothes, conservatively cut. As she stared she became aware that he had removed his hand from his face and that two large dark eyes were regarding her intently. The eyes were set deep in his skull and the scarred tissue around them was purple and white in patches. His mouth was twisted sideways as though he was leering at her. She looked away in confusion. Then, ashamed that she had done so, she said hurriedly: "At any rate, Philippine will look after Mrs. Sutton, won't she?"

Roger made no answer. The coffee arrived and he drank it down in great gulps. Then he got up before anyone could think of anything else to say. "Thanks, Mohun. See you on the plane," he muttered, and walked rapidly away.

At that moment they could hear the roar of the engines outside and Peter also got up, as the loudspeaker blared the announcement of imminent departure.

"So long," he said lightly. "Be a good girl, Fredericka, and remember all Doc Mohun's orders."

She smiled and he started to walk away. But, at the door, he stopped to put out his cigarette, and then came back to say: "Keep an eye on her, Carey. She needs watching."

"I'll do my best," Thane agreed. "Only, for God's sake, hurry back. I'm beginning to feel like the boy on the burning deck, or the one who kept his finger in the dike, or what have you—"

But Peter had gone before he finished speaking.

"Well," Thane announced, "that seems to be that. Now," he added thoughtfully, "just what did he mean about keeping an eye on Miss Fredericka Wing? Is Sergeant Brown falling asleep on the job?"

"Oh, no, he's wonderful." She was able to answer this question with genuine enthusiasm. Then, aware that Thane continued to look at her steadily with a very police-like stare, she went on hurriedly, "I—I guess Peter just thought I was a little lonely or—or something."

"I see. Well, now, I have to go back to the Farm and to the hospital. As a matter of fact Connie's fed up with me about this damn case. Could you, do you think, go along to the house and have supper with her?"

"Oh no—really—"

"Oh, yes, really. Please. As a matter of fact it would ease things for me if I could just have you along when I break the news to her about being out tonight, too."

Fredericka remembered how much she had liked Constance Carey when she met her at the bazaar and it did not take her long to decide that she would much rather have supper with her than go back home before Jim Brown was well and truly back. She'd asked him to get supper, so she'd no doubt get it for himself. Besides if Thane were to drive her home now he might easily discover the absence of his henchman; and that she must prevent at all costs—"I'd love it," she said quickly, "if you don't think I'd be just one more thing—"

"No, I can promise you that. Connie likes company

and I had thought I could be home tonight so she hasn't made any plans to entertain herself. You see, Peter's sudden departure has upset all our calculations a little."

They were now speeding along the highway. Quite suddenly Thane braked the car and swung off on to a little-used country lane. "We live quite far outside South Sutton as you'll see. It has its rural advantages and a swell view but, at times like this, even I can see that there are some obvious disadvantages. It's damn lonely for Connie. We've only got the one car which really belongs to the police force and a bicycle isn't all that much fun in hot weather."

Fredericka looked around her with interest as they drove into a small yard neatly laid out with a white picket fence and a flourishing garden. The house which was also painted white seemed to be turning its back on them but there was no hint of untidiness around the back door entrance as Thane plunged in unceremoniously and led the way, hurrying on ahead. Fredericka looked quickly at the neat new kitchen. "Goodness, Thane," she said, "it's so beautiful and shining. How did it ever happen like this?"

"All on the instalment plan." Thane stopped for a moment to look about him. Then he added cheerfully: "And I have to admit that Connie is a swell housewife. Not a flick of dirt anywhere. But just wait till you see this—" He opened a door at the other side of the kitchen and Fredericka gasped because they seemed to be looking out on to an open ledge of rock. The whole long living room hung over a cliff that dropped away sharply beneath them, and the side of the room opposite them was one great window. The woods came down to the left and right but the trees had been cut away from the cliff's edge in front to give a clear view of the soft sunset sky, the sleepy town lying just below them, and, beyond it, the green valley with its wide river reflecting the pink glow of the sky.

Fredericka forgot Thane completely as she walked past him to stand in the window.

"It is heavenly, isn't it?" a woman's voice asked quietly. Fredericka swung around. She had not seen Connie sitting on the long couch by the fireplace. Now she had put down her book and was standing up with a look of eager expectation on her face. Fredericka felt the other woman's friendliness and warmed to it as she had when they first met. "Incredibly beautiful," she answered simply. "You—you lucky things—"

"You're staying for supper with us, aren't you?" Connie asked at once, but Fredericka noticed that she looked across at Thane shyly, as if for approval.

"Not *us*, darling, *you*, I'm afraid."

"Oh, Thane, not again, or rather *still.*" She stopped and then added quickly, "But I'll have to forgive you since you've brought me Fredericka."

"I'm so glad he did," Fredericka said with genuine pleasure. "I've been wanting to see you again ever since the bazaar but I've been tied to the shop and well, what with one thing and another—"

"Yes—one thing—and another," Connie agreed, laughing a little uneasily. "I've meant to pay a visit to you and the bookshop but I'm getting lazier and lazier. You can see how far out we are, though, and I'm not what one would call a keen cyclist." She turned to her husband: "Must you go this minute or can you stop for a drink?"

"This minute, I'm afraid, darling. But I promise to be back early, so I can visit a little with Fredericka before I drive her home."

"Oh Thane," Connie's voice had now become tense and strained, "isn't the end of this miserable business in sight yet? It seems to get worse and worse. Do you know how Margie is?"

"I'm going to see her first. But we've got to face it, darling; I'm afraid there just isn't any hope. The doctors say she would have been dead two days ago if it wasn't for her youth." He paused. "But I think I can honestly say that the end of this case is in sight—just, if we can only get around this last corner. We've got very real suspicions but as yet no proof."

Fredericka started to speak and Connie put out a restraining hand toward her. "Don't ask him," she advised. "He only wants you to; and I can tell you that he'll be both evasive and maddening. *Never* marry a policeman!"

After Thane had gone, Connie busied herself with supper. Fredericka, when her help was refused, sat by the window watching the stars come out in the darkening sky. How long the day had been between sunrise and sunset. But now her early morning's contentment had returned. Thane was her friend, and Connie—and Peter. They didn't suspect her. When all the ugliness of this evil thing had been wiped away, she would still have these friends and the beauty and peace of this New England country summer.

As they ate their meal, night came down quickly and Connie lit a lamp on their table. It made a small warm glow in the darkness; like a camp fire in the woods, Fredericka thought. When their meal was finished they sat on, talking quietly and easily about themselves. Fredericka told Connie of her writing and why she had come to South Sutton. Connie confessed that she had been a New Yorker, too, and that she had given up a job in an advertising firm to marry Thane when they had met during a summer course at Columbia a year ago. Then, inevitably, they came back to talk about South Sutton and the murder of Catherine Clay.

"I think there are plenty of people in the village who think I am a witch—even that I am guilty." Fredericka now expressed the thought that had been worrying her all day and felt better for it.

Connie laughed again. "It's inevitable in a one-horse town like this. Unfortunately for you this business had to happen the minute you arrived—and in your hammock. Seriously, Fredericka, you can't blame them for rolling all the horror up with you— It's so much more convenient to put it on to an outsider."

"Oh, I know."

The day's anxieties rushed back into the peaceful room. Sensing this, Connie said quickly: "Anyway, you know how *we* feel and I know Thane's no fool and that he's got his eye on the guilty one right now." She hesitated, then she said slowly: "And I know for certain that he's *not* looking at you."

"Who, then? Who do you think did it?" Fredericka asked. "I've made a list of suspects and I've been through it over and over again, adding, subtracting, multiplying and dividing, but nothing makes sense."

"Murder doesn't make sense in spite of all the books say." Connie stopped suddenly and a silence fell between them. At last she went on slowly: "You ask me whom I suspect. I don't. I *know.*" Fredericka started to break in but Connie hurried on. "Thane hasn't told me his suspicions, as you can see, but he doesn't need to— So—well, because I do know, I can't very well speculate." She stopped and then said; "Please let's get away from this dreary subject. It—it's giving me the creeps."

For a moment she seemed to be searching desperately for something to say. Then she went on: "I've been meaning to ask you what you've done with that quilt. It's a wonder that I can bear the sight of you. I never wanted anything so much in my life. I even made Thane buy ten tickets."

"Oh, Connie, I'll have to give it to you as a reward to Thane for saving the witch from burning. But I'd hate to. I'm mad about it, too; only I'm ashamed to say that I've not so much as looked at it since I won it. As a matter of fact, I think it's still sitting on a chair in my kitchen—"

Connie looked at her in unashamed horror, but before she could speak, Fredericka went on quickly: "I—I know I've been terribly careless but I've been trying to run a bookshop under difficulties. It was the very night I brought that home that I—I found the body."

Connie reached a hand across the table and grasped Fredericka's firmly. "Don't take everything I say seriously. The quilt was only a change of subject," she said quietly.

They both managed to laugh and then Fredericka said, "You know, Connie, Thane is a first-class chief of police. I could see that at a glance, but I hadn't realized until this moment what a swell policeman's wife you are. So subtle, too!"

And, at that moment, Thane's car drove into the driveway.

13

Thane Carey braked the car sharply when they arrived back at the bookshop, and Fredericka decided that he had forgotten her presence completely as he honked the horn insistently and then leaned out to call Sergeant Brown.

"Why don't you come in?" Fredericka asked quietly. "You'll wake the town with that racket."

He turned to her as though he had been roused from a dream. "I can't stop," he explained hurriedly. "Must get back to Connie, and, moreover, there may be a call from Peter. Any messages?" he added lightly.

"No. No thanks," Fredericka said stupidly and then felt herself blushing. She was grateful for the darkness.

Sergeant Brown came down the path toward them.

"Good evening," he said politely to Fredericka who was now standing by the car, and then he turned to Thane who was about to drive off. "Hi, Chief," he said, and then asked anxiously, "any news?"

"Oh, Jim," Thane said. "No. Nothing to report. I just

wanted to be sure you were still on the job." Then, before anyone could ask any more questions, the small car had roared away into the night.

"And that's that," Jim remarked as they turned together to go up the path.

"I'm glad you are here, Jim," Fredericka said. "I'd hate to have come back alone to an empty house, and I'm not ashamed to confess it. I'm beginning to get a bad case of the jitters."

"It might seem lonely-like here I suppose, but you've got a cosy place all right. And plenty of visitors. I got back at five and, since then, the Reverend Williams has been in and left a book, said to tell you he'd decided not to buy it, after all. Mrs. Hartwell stopped by, and James Brewster and Philippine Sutton have just left. I was beginning to think about making some coffee—that is, if it's allowed."

"Of course, and I hope you got some supper."

"Yes, thanks. As a matter of fact I expected you so I had two suppers. I'd begun to get worried. Anyway I waited for you for coffee."

"Your family all right?" Fredericka asked when they were sitting at the kitchen table a few moments later, to drink the sergeant's black brew.

"Yes and no, I guess you'd say in answer to that one. Susie—that's my wife—s' okay but the baby's all choked up. I told Susie to get the doctor but she said she could cope. You know how women are—" he stopped suddenly.

Fredericka laughed at his embarrassment. "As a matter of fact I'd say she was a rare one. Most mothers I've observed call the doctor for a safety-pin scratch. They seem to think babies are made of porcelain," she said and was aware how elderly she sounded.

"Susie's not like that," Jim said complacently. But before he could enlarge on Susie's virtues, they both heard the sound of a car outside. "More visitors," he muttered as he stood up and went to the front door. A moment later Fredericka heard him say: "Hi, Phil." And then: "Isn't it past your bedtime?"

The screen door banged. Fredericka got up and, as she went out into the hall, Philippine came toward her. There was no sign of James.

"Oh Fredericka," she said breathlessly, "I'm sorry if I'm terribly late. I—I had to come. It's Margie. She's died. I felt I had to talk to you. You're the only one who seems *normal* in this whole town."

"Guess you want some coffee," Jim said gently, steering them both into the kitchen.

"Where's Brewster?" Jim asked when they had sat down.

Philippine held the steaming cup between her small hands and drank it gratefully like a thirsty child. "After we left here," she said, between gulps, "we decided to go back to the hospital. Then—then, when we heard, about Margie, I mean—James thought we ought to take Martha Hartwell and Margaret back to the Farm. They'd been there most of the day—both of them—saying nothing, doing nothing—not even crying. But I—I just *couldn't* go back with them. I wanted to talk to someone sensible so I took the jeep, and James took them home in his car—"

Fredericka said nothing for a moment. It was hard to find the right consoling words. Jim coughed self-consciously and then, in the silence that followed this burst of sound, they could hear the ticking of the kitchen clock and the subdued chirping of crickets outside.

After a few uncomfortable minutes, Jim could not bear the tension. He pushed back his chair and stood up.

"Well," he said slowly, "I guess you two would like to have a heart-to-heart. I'll clear things up here and then walk around for a smoke and a look-see. Why don't you go into the other room? It's more comfortable in there."

Fredericka and Philippine got up obediently and walked, as if by clockwork, into the office. They sat down stiffly and then there was another silence until Philippine got up and searched aimlessly for cigarettes. Fredericka handed her one from a packet in her pocket. Philippine lit it, and as she did so, Fredericka noticed that her hand shook uncontrollably.

"You're terribly upset, Philippine," Fredericka said quietly, and then added, "I'm glad you came to see me— that is, if I can be any help." The last words were a question.

"Oh my God," Philippine said, drawing in her breath and letting a fine trickle of smoke out through her small even teeth, "I've got to talk to you—*got* to. Will—will Jim leave us alone?"

At that moment the telephone shrilled from the desk beside them and both women jumped. "We're a couple of coots," Fredericka said with an attempt at her ordinary voice. She reached an arm for the receiver and said: "Hello" rather fiercely.

"Is that the bookshop?" a woman's voice asked.

"Yes."

"Is Jim Brown there?"

"Yes, yes, he is. I'll just call him."

Fredericka was aware that she felt both disappointed and relieved. She had dared to hope that it might be Peter calling from Washington, but for some reason which she didn't stop to analyse, she didn't want to talk to him in front of Philippine. She hurried out of the room with a muttered word of apology.

Jim looked worried as he came in and picked up the receiver, and increasingly worried as he carried on a monosyllabic conversation.

Both women listened and both tried not to listen. After a series of yes's and no's, Jim finally said: "I left Dr. Scott's number written out there by the phone." There was some reply to this and then he said firmly: "Look here, Susie, you know I can't. I've been off all day and I'm on duty. You know that." It was obvious that Susie didn't. There was a splutter of sound in the receiver. "Get Maud to come over, then," Jim said desperately. "Gee, Susie, I can't *help* it." There was another eruption of sound and then, with a gesture of helplessness, Jim laid the receiver back on its stand.

"I couldn't help hearing, Jim," Fredericka said quickly. "What's the matter? Is it the baby?"

"Yes, Miss Wing. Susie's wild—says he's took bad."

"Did she call Dr. Scott?"

"He's out."

"He was up at the hospital when I was there a few minutes ago," Philippine said quietly. "Why don't you try to catch him there before he leaves."

"I will then." He looked to Fredericka who nodded toward the telephone.

Jim managed to get on to Dr. Scott who promised to go in to see the baby as soon as he possibly could. But as this would not be for another half an hour, he gave Jim brief instructions for the immediate care of the baby.

When the anxious father had hung up the receiver for the second time, he asked Fredericka if he could call his wife and pass on the doctor's message. Fredericka agreed at once, and then another thought occurred to her.

"Look, Jim," she said quickly, "why don't you run home and be with your wife until Dr. Scott comes? I've got Philippine here." She turned to the woman beside her. "You can stay for a bit can't you?"

"Of course," Philippine said. Then, after a moment, she added suddenly, "But look, there's no need for Jim to come back at all until morning. I can stay the night with you, Fredericka. I mean, if you'd like me to." Then seeing Fredericka's hesitation, she said, "I don't need a bed. I can sleep on the couch. I'd *much* rather, than go back to the Farm."

"But you can't do that, Philippine. It's so lonely down here. You wouldn't sleep a wink, would you?"

"Of course. You forget that I've not lived a sheltered life—" For a moment Fredericka thought she was going to add "like yours" in one of her sudden flashes of bitterness. Instead she went on quickly, "Don't stand there and stare at me, Jim. Scram." She pronounced the word *shcram,* but Jim did not mistake its meaning. After a quick look to Fredericka for her approval he hurried out. Everything had happened so suddenly that Fredericka felt dazed. She lit a cigarette and tried to collect her thoughts.

"You don't mind, Fredericka? You are just as glad to have me, are you not? I would so much—oh so much—rather be here—than—than—*there.*" She waved a vague hand in the general direction of the Farm.

"Mind? I think you're a saint, Philippine. I'd be, well, reasonably willing to stay alone only—well, I promised—er—Thane Carey that I wouldn't and well, I admit that these last weeks haven't exactly strengthened my courage."

"I know. Mine either. It's such a horrible business—and so close to us. But it isn't so bad any more. That's really what I want to talk to you about. It will help me to do so and I think it may help you, too. We really are alone now, and I want to tell you what I know. You've no idea how much it will help me—oh so much it will help me—to tell you who are not close to it."

"What is it, Philippine?" Fredericka sat forward in her chair, as the other woman's voice became hoarse with the intensity of her feeling.

Philippine lit another cigarette from the end in her mouth and then said slowly and very distinctly. "You see, now that Margie is dead, we have nothing to fear any more."

"What do you mean?" Fredericka fairly shrieked her question.

"I will tell you," Philippine went on, and her voice had now become gentle, "only just please to sit back in your chair. It is so miserable and sad what I have to say."

"You mean—surely you *don't* mean that Margie killed Catherine Clay? But, Philippine, it just isn't possible."

"Why not?"

"She was a tiresome child, but *murder*—Oh, no, Philippine."

"Listen." Philippine now sat forward in her turn. "I am not guessing this. I know it. I have known it from the first, but I couldn't say anything. I felt sorry for the child because she is too young to know what she does. And, besides, I myself hated Catherine Clay." As she said this, her face hardened and her brows drew together fiercely, but she hurried on, "I have seen enough and plenty of death myself—in the war—in the camp. What does it matter—one more dead who is better dead?—who makes everyone, I say *everyone,* miserable—her mother, her brother, Margie, James—yes, all of us." She stopped abruptly and then went on more quietly, "But yes, it was Margie who killed her—that I know. And for that I bless her."

"But how could she? How do you know?" Fredericka asked.

"Catherine was killed on a Saturday—the day of the bazaar. That morning I told Margie I was going out collecting, but when I got started I remembered that I hadn't done up some orders for herbs, and I thought I'd better do them first or Margaret would, and she ought not to stand up so long, especially as she insisted that she would go to the bazaar. She's not been well, you know, and she'd already done all that extra work for her booth. Besides, I knew I could probably get Roger to go with me and help me with the herbs later on because he'd want to get as far away from the crowds as possible. So—well, I went back. I had on rubber-soled shoes and I went into the lab quietly, thinking more about the work I had to do than anything else." She paused for a moment and shut her eyes as if in an effort to shut out the sight that her next words would recall. "Margie was there," she said simply, "she was making—making," she paused, *"capsules."*

"Oh!" Fredericka said only the one word and it faded away in the silence like a note of despair.

"Yes," Philippine went on after a moment, "I did not think anything of it then, you see, because I have taught her to fill up these capsules. We use them for our herb medicines and all these things. But later—afterwards—I remembered this and the whole scene came back to me when Thane asked us about the little silver box of vitamin capsules. I remembered, I think, because she had looked so guilty when I found her, and she had not expected me to come back. So then I asked her about this. At first she would not say, but then she knew that I knew too much and so she told me how she put the yellow jessamine into the capsules and put them in the little box and put it back into the dining room where Catherine had left it. I blame myself because that poison I had told her about and perhaps I should not have had it there,' but we need it for our experiments—and how could I know? I never did dream such a thing—"

Fredericka felt the weight of Philippine's words like a physical pain across her forehead. She closed her eyes. Of course. It was all plain now: this explained Margie's fear and strangeness—her anxiety. "She tried to get back the silver box from me," Fredericka heard herself say at last.

"From you?" Philippine asked.

"Yes. You see, Thane Carey's man found it outside here and he left it with me to see if I could find out who it belonged to. He took out the remaining capsules, but perhaps Margie thought they were still in it, and that they would be used as evidence, especially after what you had seen."

"That must have been how it was," Philippine said slowly and thoughtfully.

"But," Fredericka went on, thinking out loud, "But, Philippine, I just *can't* believe it. She was such a blundering child. Perhaps she did hate Catherine, but to *kill* her!"

"That was what I thought at first. But then when she confessed to me, she poured it all out—all the hate and misery and things shut up inside of her ever since Catherine came back."

"What things?"

"Catherine was cruel. More than cruel. She was a beast—like those Nazi fiends we all know about—but I more than you. It was cruelty of the mind—the spider to the fly in its web. Margie was afraid of Catherine and showed her fear and that made it worse. Little beastly things she did, always. Oh, I saw her but she was too clever. We could not stop her, any of us. And the cruel things she would say— And then, you see—Catherine she was beautiful like a film star, and Margie was an unattractive adolescent girl. She had no beaux and not very many friends. She was eaten alive with jealousy of Catherine. She hated her and the hate in her grew and grew until—until this. And I, I do not blame that child. As I have said already, and I would say over and over again, the world is better without that woman—she was *evil!*" Philippine spat out the word with such venom that Fredericka drew back as if she had been struck.

After a moment Philippine went on more quietly: "So, when Margie told me and I knew the truth, I told her that I would not tell this to anyone. I told her that if she did not say anything when they questioned her that no one could make her say anything. But, you see, she is a good child, really. She couldn't live with herself any more. This illness. I think it is because she wanted to die. Oh, Fredericka—it is all such a terrible wicked wrong and needless thing."

"But she couldn't have had such an illness just from *wanting* to die," Fredericka said.

"Well," Philippine said slowly and with obvious reluctance, "there are those herbs in the lab. I should have taken away all the poisons, perhaps. But how did I know what she would do? I do not know now what she did take. I could not find anything missing. It is strange because if she really wanted to kill herself she could have had the yellow jessamine. But that she did not touch again. She kept all her private things here somewhere in her aunt's house. I know because her mother is so strict. I tried to see if I could find anything that might have explained it. That was the day I came for her insurance and I kept thinking if we could now *what* she was doing to herself then we could have known what remedy."

"You really did think, even then, that she was poisoning herself in some way?" Fredericka asked.

"Yes. That is, when she began to have the odd symptoms and be so very ill. But I could find nothing."

"Why didn't you tell Dr. Scott? Oh, of course, you couldn't without letting him know *why.*" Suddenly Fredericka remembered the bottles and jars that she had discovered in the shed. "Philippine," she said quickly, "I wish you had told me then, I mean that day when you came over. Margie did have a secret hiding place in an old shed, a sort of disused greenhouse, down by the alley. Thane's men found a collection of oddments there and Chris told me they were Margie's. I meant to ask her about them, but she was so odd these last days and I never managed to."

"That's it—that's her secret hiding-place—Of course. I'm sure that's it." Philippine jumped to her feet. "Come, Fredericka, we must see those things. Now. At once."

"Oh no, Philippine. It's—good heavens—it's after midnight. It's dark as pitch out back. Philippine, it's madness to go poking around out there tonight. Please let's go to bed. Whatever there is will keep until morning. What difference does it make now, anyway? Margie's dead. We can't get any remedy now." Fredericka's words fell over each other as she tried to hold Philippine back. "Oh, Philippine, don't persist in this madness. I tell you, it's black as night out there. We'd break our necks. I'm—

I'm *terrified* to go out there now." The memory of the
other night was too real.

"What is there now to be frightened of, Fredericka?
As you say, Margie's dead. But don't you see, we've got
to get those things before Thane takes them away. He's
sure to now. And then he'll put two and two together and
know the truth. Don't you see we've got to protect Margie? It's most terribly important."

"I can't see what harm it is for Thane to know now.
Surely you'll tell him, won't you?"

"Of course I won't tell him. What of her mother and
the Suttons and the business? Everything's at stake. And
I promised Margie. That's as important to me as if she
were still living."

Fredericka stood up. "It's utter madness. The police
are bound to find out sooner or later and I'm not going
to explore that jungle before daylight. I'll set the alarm,
if you like, and I'll go out with you at six A.M., before Jim
gets back. But I won't go now."

"Very well then, I'll go myself—alone. I did not know
when you say you are timid that you are *so* timid. It is
nothing except the darkness and I've got a torchlight in
the car. I'll get that." Suddenly her voice dropped. "Oh,
please, Fredericka, I suppose I'm really a little frightened
to go alone. But I must, otherwise I can't sleep. Please
come with me; it'll only be a minute and then we can go
to bed and know that everything is all right."

"I can't see how it will be all right," Fredericka persisted. "Thane and Peter will ferret this thing out even if
you don't tell them. They won't leave the case open.
They'll have to know the truth in the end."

"Oh, Fredericka, I thought you would understand.
What can Thane and Peter do without proof? The family

and the Farm are my whole life now. Margie is dead. It is all over. In time it will be forgotten. Perhaps it is madness. Perhaps you are right. But please, anyway, just come with me. You see, *I must.*"

She put her small strong hand on Fredericka's arm, and suddenly Fredericka was too tired to care. What did it matter? It was all part of the nightmare and the sooner it was over, the better. Peter seemed very far away. "All right," she said quietly.

"You will? Oh, bless you, Fredericka. I'll fly and get the torch."

When she had gone, Fredericka stood still in the silent room, trying to collect her thoughts and to absorb all the things Philippine had told her. Then, reluctantly, she walked across the room to the door. As she heard the quick returning step on the front path, a sudden thought occurred to her and she hurried out to meet Philippine. "Have you got the torch?" she asked at once, and when Philippine held it up she went on quickly, "Oh, thank goodness, you see there's an open well out there. We haven't got it properly covered yet. I'll have to go first and then I can show you where it is. Do keep the torch low and flash it ahead of me. I've no desire to walk into the thing myself."

"Of course, but that is nothing, nothing at all, Fredericka," Her voice sounded excited—almost happy, Fredericka thought, and her own anxiety increased. "Yes," Philippine went on quickly, "you lead the way and I'll follow just behind you and flash the torch ahead of us, like you say. Good, Fredericka. Oh, good."

The back door slammed behind them. This is madness, Fredericka thought, utter madness. She's lost all sense of reason. But if it has to happen, it's best to get it over and done with. Otherwise she'd be at me all night. She stepped out boldly into the small bobbing circle of light on the grass.

14

After a few steps, Fredericka allowed herself to look up from the magic circle of light moving ahead of her. The sky was overcast now and the stars that she had watched so happily from Thane's living room window, had disappeared. How long ago that seemed; and how normal and sane and infinitely remote from this world of madness and delirium.

Philippine spoke from just behind her. "Can you see now? Is it all right if I hold the torch like this?" she asked.

"Yes. Yes. It's fine. The path's easy to follow if you keep the light just as it is."

"Good. I will then. And I follow you."

They moved slowly forward in their private pin-point of light. It seemed to intensify the darkness that walled them in. There was no escape, Fredericka thought wildly, fighting back a feeling of panic. She could hear Philippine's quick breathing behind her. "Are you all right?" she asked in a louder voice than she intended. Then she tried to continue more normally, "The well's just ahead. Good grief, they've left the cover off altogether!"

"Yes, I see it. It's O.K." Philippine barely whispered the words. Then she leant forward and muttered in Fredericka's ear. "But, *mon Dieu,* we are being followed! I know it! I can hear someone behind me! Footsteps! Listen— Who could possibly?—Oh—My God . . . Now—damn—I—I've dropped the torch!"

The light went out suddenly and the suffocating darkness closed around them. Fredericka turned back to Philippine and reached out her hand but, as she did so, something crashed down on her head and she pitched forward to fall down—down—down into a black sea of oblivion.

When Fredericka opened her eyes she closed them again quickly to shut out the light that blinded her and was a knife thrust through her temples. Then, after a moment, she tried again, slowly and cautiously. The effort was painful, not only to her eyes but to her whole body. She must know where she was and what had happened to her, and why she was in such agony. But it was no use, she could not think—could not even keep her eyes open. She closed them and drifted off again into unconsciousness.

It was a long time later when she again struggled to open her eyes. A familiar voice was calling her name and some instinct told her that she must answer. It was important to make herself heard. But at first she could not speak. Then she moved her body slightly and the pain was so great that she cried out wildly.

"Thank God," and then, "Oh—thank God you're alive," the voice said. But it seemed to be coming from miles away—somewhere far above her.

She tried to raise her head and felt the sharpness of rock dig into her shoulders. Then, gradually, she eased her back forward from the hard wall behind it, and looked up to see a round gray hole broken by a darker shadow against its rim. As she tried to puzzle this out, the shadow moved and the voice spoke again.

"Fredericka, can you hear me?"

"It's Peter," she cried feebly, before she closed her eyes again. Now everything would be all right. She was alive and Peter had come. But he couldn't take away the pain. Pain and darkness. Darkness and pain. Anyway she had spoken. He had heard her. Now there was no need to struggle any more.

When Fredericka next opened her eyes, the pain was still there stabbing at her head but the hardness of rock behind her had become strangely soft. She looked up cautiously and saw a pleasant female face bending over her. She tried to speak but no words came.

The face disappeared and then another one took its place.

"Peter," she whispered.

"Yes. Don't talk now. Rest is what the doctor's ordered and you look as though you could do with it."

"But what—what happened?" Then as memory came back slowly she forced herself to say slowly: "Where's Philippine? Is she all right?"

"Yes to that one, too. Now go to sleep. You are bruised and battered." He grinned. "My God, if you could see your face! And nothing more serious than a bashed head, a broken left arm, and a broken right ankle. You'll recover. But not another word for twenty-four hours."

Before Fredericka could find the words to speak again, he had disappeared. Then the woman came back, and this time she said: "I'm going to lift you up a little to drink some hot milk, but I'll try not to hurt you. Then you'll go back to sleep again, and when you wake up you'll feel better—much better."

"All right," Fredericka said, as though each of the two words was of the greatest importance.

The woman slid an arm under her shoulders and lifted her gently. Fredericka found she could hold the cup in her good hand and she drank gratefully. Then she was lowered back on to the pillow and fell instantly to sleep.

This time when Fredericka woke up, the sun was streaming across her bed and the air coming in the open window beside her smelt of hay and tansy. She felt hot and sticky but the pain had gone. She moved her body cautiously and felt stiffness and soreness—no more. She looked around her with interest at the very white room and the large open screened window. Hospital, she decided, and—remembering the woman's face—that must have been a nurse. She felt immensely pleased with her intelligence. Next she looked at all of herself that she could see: a right arm covered with black and blue marks and scratches, a left arm in a plaster cast. With a great effort she untied the curious white sack that was her nightdress and found more bruises on her chest and shoulders. She pulled herself up to a sitting position and began to want a cigarette—badly.

The door opened a cautious crack and Peter's head appeared.

"Have you got a cigarette?" she asked a little irritably.

"I have. And you're better—if a little undressed." He came in, gave her a cigarette, lit it, tied the tapes of her nightdress carefully and then sat down in the chair by the bed. "You deserve to be dead, you silly little fool," he said agreeably.

Fredericka made no attempt to reply. She was enjoying the cigarette and it did not, at that moment, seem to matter very much what Peter or anyone else had to say about her.

He got up and went to the chest of drawers on the other side of the window. Presently he returned with a hand mirror. "Here," he said. "A survey of the ruins, please."

Fredericka took one look and put the mirror down quickly. Her face was covered with long red scratches. One eye was black and swollen; the other stared out from a deep cavern of a mysterious dark colour and her forehead had a large egg-shaped lump just to the right of centre.

"Well, I don't see why you had to show me," she said crossly.

"It was good enough to be shared," he answered pleasantly. "And you'd have had to know sooner or later, females being what they are."

"And now that you've had your fun, am I to be told anything? I want to know more—all in fact. Just why am I a silly little fool? I think I quote correctly?"

Peter put back his head and roared with laughter.

This was too much for Fredericka. She hated him. Never had she hated anyone quite so much.

Finally he stopped laughing and reached for her free hand. "I don't care how you look and I like you to be disagreeable. It's so comfortingly human of you. I'd imagined you to be—but we won't go into that now—"

"You'd imagined me to be what?" Fredericka couldn't help asking, but she took away her hand and then said quickly, "Oh Peter, don't tease me any more."

"Now let me see. You've lost some of your—well, primness—down the well perhaps. But I thought you wanted to know what happened on Sunday night—or rather what's happened since. It is now Wednesday morning, in case you're interested."

"Wednesday morning," Fredericka gasped. "The bookshop—" She started up in her anxiety.

"Calm yourself, woman. The bookshop's O.K. Connie Carey's taken over and with this new chapter of antics, you've increased the customers by about one hundred percent." He laughed suddenly, then he went on: "Connie makes them buy, too. If they get their view of the scene, they have to pay for it, and extra for the well."

"The well?" Fredericka asked.

"Yes, that's where you were. I pulled you out, like little Johnny Stout."

Fredericka leant back against the pillows with a sigh of relief. "Even though I do hate you, I have to admit that you are good to me—all of you," she said simply.

Peter reached over and patted her hand gently. "You're worth it," he said, "even if you do despise me so much."

Fredericka turned her head away quickly. In spite of herself, sudden tears pricked against her eyelids. It's weakness, she thought fiercely, just silly stupid female weakness.

If Peter noticed, he made no comment. "What I want really is *your* story. It's much more important than mine, and I've told you the important part already."

"Please," Fredericka said with some effort, "let me have a minute to think it all out. You tell me the rest of yours first."

"Right, then. Here it is in brief. I got back at seven

A.M. on Monday morning after having turned Washington upside down for a couple of hours, and, though you will never believe it, I went straight to the bookshop with the idea of cadging a breakfast—" He held up a hand when Fredericka started to break in. 'No, you wanted my story so you shall have it *in toto*. I made one hell of a racket trying, as I thought, to wake you up. Then I suddenly panicked because I realized all at once that Jim Brown wasn't there—the doors were all unlocked, too, and that wasn't like our town gal either. I went in to the office and was just picking up the receiver to call Thane when Jim Brown walked in. I turned on him and he was the sickest and saddest guy I've seen for a long time. He told me all—or at any rate all he knew. But he knew enough to scare the pants off me. Well—we didn't wait to call Thane, we began a systematic search of the place. And it wasn't long before we discovered Philippine's body—"

"Body? But you said—"

"I repeat. You are not to interrupt unless you want the whole floor—She was alive, but apparently in a very bad way. She seemed to have a bash on the back of her head but not all that bad. Still, she looked like a corpse all right. Jim carried her back into the kitchen and I let him in on the contents of Lucy's secret cupboard. So, while he was pouring brandy down Philippine's throat, I went on looking for you. But, hell, I couldn't find you anywhere. I confess I didn't feel too happy—even though you are such a care and worry to me—"

"Peter. Do you have to drag this out so— *Please."*

Peter grinned. "I am telling my story as you wanted me to. And in my own way. I went back to the house. By that time Philippine had come to, and she was, as she always is when conscious, both sensible and coherent.

She confessed that you had both agreed to let Jim off and then she said that you two got talking and that you told her about that secret cache of Margie's in the shed out back—"

"That's right."

"Is it? Good. She said she felt that she must have a look at Margie's things even at that late hour, but you objected because you were frightened—"

"I—well, yes, I have to admit that I was—"

"And with good reason, I may add. I was wild with her by then and called her all kinds of names for such an escapade—utter madness. Then she poured out a story about how she thought Margie had a guilt complex and had been taking poison and she wanted to protect Margie's name—and, I suspect, the business—by having a look at Margie's private possessions before the police could—"

"Well, but isn't that true? I mean didn't Margie commit suicide?"

"Are you absolutely insane, Fredericka, or have you a few grains of sense left? If Margie was the guilty one, who the devil hit you over the head—*after Margie was dead?*"

"I never thought of that," Fredericka said weakly.

"Philippine then went on to tell me how you two bright little gals started out with your torch—"

"Hers—"

"What difference does that make? It was the one that bashed you both over the head." Peter's patience seemed to have worn thin. "Then she told me about feeling someone come up from behind, dropping the torch in panic and then being hit on the head, and knowing no more. She said you were ahead of her and had just warned her about the old well— That gave me a bright idea and I dashed out—and sure enough I found the well, all neatly covered up with boards. I ripped them off in a hurry and there, sure enough, was our Fredericka, all crumpled up in the bottom which, thank God, was full of old cuttings that Chris must have been dumping in for years—and so where you landed was dry—"

"Not very—"

"Enough so you didn't drown. I called and—you answered. It was a good sound, I confess. Well, it didn't take long to hoist you out and get you here. By that time, of course, you'd passed out again. Jim helped. Philippine also went out again on the sofa, but eventually she was able to drive herself home while we were getting you to the hospital. Thane came to rejoice with me. And that, boys and girls, will be all for this morning. If you listen in at the same time tomorrow!"

"Oh, Peter, *shut up!*"

"I have. It's your turn now."

"Everything's exactly as Philippine told you. I can see that I wasn't very bright, but for one thing I didn't want to admit that Philippine was braver than I was when there didn't seem to be any logical reason to be scared after what Philippine had told me about Margie."

"Exactly what did she tell you?"

"Just what she told you, I expect," Fredericka said. But when he urged her for details she tried to remember all that Philippine had said and repeated their conversation word for word.

"Yes. That's pretty much what she told me."

"It makes sense."

"It *made* sense, you mean. You seem to forget that there has been as near another murder as makes no difference."

"Some difference, I think. But why don't you say 'as near two other murders as makes no difference'?"

"What? Oh yes—two, if you like—" Peter agreed absently. "The present puzzle is about Margie's pathetic little secret hiding place in the shed. The police found some sort of makeup kit, a few bottles of cosmetics, several letters from firms advertising cures for skin diseases to which she had obviously been writing, and some comics, but nothing else of the slightest interest—"

"That's all I remember seeing there, but my visit dates back to the day after Catherine's murder. I haven't been near the shed since then. Thane told me about the stuff and I was going to speak to Margie about it but never did. And then when I talked to Chris, he said Miss Hartwell was in favour of her having the stuff there so, of course, I left it alone, just as Thane did. Anyway I wouldn't have touched it without his O.K."

"Why did you feel you had to get his permission?"

"I don't know exactly," Fredericka said slowly. "I guess it was just that he had told me about it—well, he didn't really say anything more than that he'd found some curious oddments about the place. But I thought when I found Margie's junk that that was what he meant. I suppose it's because I'm Watson, well trained by Holmes, that I didn't want to get rid of it just because he did know about it. It could have been a *plant* or something."

"Good girl," he muttered. He looked at his watch. "Your nurse gave me one hour and I think I hear an ominous starched rustle outside, so I'm going before I'm chucked out." He stood up and then leaped over and kissed her lightly on the forehead. "I repeat," he said softly, "good girl—but perhaps just a little silly, my dear Watson."

Fredericka again turned away toward the wall to hide the tiresome tears. Then at the door, Peter stopped in his flight to say: "Fredericka, you must rest and sleep and eat. Your arm and leg will slow you up for a bit but you're absolutely O.K., and we hope to get you back to work in a day or two. I ought to say 'Forget this nightmare,' but I know you can't forget it, and so, selfishly, I want to say just the opposite. Try to remember everything. Think of every damn little incident. When you remembered Chris's stamps and those letters, you gave me a most valuable clue— So, as you lie here, *please* think over every moment of every day since you've been here. And think especially of last Sunday night—every miserable inch of it."

"I will, Peter," Fredericka said quietly. "Anyway I'll try." Then a sudden thought occurred to her. "That clue. Did you find out anything in Washington?"

"Yes, something, but not enough. I know who murdered Catherine Clay—who probably murdered Margie, and who attacked you and Philippine. Oh yes, I know all right. But I haven't *proof.* It's there you can help me."

"Peter. If you know, why don't you tell me? I could think it out much better if I knew what I was trying to find."

"No. I don't think so. You'd invent things—not intentionally, but because you'd be cutting off toes to make the slipper fit, like Cinderella's sisters. Besides, you haven't got a poker face, my dear Fredericka, and I don't want you to be attacked again. Another time it might be more successful. Anyway, we're going to keep you here under guard just in case. You see, the murderer must feel, just as I do, that there's probably something important you might remember—I'm sorry, but the rule is NO VISITORS."

"What are *you,* then?" Fredericka asked, a little crossly. All her annoyances seemed suddenly to be of major importance. This secrecy, her own tendency to tears, her helpless heavy arm and foot, and now her imprisonment, and all this officiousness.

"I'm Police, and *very* special." Peter grinned: "And I'll probably bother you a lot. If you have any inspirations, though, *please* get the nurse to call the station, and they'll have instructions to relay the good news to me. And I—wherever I am—will come loping over here with all possible speed—"

"Now that's something to look forward to," Fredericka grumbled. She was still annoyed with Peter and the world, and her head had begun to ache again.

Peter Mohun made no attempt to reply. But he was still smiling as he turned quickly and disappeared.

Fredericka lay still listening to the hollow sound of his footsteps as he walked away down the corridor. Hasn't got on his Silent Sleuth shoes today, she thought. But no less pleased with himself, and mysterious. Well, he can do his own thinking. . . .

An hour later Fredericka opened her eyes to see the nurse bending over her.

"You've had a nice little sleep. And now a good wash and then I'll bring your lunch."

Fredericka's head still throbbed dully, but she managed, with the nurse's help, to raise herself to a sitting position. Then, as the woman bustled around and fussed over her she began to feel better.

"You've washed away my headache, and, I hope, my bad temper," Fredericka said at last.

"You've a right to headache, bad temper, whatever

you like," the nurse said surprisingly. "I guess the town'll stop their silly gossip now. Or perhaps they'll say you bashed yourself over the head and threw yourself down the well. I wouldn't put it past them— Well now, I'll just get you some food. Hungry?" When Fredericka nodded a little uncertainly, the woman whisked off and Fredericka watched her wide retreating back. Then she leant back on her pillows feeling spoilt and grateful. Murders, South Sutton, even the bookshop seemed very far away.

"Miss Sanders," the woman announced as she put down the tray, on her return.

"I'm Fredericka Wing."

The nurse laughed. "Oh, you don't need to tell me that. Now you just eat your lunch. Here, I'll cut up your salad for you. Not very ladylike, perhaps, but it's easier that way until you get used to managing with one hand, or perhaps I should say a hand and a half."

Fredericka made no reply because all at once she had begun to think. The murders, South Sutton, the bookshop—and Peter—had come back into the quiet room. She frowned down at her food in her abstraction. When at last she looked up again, Miss Sanders had turned away from the bed and was straightening things in the room.

"I'm sorry, Miss Sanders, I never said a word of thanks and you are so very kind. I'm supposed to try to remember everything that's happened to me and, all at once, I began to—"

"It's a lucky thing you are alive to remember," the woman said firmly. "No thanks to the police that you are," she added darkly. "I can't think what they were up to, leaving you unprotected like that."

This reminded Fredericka of the woman's earlier

disapproving remarks and she asked: "There was something you said a while ago about people in the town. Is it true then that they thought I was the murderess?"

"Oh yes. And the *stories* they told. You wouldn't believe it. Just because you didn't happen to be a native."

"I should think that there were plenty of people who would answer to that description. The students, the faculty, Catherine Clay herself—and Philippine and Roger Sutton, for that matter."

"The students and the teachers don't count. Catherine Clay and Philippine and Roger—they're all attached to the Sutton family whether they live here or not. They're rated as natives all right—but you are a real outsider."

"Oh—dear—"

"Now don't fret yourself. No one suspects you now unless they're all lunatics. And I expect when you're up and about again, you won't even feel like an outsider any more. It usually takes more time, but I daresay all this fuss has speeded things up a bit."

"Aren't you a native, then?" Fredericka asked.

"Good gracious no. I've only been here five years next March."

They both laughed and then, when Fredericka again became silent and thoughtful, Miss Sanders picked up the tray quietly and started for the door.

Suddenly Fredericka sat bolt upright and started to put her foot out on to the floor until its heaviness reminded her that she couldn't. Then she fairly shouted at the retreating figure. "Nurse. Oh, Miss Sanders."

The woman turned round and the china on the tray clinked ominously. "Good gracious, you startled me. Whatever is the matter?" she asked a little abruptly.

"Please will you telephone the police station and ask them to get a message to Colonel Mohun. It's *most* important. I want him to come and see me *at once.* I—I've just thought of something."

For a moment Miss Sanders struggled with an overwhelming desire to know what that something could be. Then training and character won, and she said, quietly, "Yes, Miss Wing. Right away as soon as I can drop this tray and get to the telephone."

"Thanks— Oh, thanks," Fredericka said, and then couldn't resist adding: "You will hurry, won't you?" But fortunately Miss Sanders had already left the room.

15

As Peter Mohun walked away from Fredericka's room down the long corridor that smelt of soap and disinfectant, the smile disappeared and a look of concentration took its place. Outside, he stopped for a moment in the shade of a giant maple to light a cigarette—then he walked on slowly and climbed into his car. As he drove back toward South Sutton, the sun beat down on the canvas top of the old Ford and beads of perspiration stood out on his forehead. He kept his right hand on the wheel and fished for his handkerchief with his left. Then he absently mopped his head and neck, but the look of concentration did not leave his face.

It was just as he was approaching the town along Beech Street and was about to stop at the police station that the inspiration came to him. He did not stop. Instead he went on at breakneck speed to Miss Hartwell's bookshop, drove the car around into the alley, and parked it quietly. He noted with satisfaction that there was no one else about as he got out quickly, walked along until he found Margie's foxhole, eased his large body through the gap, and went straight to the old greenhouse.

Inside it was very hot. The sun's rays were now directly overhead and the nearest tree offered little shade. Peter went back to prop open the door with a stone and then began systematically to explore every inch of the floor and walls. Finding nothing of interest except a large collection of empty jars, he picked up each of the two bottles and the jar on the shelf, observed the name on the label, then opened and smelled each one, and returned it to its place. They were all standard brand products labelled and heavily perfumed. He stood still and stared at the shelf. Between the two bottles was a greasy ring that showed plainly in the dust. Peter took the jar and found that it was smaller than the ring. His look of concentration increased as he searched about for the right jar and found none. He then looked at the makeup kit which was also revealing. Finally he dispensed with the pile of comics and the letters. They were all much alike. One was headed "Perfection Beauty Creams Company," with an address in Chicago. He read:

Dear Miss Hartwell

In reply to your recent inquiry, we judge from what you say of your case, that our cream number 43 is exactly what you need. We are sending a small sample jar under separate cover but beg to advise that in a serious condition, as you describe yours to be, you will need a large jar and constant application. We shall be happy to send this at once post free on receipt of check or money order for three dollars.

Yours very truly,

The signature was obviously a rubber stamp and very blurred.

"Poor kid," Peter said aloud, as he put the letter down and glanced through the other similar ones.

"Oh, it's you-all, Colonel Mohun." A soft voice spoke behind him and Peter turned quickly to see Chris peering in at him.

"I'm sorry, suh, I seen the door standing open and I thought it might be them kids."

"Nothing to be sorry about, Chris. I'm just having a look around." He took out his cigarettes and offered one to the old man. "It's hot as hades in here. I'm about ready to get outside."

They walked up the back path toward the house and Peter asked: "Did Margie use that shed much, Chris?"

"She sure did. Come in and out that little hole back there night and day she did. Pore chile."

"Even last week, Chris?"

The old man took off his hat and scratched the back of his head. "Yes, sir. I remembers now. She was here jes' before she was took sick. I told Jim not to take no notice of her. Miss Hartwell she let her have that place for playin' in. Didn't make no harm."

"No, of course not."

"I never did tell no one about it whatsoever. Her Mom got real mad about her puttin' those potions on her face so Miss Hartwell and I we kep' it in strict secrecy until those policemen had a look round and foun' out about it. But they didn't take nothin' away and that chile come right along day and night like I told you. She did love that little hidey-hole." He sighed heavily.

As they approached the house Connie heard them, and came out the back door.

"Hi, Peter," she greeted him. "Had any lunch? And what about you, Chris?" she added.

Both men approved this implication that she could supply it and sat down on the edge of the porch. Connie went back into the house.

Peter stared down at an ant tugging away at what appeared to be an enormous egg. He moved a stick out of the way of its progress without realizing that he had done so. Then suddenly he stood up. "Look here, Chris," he said, and a note of eagerness had come into his voice.

"Yes, sir," Chris answered, getting to his feet with obvious reluctance.

"I want you to help me. I think—yes, I'm as good as dead sure that somebody has buried something around here. I want you to do a search of the grounds with me—every inch."

Connie reappeared. "All right, sleuth, but first you both eat." She put down a tray with a plate of sandwiches, and two large cups of coffee.

"O.K.," Peter said, "oh and—thanks. I say, what about you?"

"Fat chance. Even at lunch time I've got half a dozen customers."

The screen door slammed on her retreating back. The two men finished off the sandwiches and coffee quickly and then Peter said, "We'd better start out back by the shed and work our way up toward the house."

"Excuse me, sir, but jes' what am you fixin' to find buried in these here grounds?"

"That's the devil of it, Chris, I don't know, but I think its a medium-sized round box or jar, but even at that I'm just guessing."

Again Chris removed his hat and scratched his head. "I jes' remember seein' a place near that sycamore back there where I thought a dog must have buried hisself a big ole bone—all scuffed up like."

Peter placed a heavy hand on Chris's shoulder. "Good man," he said quietly, but there was no mistaking his excitement.

A few moments later they were digging away at a spot well hidden in the shrubbery and about midway between the shed and the old well. Before long the trowel that Chris was using hit something solid.

"Careful. Here, let me have a try now," Peter said quickly. He dug with his bare hands and unearthed a small broken jar from which oozed a large amount of thick face cream, now covered with earth, but still unmistakably pink.

"Well, I never did," Chris said.

Peter stared at the bits of glass and pasty liquid for a moment. Then he took out his handkerchief and lifted it out of the earth without touching it with his hands. "So that's what it was. My God!" he said. He wrapped the treasure in his handkerchief, dropped it in his pocket and dashed off toward the back gate. A second later, Chris, who was still standing with his mouth wide open, heard the sound of a car backing out of the alley. It roared away into the distance and then silence returned to the garden. Chris scratched his head once more and went back to his work.

Peter drove straight to the police station where the sergeant in charge told him that Thane Carey was at the Farm.

"Good," Peter said. "I'm heading there, too."

"There's a message for you, Colonel—just come in—It was Miss Sanders over at the Hospital. Miss Wing would like you to go over there as soon as you can."

For a second only, Peter hesitated. Then he said, "Can't do. Must get to the Farm."

"Shall I give her a ring and let her know?"

"No, I don't think I'll be long. Better leave it."

"O.K."

Peter started to go and then turned back. "Where's Jim Brown?" he asked.

"Just gone home for a late lunch. He's been at the Farm. When the boss went out there just now, he sent Jim back."

"And the other men?"

"Oh you mean those guys from Worcester. Gone back."

It was evident that there had been no love lost between the town and country police. Peter grinned. "O.K.," he said "I hope Jim's had time for his meal. I'm afraid I need him."

The sergeant opened his mouth to speak but Peter, sensing a question, hurried out in the hot sunshine. A moment later Peter stopped at Jim's house, a small bungalow a few hundred yards beyond the station. Jim's wife came to the door, in answer to Peter's loud knocking and went to call her husband with obvious reluctance. But a second later, Jim was beside him in the car.

"Fireworks at last?" Jim asked as they started up.

"I think so."

"How's Miss Wing?"

"Busted arm and foot—some shock—otherwise O.K."

"I say, Colonel Mohun, I'll never forgive myself for that."

"As it turned out, Jim, it solved the case for us so—just forget it, kid."

They drove on in silence until, as they approached the Farm, Peter said: "You're armed, of course?"

"Yes. I'd just taken off my belt to make room for my dinner when you came. But reached for it automatic-like when I saw you through the window."

"Good. Sorry about that meal."

"It'll keep."

They were now moving slowly up the driveway. "I'm going to stop short of the last curve and out of sight of the house. And I'm attempting to make our approach a quiet one but perhaps you hadn't noticed."

Jim laughed. "These old flivvers can go but they sure do make a row about it. Saw your new buggy down at the garage. Nice job."

Peter smiled. "Funny how news gets around in South Sutton, Mass.," he said. "It's a lucky thing I've got that car in hand. Look here—this is what I want you to do." He stopped the Ford in the middle of the drive just before the wide curve that led up to the front door. Then the two men sat quietly for a few moments while Peter outlined his plans.

As Peter walked alone up the road to the house there was no sound except the shrill notes of the crickets and the subdued crunch of his own feet on the gravel. Midsummer peace, he thought, and peace it might have been if Fredericka's devil hadn't decided to have them all for—how long had it been? She'd sneezed on that first Sunday, a week later she'd found Catherine Clay dead in her hammock, after another week Margie Hartwell had died— No wonder South Sutton had taken a dim view of the advent of Fredericka. And yet, if it hadn't been for her there would still have been the deaths and, quite likely, no solution. There was no doubt about it, South Sutton owed a great deal to Fredericka

Wing and her warning sneeze. And Peter Mohun—there was no doubt about that, either.

There was no one about as Peter walked up on the porch and pushed the screen door gently. It flew back from his hand with a protesting shriek of its rusty spring. He cursed silently.

"Who's that?" someone called.

"Only Peter Mohun," he answered.

"Oh, Peter—come on out to the back porch. You're in time for iced tea."

Peter walked through the hall and the long living room to the screened porch and paused in the open doorway. Thane Carey was sitting in a large armchair and Mrs. Sutton on the couch near him. She was darning socks. A tray with a pitcher of iced tea and some tall glasses stood on a table between them. There was no one else in the room.

The effect of this quiet domestic scene on Peter was one of acute anticlimax. He stood for a moment and stared at them blankly. Then he said hoarsely, "Carey— I'm sorry Margaret—but Carey, I must have a word with you—at once."

Thane Carey stood up and came toward him. "Outside. I'm keeping an eye on the one door of the lab," he said quietly.

The two men disappeared. A second later Margaret Sutton put down her sock and followed them.

The minute they were out of the house, Peter said: "I've got the evidence but I can't stop to explain. Where is she?"

"Are you looking for Philippine?" Mrs. Sutton asked quietly.

Both men jumped and swung around to face her. Margaret Sutton looked first at Thane and then at Peter.

When neither of them spoke she went on slowly: "Oh, I know. I have watched you watching her, Thane, but I knew long ago—even before you did, I'm afraid. I thought— Oh dear, what difference does it make now what I thought. She's been in the lab all day. She's still there, isn't she, Thane?"

"Yes."

"You're going to arrest her, then?"

This time it was Peter who said, "Yes. We must. And at once."

Margaret Sutton put her hand on Peter's arm and he looked up at her quickly. How old she looks, he thought, and how inexpressibly sad and tired. "May I ask you one favour?" she said. "Let me talk to her first. She's not to blame." She looked steadily at the set faces that stared back at her.

The two men looked at each other and then Thane answered her. "Of course, Margaret, if you insist. But we will go with you—and we are both armed. You understand that?"

"Yes. I understand. But it isn't necessary."

They walked slowly along the path to the laboratory. Inside they stopped and listened. Then Mrs. Sutton called, "Phil, where are you?"

"Here in the herb room, Aunt Maggie. Do you want me? I'll come in a minute."

"No, I'll come to you." She turned to the men behind her. "I'd like to go alone."

"No—" They both answered her at the same moment.

"Very well."

As they entered the room, Philippine turned from the table. "I'm afraid I've been antisocial today, Auntie, but I got so behind in my work," she said, and then stopped when she saw the two men.

"Have you anything to say to me, Philippine?" Margaret Sutton asked quietly.

"Anything to say to you? No, I don't think so. What—what do you mean?"

"These men have come to accuse you of the murder of Catherine—and I told them that I wanted to talk to you first."

"The *murder.* This is madness," Philippine said calmly.

Peter looked at her face closely and could see no hint in it of either fear or anxiety. He stepped ahead of Margaret and spoke quickly: "It's no good, Margaret, Philippine will fight for her life until all hope is gone. Won't you?" He flung the words at the woman who now faced him.

"I have no need to fight, Peter. I am innocent."

My God, I've never seen such superb acting, Thane thought as he watched her.

"Very well then, how do you explain this?" He reached in his pocket and produced the stained handkerchief containing the fragments of jar and face cream.

"What is it?" Philippine asked with an expression of distaste.

"It is a jar of poisoned face-cream, or so I believe. Buried by you in Miss Hartwell's back yard on Sunday evening after you had, as you thought, dispensed with Fredericka Wing. I didn't stop to send it to the lab. I don't need to, but Thane will get a report in due course. What's more, I think this time, unless I'm much mistaken, you overlooked the little matter of fingerprints."

"You're insane—all of you," Philippine said quietly. "I have no idea what you are talking about. I do know and I have told you that Margie Hartwell poisoned Catherine—then if, as you say, that face cream is poisoned she must have poisoned herself that way. I wondered what she had done."

"But Philippine," Mrs. Sutton said suddenly, "Margie wouldn't poision herself with face cream. She wouldn't hurt her poor face any more. Oh no, Philippine. You see—I saw—"

She stopped suddenly, and before she could go on, Philippine spoke and Peter now observed that for the first time her face had gone white and that her voice was hoarse and strained, "If you must go on talking this nonsense, I suggest that we go into the house and sit down. Aunt Maggie ought not to stand on that ankle."

"A good idea," Thane said quickly. He nodded at Mrs. Sutton and she turned without speaking and led the way to the door. "You go next, Philippine," he said, "and Peter and I will follow."

The little procession moved toward the door and outside on to the path. Then, without warning and with the speed of lightning, Philippine pulled a small revolver from the large pocket of her white coat and stepped aside to face them. The move was so unexpected that neither Thane nor Peter had time to move.

"Stand where you are," Philippine said fiercely, "all of you, and if you move a finger I shall shoot—and to kill."

Peter tried to reach his revolver and a shot whisked by his left ear. He cursed himself for an idiot.

"I meant what I said," Philippine continued quietly. "Now put up your hands, please." Thane and Peter made no further effort at resistance and Philippine took the revolvers from their pockets and put them into her own. Then she backed away toward the jeep that stood behind her in the driveway.

"My God, I never wanted to kill as much as I do now," Thane muttered.

Philippine had now reached the car, and was slipping in under the wheel when suddenly Margaret Sutton, whom everyone had forgotten, stooped down and picked up one of the large stones that edged the flower bed by her feet. As she flung it toward the figure in the car, a second shot rang out and the older woman fell forward on to the grass verge of the driveway. At the same instant the jeep leapt forward with a deafening roar, Peter ran to Margaret, and Thane grabbed another rock and charged helplessly after the departing car.

Peter watched the stain spread on Margaret's white collar and felt for her pulse. Then he stood up and called after Thane. "It's no good, Carey. Come and help me here." Then as Thane came toward him, he added: "Margaret's only got a shoulder wound, but it's no thanks to us. However, I did take one precaution."

A second later the crash came. Mrs. Hartwell appeared from the door of the house like a jack-in-the-box and Thane and Peter lifted Margaret Sutton gently and carried her into the living room.

"Philippine can't have survived it, I'm afraid," Peter said. "I left my lovely Ford in the middle of the drive—just around the corner and she was going at a good clip. Anyway, Jim's there to pick up the pieces. But we were a couple of mugs, Thane. I never dreamt she was armed and neither, I think, did you."

"Hadn't a clue. My God, what a dame!"

"You said it, wise guy, you said it. A cool customer—and how."

They left Mrs. Hartwell to sit by Margaret Sutton while Peter went to call Dr. Scott and Thane hurried off down the driveway.

16

What had Peter said? *"I'll come loping over with all possible speed—wherever I am—"*

Well he hadn't come. Fredericka had tried to read, but it made her head ache. She had looked at her watch at least a hundred times and she had called Miss Sanders almost as many. But there was no sign of Peter.

As the afternoon wore on, the room grew heavy with the summer heat and Fredericka's arm and foot in their plaster cases throbbed and itched maddeningly. She turned over her pillows once more and lay back against them. The room was so white and clean and bare and smelt so persistently of disinfectant. There wasn't even anything to look at except a small and very lazy fly making its unhurried way across the ceiling. She closed her eyes and groaned.

The door opened and she sat up eagerly. But it was only Miss Sanders with a tray. "I brought you some iced tea. It's getting hot again and this room always does seem to steam up in the summer. I wouldn't have put you in here if I'd had any say about it."

I'm just *patient* to her. I'm not Fredericka Wing with the solution of the South Sutton murders in my helpless hands. I'm not Peter's Dr. Watson to her, or to anyone else. I'm just nobody at all. Oh, dear God, where *is* he? Suddenly she was aware of the silence in the room and she said quickly, "Oh, Nurse, bless you for that tea, and forgive me for not saying so at once. The fact is I'm fed up with waiting. You see I've remembered something and I know it's important to Colonel Mohun to know it. And now—now he just won't come—"

It was apparent to Miss Sanders that her patient was near tears. "There's no need to carry on so, Miss Wing," she said firmly. "You'll only get yourself into such a state that you won't be able to talk to Colonel Mohun when he does come. Now drink up your tea, like a good girl."

Fredericka fought back the silly tears: "Please can't you stay with me a few minutes, Miss Sanders? I can't read and there's nothing to look at, and I hate to think."

Miss Sanders lowered her large body into the chair by the bed. Fredericka sipped her tea slowly and tried to think of things to talk about but conversation lagged, and presently her nurse got up. "I mustn't sit here. I've all my other patients to see to I'm afraid. Shall I get you some aspirin for your head?"

"No. No thanks. The tea was wonderful. I'll be all right now."

Miss Sanders, obviously relieved, took her unhurried departure, and again Fredericka was left alone with her thoughts.

It was dark when Peter finally came. Fredericka had, at length, fallen into an uneasy sleep, but she woke to hear slow footsteps coming down the corridor. That could not be Peter, she decided, and turned over to try to sleep again. Then the door opened and she sat up, blinking at the sudden light. Then she saw his face, and she was startled out of her own mood of hurt and self-pity. He wore no coat and his shirt was torn and stained with sweat. His hair was uncombed and his face was gray and lined. He looked old and utterly exhausted as he sank heavily into the chair. For a long time he said nothing.

Fredericka reached out her good hand and touched him gently on the arm. "Are you all right, Peter?" she asked helplessly, knowing that he was not all right.

"Yes, in body," he said slowly. "Do you suppose this place could produce a brandy?"

Fredericka pressed the silent button that was the modern vision of a bell and they both waited without speaking until, after what seemed a very long time, a young nurse put her head in the door.

"Miss Sanders?" Fredericka asked impatiently.

"She's off now—since eight o'clock."

"Oh— Please could you get some brandy. I'm afraid Colonel Mohun—in fact we're both—rather ill—"

The nurse looked at them suspiciously for a moment and then disappeared.

Peter stared at Fredericka blankly and then said slowly, "The sight of you is good. There was one moment when I didn't think I'd ever have it again. . . ."

Fredericka reached for his hand and held it tightly in hers until the nurse returned with two small medicine glasses of brandy on a tray. She put this down on the bed table with a look of bewildered disapproval.

"Is there anything else you want, Miss Wing?" she asked Fredericka, but she looked at Peter, who shook his head and waved her away.

"Thanks so much," Fredericka said quickly, and,

when the girl had gone, she added: "Drink both of them and don't try to talk. There's no hurry."

When he had taken all the brandy, slowly, and with obvious pleasure, he offered Fredericka a cigarette and took one for himself. Then he said quietly: "It's all over."

"I thought it must be from the look of you. Can you talk about it?"

"Yes. In a minute. Tell me first what you wanted me for."

"It seems unimportant now, but I did think it might be the evidence you needed. You see, I tried to do what you told me to. I went backwards in my mind over everything and particularly that last night. And then I realized that it couldn't have been a third person who hit me. It must have been Philippine."

"Yes. It was. But how did you work it out?"

"Well, you said I had been hit with her torch—I suppose it must have had bits of me on it and bits of her. That seemed reasonable until I remembered that she had said, "I've dropped the torch," or something like that, and then *instantly* I was hit. There just wasn't time for anyone to have picked it up. So if it was that torch that hit me, she couldn't have dropped it at all but must have just switched it off and used it herself."

"That's exactly what she did do. It was careless of her. But the attack on you was not carefully thought out. She had to remake a lot of plans because of you. Moreover she must have felt that she could afford to be careless since she intended to do the job up brown and silence you completely. She had no idea that the well was dry, you see. Otherwise she'd have finished you off before she pitched you into it."

"Oh, Peter!" Fredericka clutched his large hand more tightly. "Somehow I feel I would have known that it was Philippine much sooner if only I hadn't—oh, dear—I *liked* her so much."

"That was the secret of her amazing success. Everyone liked her—except, of course, Catherine Clay. She could bank on being liked and indeed cultivate her own likableness as she cultivated her poisons in that laboratory of hers—"

"Did she poison Margie, then?"

"Oh, yes. And in the most diabolic way. You see that story that she told you about coming on Margie filling capsules in the lab was true, *the other way around.* It was Margie who discovered Philippine and, being Margie, she asked questions. Whatever answers she got satisfied her at the time and Philippine wasn't unduly worried then, because she intended to have Catherine's death look like an overdose of dope either by accident or design and that would have been by injection not capsule. She intended to recover the little silver box and any remaining poisoned capsules after Catherine's death and before the police found them. If she had succeeded, Margie would never have thought anything more about surprising Philippine in the lab."

"But Philippine couldn't get at the corpse."

"She may have done. I believe she trailed Catherine around because I found out from Roger that they were not together on their herb hunt but went in separate directions. Unfortunately for Philippine's plans, Catherine had dropped the box in the long grass near your back door. Philippine may well have looked for it and not been able to find it."

"And then it turned up—too late."

"Yes. But it might not have been too late even then. It was Margie who told Philippine that the box had been found. And, in fact, the silly child remembered then that she had seen the box in Philippine's hand that day in the lab and said so. At that time no one had suggested poison in the vitamin capsules and Margie didn't put two and two together. But Philippine knew that she must recover the box with the extra capsules and, failing that, that she must get rid of Margie who would be able to connect them with herself. She decided to use Margie to recover the box by refusing to believe that it was the same one. Margie tried to get it from you and failed, as we know. Then the fact of poisoning became known. Margie must have put her two and two together and Philippine then had to carry out her plan of getting rid of Margie who might, at any moment, turn informer."

"But why didn't Margie turn informer at once?"

"I'm not certain. Philippine is too far gone to give us a confession so this is mostly conjecture, but I would say that she had some hold over the child. She may even have made Margie believe that if she went to the police with her story, they would believe Philippine's word against hers. Philippine probably threatened to say that she had found Margie in the lab with the box and capsules and pin the murder on to her as she did do, later, in her story to you. Margie's passionate hatred of Catherine was well known. Philippine's was not."

"Oh God! If we'd only known. Oh, Peter, I was so much to blame."

"No more than any of the rest of us," Peter said bitterly, but he let go of Fredericka's hand and gripped both arms of the chair fiercely. "It's the *way* she killed the child that is so terrible. I suppose if we'd seen the Nazis at work in a concentration camp as she did, it wouldn't seem so demoniac—"

He stopped speaking and, after a moment, Fredericka said quietly, "Oh, Peter, please tell me what she did do. I—I can't stand it either."

"She must have told Margie that she had at last discovered a face cream that would cure her acne. Margie believed her implicitly because she thought Philippine a sort of wizard with her herbs and potions. What Philippine had discovered was that some one of her damned old herbs could poison through the skin—I confess I'm guessing now, but Thane's chemist will soon know all—"

"Oh, Peter—no!"

"Oh, Fredericka—*yes,*" Peter answered grimly. "You see the beauty of this hideous plan. She used the poison that would kill the child as a bribe to keep her quiet while it was killing her. The difficulty was that the poison was slow. I believe she told Margie that she would give her this miracle cure in return for the child's silence. Margie kept her part of the bargain—"

"I can't believe it of Philippine, Peter. I just can't." Fredericka was silent and thoughtful for a moment, then she asked, "Was there any reason why she couldn't give the child a quick sure death like Catherine's?"

"Oh, yes. She couldn't without being caught and she didn't intend to be caught. When her plan to make Catherine's death look like too much dope failed, she knew that the yellow jessamine poison would lead us straight to her laboratory. And she knew that the possible suspects, from our point of view, were very few. But she had sense enough to know that we were helpless without evidence and that we hadn't a shred of it. If she had taken an obvious quick method of killing Margie, we'd have been on to her at once. Oh, yes, we had our eye on that damn bottle of yellow jessamine all right, but this face-cream business was a brand new wrinkle— She was, in fact, too clever for us. My God—how we guarded that kid's food and drink. I expect Philippine had some good laughs over that."

"But Peter, you haven't explained why she wanted to kill me. I can't see it. Until two hours ago I hadn't a clue—"

"Yes you did—a beautiful clue. But you didn't realize it. The jar of poisoned face cream. That was the one piece of incriminating evidence and she knew it. But she couldn't find that any more than she could find the box with the capsules after Catherine's death."

"So when I said Margie had used the shed or greenhouse or what-have-you for a secret hiding place and there were some cosmetics and junk there, she knew where the face cream must be."

"She did indeed, and she had to think fast. I believe she came that night to the bookshop determined to find the stuff but without any formulated plan."

"Yes. I remember now that, before that, when she came for Margie's insurance card and pyjamas in the storeroom, she did seem to be looking for something. In fact, she admitted as much. And now I can see the real reason, of course."

"If we'd only known that—"

"But it didn't amount to anything really—I never thought of it at the time."

Peter sighed heavily and then went on slowly: "By last Sunday night when Margie died, Philippine was beside herself with anxiety. She had ransacked the Farm and, as you say, she had had a good look at the Hartwell's storeroom at the bookshop. But she thought she must have another look at once. So, without any idea beyond finding the stuff and getting rid of it, she abandoned James and came to call on you."

"I see. And, in a way, circumstances played into her hands. Jim Brown wanted to go home to his wife and baby. But when that happened I'd have thought she would simply have waited until I got to sleep and then had a look-around."

"Perhaps she intended to do that but when you practically told her where the face cream was, she didn't dare risk having you wake up and find her out getting rid of it. She was almost insane by then, I imagine, and on the spur of the moment, she thought up this lunatic scheme of killing you and faking an attack on herself."

"She almost got away with it."

"Yes—almost."

"And if she had, you'd have gone on suspecting her, I suppose, but would have had no evidence to pin it on to her."

"Theoretically, yes. But, in fact, if she had killed you, we'd have got her somehow."

Fredericka felt suddenly cold. "I think on the whole I'd rather be here," she said with a poor effort at laughter.

"And I'd rather you were, too—on the whole. But I might have spared you everything if I'd had even one grain of sense. I underestimated her—an unforgivable sin in my profession." He stopped and then said abruptly: "And now I'm dead beat and so are you. Tonight we can sleep, both of us. Tomorrow is another day. I'm going to try to get you out of this hole. Connie wants to be your nurse and assistant in the bookshop until you learn to manage it in some wonderful crab-like way."

"But Peter! Oh—please don't go. You haven't told me anything—I know from what you say that you've caught Philippine, but *how?*—and *where?*"

"That's just what I *didn't* want to tell you tonight but

I suppose I'll have to even if it does give you nightmares. You've been a good Watson and you've earned it." He ran a hand through his hair and for a moment he sat quietly as though searching for words.

Feeling the weight of his tiredness and depression, Fredericka forced herself to say: "Look, Peter, I can wait until morning if you really want me to. I know you're worn out. Perhaps I'm being unfair."

"No. Let's get it over with. It's so damn grisly, though. Thank God you weren't in at the kill."

Fredericka wished she had been, but didn't dare to say so. She lay back on the pillows and waited patiently for him to light them each a cigarette before he went on.

Then, quite simply, Peter recounted the story of his day's adventures from the time he left Fredericka. When he told her of his search among Margie's treasures in the old shed, Fredericka broke in to say suddenly: "Of course. That night she scared me stiff I suppose she was just paying a regular visit to her hideout."

"No, I don't think so now. I believe it was Philippine. That was the very night after the murder, you remember, and Margie would have been too scared. We were fools to think it could have been her."

"And Philippine was having another look around for the silver box?"

"Yes—I think so but, again, you threw a monkey wrench in her plans. She couldn't hang around after you discovered her so, cleverly, she pretended to be Margie."

"I see."

"And Margie's junk in the old shed meant nothing to any of us—a kid's secret hiding place—and we left it alone. So it was natural that Margie should take her jar of magic cure to her hidey-hole. And I'm sure she went there and used it until she was too sick to use it any more. By then, of course, it had done its work."

"So you sat and talked to Chris and did some heavy thinking?" Fredericka prompted.

"Yes. Then I saw daylight. After Philippine thought she had got rid of you, she still had to find whatever it was she was looking for before she could do the faked attack on herself. So she shoved you down the well, put that mass of boards on top and went on to the shed where she found the treasure she was seeking. Then— what did she do with it?"

"Threw it in the well on top of me?"

"Oh, Watson, you're slipping. When we found you, which we were bound to do because she intended to tell us about the double attack, we'd find the face cream sure as fate. No, the quickest way to get rid of it was to bury it. Later she could come one night to recover it and do away with it for good and all."

"I see," Fredericka said slowly. Then when Peter fell silent, she added: "But please go on, I'll try not to interrupt again."

After a moment, Peter lit another cigarette and went on slowly. When, at last, he came to the end, Fredericka said quickly, "Margaret?"

"She'll live. Dr. Scott says it's a shoulder graze. But Philippine did a better job on herself. The jeep and my flivver were a mess. Jim pulled her out of the pyre. She's still alive but she hasn't been moved from the Farm. I don't think she'll ever recover consciousness. Perhaps it's just as well."

"Oh Peter!" was all Fredericka could find to say.

"And now," he said tiredly, "please may I go home?" He got slowly to his feet and looked down at Fredericka's anxious face. "Don't fret any more. There's nothing more to fret about. Peace has returned to South Sutton. Of course you were a fool to get sandbagged and dumped down that well. But you've been the best Watson I've ever had. And right now I'm a little sore but I'm still grateful to you for making me tell you what happened. It's off me—thank God—and I'll sleep. All thanks to you, Fredericka, and I can only hope you will, too." He took her good hand in his two large ones and stooped to kiss it lightly. Then he was gone.

17

On the morning after Peter's late visit to the hospital, Fredericka was wakened at a very early hour by Miss Sanders, who put down her breakfast tray on the bed table and instantly began to talk.

"Philippine Sutton's smashed herself up— Did Colonel Mohun tell you?" she began.

Fredericka, who was never her best in the early morning, felt that she could have done with a more cheerful greeting. She made an appropriate noise sounding like an affirmative answer, and poured out her coffee.

"Yes. And they say it was that woman who caused all the trouble in the family. You never would have thought it now, would you? Well, I always did say, never trust these good women—they're just whited sepulchres, that's what they are—" She paused for breath and then a sudden thought occurred to her, "You don't think it was Philippine who tried to do you in, do you?"

Fredericka began to revive as she drank the strong black coffee. "I don't *think*, Nurse, I know. I just wish I'd remembered about whited sepulchres a little sooner." She lifted her injured arm in its heavy case of plaster. "I'm not going to be good for much for a while."

This had the desired effect of diverting Miss Sanders. She bustled about tidying the room, all the while offering a stream of nurse-like reassurances. "You'll hardly notice those casts in a day or two. A crutch for the foot; and you soon get used to being one-handed. Now my sister-in-law—"

Fredericka cut in quickly with the question she had not intended to ask, "I don't suppose Colonel Mohun has telephoned, has he?"

"No, but Mrs. Carey has. It slipped my mind with all this excitement. Here, I've got the message somewhere. They sent it up from the office with an O.K." She searched in all her pockets. "Dear me, I must have left it outside. Anyway I know what it said. Dr. Scott's letting you check out this afternoon, and about four o'clock Colonel Mohun is coming to collect you and take you back home. Then, if you feel up to it, you're all to go out to the Careys for supper. Sounds like a nice evening, don't it?"

Fredericka laughed. "Yes," she agreed, "a very nice evening."

Miss Sanders was now preparing to make her departure. "It'll be a comfort not to have to worry about being sandbagged from behind, won't it?" she asked over her shoulder as she rustled toward the door.

"A great comfort," Fredericka agreed. It would be, too, she thought, when the woman had gone. How different South Sutton would be without the strain and anxiety of these past weeks. She poured out another cup of coffee and sipped it happily. The best of the summer lay ahead and she wouldn't be an invalid for long. The ill wind—this hideous Murder-In-The-Country she'd been wishing on them with all her senseless chatter on the night of the bazaar—had blown her good things, she thought guiltily. There was no doubt about it. She had gained not only customers but friends like Connie and Thane—and Peter. But she mustn't think too much about Peter—

At this moment, Miss Sanders reappeared. "Parcel for you," she announced, "and if you've finished, I'll just take your tray."

"Yes, please." Fredericka opened the package eagerly and then laughed. A pile of paperbacked murder mysteries tumbled out on the bed. Miss Sanders, who had stood by to watch the opening, reached over and picked up a folded sheet of white paper.

"Here's some sort of note," she said.

Fredericka fairly snatched the letter. She read:

Dear Fredericka,

I have made this large purchase at *your* bookshop and from your efficient new assistant. I asked specially for murders with a country setting, and Connie says she's done her best. So please get to them right away and I have every hope that this overdose will cure you forever—and Amen—

I'll collect you around four and hope you feel up to an evening at the Careys. Connie's not having anyone else so it oughtn't to be too tiring for you. We've all recovered sufficiently to want to iron out the wrinkles in this case and then file it clean away—Quite yours,

Peter

For some reason Fredericka flushed and Miss Sanders looked at her critically. Then she smiled: "Well, I'll leave you to it. Now you won't be sitting on that push button all morning like you did yesterday afternoon."

"Oh, Nurse, I *am* sorry." But Miss Sanders had left before she could hear this unnecessary apology.

In spite of the murders, Fredericka's morning dragged and the bed grew hot and sticky. By noon she had had enough of it, and of the books. "I guess I am forever cured," she said out loud to the empty room. She decided to get dressed, ask for the crutch Miss Sanders had promised her, and do a little experimenting with it. By afternoon she was fairly sure of herself and feeling very much recovered. She even went calling on some of the other patients down the corridor. Then, when she returned to her room at three the young substitute nurse came in to tell her that Mrs. Sutton, who was in the other wing, had asked to see her.

Fredericka limped after the nurse, more rapidly than she would have believed possible. She found Mrs. Sutton propped up against some large pillows, looking very frail and white.

"My dear Fredericka," she greeted her, "when I heard you were here, and leaving so soon, I felt I must see you for a moment."

Fredericka smiled as she stood her crutch against the wall and lowered herself into the large chair by the bed. Then she reached across and took the thin hand in hers in a sudden gesture of affection.

"It's all over," Mrs. Sutton said quietly.

"Yes. And once you're rested, everything will be all right again."

"I expect so. But I shall miss Philippine." She stopped and her next words came with obvious difficulty: "We mustn't judge her too harshly. It's the upside-down-ness of the world that brings out the wickedness in all of us—warps us in our souls, like Philippine, or in our bodies and spirits, like Roger."

How good she is, Fredericka thought, and how much she has suffered. She wanted to find the right words in answer but for a moment she could not speak. Then, in a rush, the right words came: "Thane and Peter both tell me that Roger is getting well—and that he has everything—everything you need."

Mrs. Sutton smiled and for the first time there was a fleeting look of happiness on her face. Then it vanished as she said, quickly: "But I didn't ask you to come here to console me, rather to apologize to you for what my family have done to you. I don't think Philippine intended to—I mean— Oh dear. I just am very sorry, Fredericka. And once I'm mended and restored I shall try to make it up to you."

Fredericka stood up and moved awkwardly to the bed. Then she stooped down and kissed the soft cheek lightly. "I know you will want to. But there's no need. I'm really happy in South Sutton and perhaps I wouldn't have been otherwise—" She blundered on hurriedly: "Aside from anything else, I wouldn't have come to know you so well if it hadn't been for all this."

Margaret Sutton made no attempt to answer. She smiled tiredly and then turned sideways on the pillow and shut her eyes. Fredericka felt for her crutch and left the room as quietly as she could. But when she reached the door, she turned back to see that the woman in the bed had opened her eyes and was smiling again. "Fredericka," she said firmly, "if Peter hasn't given you that message from my tussie-mussie, he must. You see that he does—and," she hesitated, "you follow its advice."

As Fredericka limped back to her room, she too was smiling. She'd forgotten all about that tussie-mussie.

"What's the joke?" Peter asked, rising from her only chair. "And where in thunder have you been?"

"Visiting Margaret Sutton, and the joke is private—for the moment."

"I'm a sleuth—you forget. You can't keep a secret from P. Mohun, Spycatcher. Just let that be a warning to you."

On the way out, Peter said seriously, "How was Margaret?"

"All right, I think. I do admire her, Peter."

"You've reason to." He was silent for a moment and then he went on slowly, "You know I think she knew about Philippine from the first and I think she forgave her for killing Catherine—her own daughter. But Margaret believes in man's natural goodness and she didn't realize what can happen when human beings become killers."

"If that is true, then she must blame herself for Margie's death. She was distressed about me, too."

"Well, even at her age, we live and learn."

"But I'd hate her to unlearn that belief in inherent goodness."

"In some ways I think it may be strengthened."

"Yes. I see what you mean," Fredericka said slowly. "Shadow strengthens light, I suppose. But the price was high."

"Yes. Too high," Peter answered and then as if he couldn't bear the subject any longer he said quickly: "Did you like my murders?"

"Not as much as I hoped. I'm a changed woman, Peter."

"Are you telling me?" Peter laughed. "Well, here we are and you haven't said a word about my brand-new Ford."

"Oh Peter. It's beautiful. I—I just didn't think."

"Well, I'll forgive you."

He stopped the car but before he got out he patted her nearest knee affectionately. He laughed suddenly. "I'm awfully pleased with you, Fredericka. Not just your recovery but, well, you have grown up, haven't you? Or perhaps I mean grown *down.*"

He got out and lifted the invalid from the car. Then he took her free hand, ostensibly to help her, as they walked up the path to the bookshop.

A thunderstorm flashed across the valley while they were eating their supper.

"I can't decide what weather I like best from our window, Connie," Thane said. "This is superb, but rather like a backdrop to Macbeth and I'd rather we'd left all that behind us. Summer afternoon's better perhaps, especially at sunset."

"I've had summer night and stars," Fredericka said, "and I'll not soon forget it."

"Stop burbling," Peter said, laughing. "If we had a dictaphone and you could hear back what you've been saying, I think you'd agree that it would make a beautiful page for one of your scribblers, Fredericka—Mrs. E. D. E. N. Southworth, shall we say?"

"Oh Peter, you beast," Connie said, getting up to clear away the dishes. "You like this house just as much as we do. You are, in fact, jealous. Besides you just can't wait to do your little Sherlock Holmes act. End of the chapter and all that."

"How intuitive you are, my dear Connie. But to show you I'm a man of iron, I'll dry the dishes for you first."

"You'll have to, as penance."

They departed together into the kitchen and Thane and Fredericka watched the storm roll away and the stars come out one by one.

"I do love this place," Fredericka said simply.

"Do you mean *this* place or do you mean the village of South Sutton lying out there for your inspection?"

"Both," Fredericka answered quickly.

"You're not going to run out on us then, in spite of everything?"

"No. Oh no. Not until I have to. And it's not in spite of everything—it's well, almost *because* of it," Fredericka answered, thinking of her conversation with Peter that afternoon.

Thane made no answer. He lit a cigarette for Fredericka, then his own pipe and puffed at it quietly until Connie and Peter came back.

"Now," Peter announced.

"Speech, speech," Thane muttered without taking his pipe from between his teeth.

"It's your show really, Carey," Peter said a little half-heartedly.

Thane now removed his pipe and sat forward in his chair. "I am quite aware that I'm supposed to bow out after that little sop to your conscience, Peter. And I will—eventually—but first I want to give you a small piece of information. I've just had the chemist's report on that face cream. It was, as you thought, packed full of another beautiful herb poison—cowbane, sometimes mistakenly called wild parsnip. It can be absorbed through the skin and can be fatal when the skin is broken, as Margie's was, in several places. Poor kid." He stopped, and then added with an attempt at cheerfulness: "And now policeman defers to Sherlock Holmes. But by way of introduction I would just like to say that

I seem to remember telling Fredericka that one day I'd like to write a murder-mystery. Well, I'm not so sure about that now. I think I'm going to take up painting." He sat back again in his chair, adding: "You can have the floor now, only just don't forget that I'm a sensitive man even if I am a chief of police. Everything that you say is apt to be held against you."

"O.K., O.K. Bouquets where bouquets is due. Now I'll just carry on from where I was about to start when I was so rudely interrupted. This case was a family affair and to understand Philippine's motive for killing Catherine Clay we have to go back to 1945. Perhaps I should say here that my sudden trip to Washington gave me this background information. And I went to Washington because Catherine Clay had received a number of letters from France, including one that came after her death and never reached Mrs. Sutton because Philippine got it from Margie, who had taken it from Chris at the bookshop. It was evident from what I learned—fortunately Chris had some old envelopes for his stamp collection with the name of a French legal firm printed on the outside—that Catherine Clay had got hold of some facts I am about to reveal and was practising a form of private blackmail on her supposed cousin."

"Supposed?" Connie asked.

"Don't interrupt. I am coming to that. Perhaps it's best to go back to where I started—the year 1945—the year of the liberation. A young girl called Alma Fersen who had been imprisoned by the Nazis was one of those released from a concentration camp. During her three years of imprisonment she had come to know intimately a French girl who had been a member of the Maquis—a girl called Philippine D'Arnley Sutton. Alma learned all about this girl. She was the only daughter of an American man, Arthur Sutton, an artist who had settled in France after World War I and married a French woman, Renée D'Arnley. Both the real Philippine's parents were dead, her father before the war, and her mother in a bombing raid during the German invasion. Toward the end of the war, Philippine herself died. There are no facts available about this. It may be that our Alma hastened the end. Anyway she knew that Philippine's name would be far more useful to her than her own in the post-war world, so she changed their clothes and assumed Philippine's identity. Alma was a fully qualified chemist which was an important fact in our investigations, because the real Philippine wasn't. I say 'our' investigations. I mean the Government ones. They'd had an eye on Alma-Philippine as on all aliens. This greatly expedited my Washington inquiries. Alma Fersen was supposed to have died late in 1944. We now know that she is only now dying."

"Has died," Connie amended. "Thane got the message just before you came."

"So be it," Peter said, and then went on quickly: "When Alma, as Philippine, emerged from the camp, she soon discovered that Margaret Sutton was searching for her niece, and it was not long before, as Philippine Sutton, she came to America to gladden the hearts of all who knew her—"

"The fact is that she did—gladden their hearts, I mean," Connie said quickly.

"Well—yes and no, to that one. She was a good business woman and she had charm. She took charge and greatly helped Margaret who had started the herb farm and had had to carry on, virtually alone, while Roger was in the war and Catherine off in New York.

"It was also in 1945 that Catherine left her husband

and came home for the first time since her marriage. She and Philippine hated each other on sight and soon after Philippine arrived in 1946 Catherine secured her divorce and returned to New York to start a beauty parlour venture. That was also the year that Roger returned home.

"By 1949, Philippine was well entrenched, the herb business was doing very well, and she was able to start her experimental laboratory. Catherine, on the other hand, had run into business difficulties in New York, tried dope peddling to recover and was eventually forced to return to South Sutton under the eye of the police. Rumour had it by then that Philippine and Roger were engaged. We now know that Roger was devoted to Philippine because of her clinical attitude toward his injury, but he did not want to marry her. Philippine, of course, wanted marriage, but she had begun to despair of this hope with Roger and had set her cap for James Brewster who was more susceptible, and, if not a Sutton, definitely well off. But Catherine also had designs on the town's Beau Brummell dating from 1945, and this added fuel to the flames of their hatred. In 1950 Sutton College established its new department of Military Government and Colonel Peter Mohun came to South Sutton."

"Enter hero," Thane put in quickly.

"As you say, Carey—thank you—'enter hero'! This brings us to 1951. Early this year, Philippine took in Margie Hartwell as helper in the lab and her mother as bookkeeper. So now our family is—or was—complete. But if we're going to bring ourselves right up to date and complete our cast of characters, we come to July, 1951 and the arrival of Fredericka Wing to take over the bookshop from Lucy Hartwell."

"Enter heroine," Thane muttered.

"As you say, Carey—thank you—'enter heroine'! If it hadn't been for Fredericka I don't think either the police or their assistant would have worked this thing out—at any rate, not so soon."

"I have to agree to that one, Peter, and to applaud your most excellent—oh, most excellent—exposition. But please, teacher, may I ask one or two questions?" Peter laughed, and Thane hurried on. "The principal motive you've given Philippine for the murder of Catherine Clay is jealousy. But you've only hinted at the deeper reason. The spark that set off the fuse was the fact that, somehow, Catherine had discovered the possibility of Philippine's true identity. She'd been writing to that firm in France who were doing a little quiet investigating for her. Philippine must have cottoned to that and wanted to kill Catherine before the investigations went too far. I gather that she was just in the nick of time. That letter that came after Catherine's death revealed all. Wasn't it also true that Catherine badly wanted money and was pressing her mother for it?"

"Oh yes—I thought I had said all that. Philippine certainly wasn't going to let any of her hard-earned cash go to Catherine. There was that, too."

"But I don't see, Peter," Connie said suddenly, "why, if you found out this Alma Fersen business when you went to Washington, you didn't come back and bag your bird quick before she went for anyone else."

"Two reasons. I hadn't final proof. You remember that Philippine got hold of that last letter and presumably destroyed it. Anyway it was never found. I had to write to France and moreover to work through the Sûreté and I've only just today had the final information. The other reason was that even *knowing* that our little Philippine was, in fact, Alma Fersen, didn't prove that

she'd murdered Catherine Clay and Margie Hartwell. I
think now that I might have bluffed her into a confession
because Margaret had actually seen her in the lab with
the capsules, too. But I didn't know that, of course, and
I was convinced that we had to have concrete evidence.
Thinking it over after the event, I believe that she
wouldn't have given in if Margaret hadn't been so sure
and I hadn't had that nasty little mess of poisoned face
cream in my pocket. She was no mean adversary, as they
say in the best books."

"What about that dope in Mrs. Hartwell's bag?"
Fredericka asked.

"I regret to say that it got there from James
Brewster's apartment via Philippine. Brewster was running a nice little racket under cover of his great respect-
ability. He kept Catherine supplied and Philippine was
aware of this, too. They knew James's place would be
searched and they figured that Mrs. Hartwell's bag was
a most excellent place for the current batch to be discovered, as indeed it was."

"But how did you find all that out. He didn't confess,
did he?"

"Oh never. He's the best cover-upper ever known
but he was so sure of himself that he neglected to jetti-
son his supplies in his office in Worcester and that's how
we got him. He'll do time, I'm happy to say."

"And another little thing he forgot to hide was the
architect's drawing of his future happy home," Thane
contributed.

"Yes. He confessed in the end that he had intended
it for Catherine originally but when he tired of her it was
replanned for Philippine. They would have made a most
excellent pair. He was, of course, another one of Philippine's motives for murder."

"He must have suspected her, surely," Connie said.

"Undoubtedly. He may even have encouraged her in the first show. But, of course, he won't admit to anything of the sort. He's a lawyer with a strong sense of self-preservation."

"He'll need it when he gets out," Thane said with obvious pleasure.

They were all silent for a time when he finished speaking and then Peter got slowly to his feet. "I promised Dr. Scott to get Fredericka home early and I have a hunch that you two could do with some sleep."

Connie yawned and then laughed. "I think you're sensible, Peter, but we do hate to have you go. May I help for a while longer in the bookshop, Fredericka? I had no idea it would be such fun— Oh and I've been meaning to ask you— Can you tell me why the Reverend Archibald has such a passion for Bertrand Russell's books—I never would have suspected it of him—?"

"Sh—Connie," Peter answered quickly, "We can't start questioning the minister."

"Perhaps he wants watching." Thane laughed. "But I can't spare a man right now. Perhaps Colonel Mohun—"

"It's time we left, Fredericka," Peter said quickly, taking her arm and handing over her crutch.

When they got to the car, Peter stopped to push down the top.

"All the thunder's over, my dear," he said quietly, "and I thought we'd like to look at the stars."

"It's beautiful, Peter, and so incredibly peaceful. I've been thinking of that all evening. All this horror and now it's gone there's peace again."

"But is that such a world-shaking thought, my dear Fredericka?"

"Oh, Peter, don't make fun of me. It's only that two people who were so much a part of the life of this place—are dead and yet even Mrs. Sutton is peaceful."

"It will take 'Mom' Hartwell a long time to recover—James probably never will."

"Oh yes— But I'm not charitable enough to waste any sympathy on him."

"And I'm certain I don't want you to, my dear Fredericka, especially as I could see plainly that he had begun to make sheep's eyes at you."

"I suppose he did care about Philippine?"

"I wonder. She had a hold on him because she knew about his little dope racket. But I must say his interest in building his estate certainly picked up *after* Catherine was out of the way."

"Do you think he found Philippine looking for the silver box when he discovered the body on that awful Saturday afternoon?"

"He may have done. It's hard to say. But can't we leave him now, please— I'd rather like to talk about ourselves—"

"Is there anything to say about us?"

"Yes, lots, and stop being coy. Now. We've settled up all the tag ends of our first case, Watson. But in the general excitement I seem to have forgotten several private matters. Now perhaps you noticed that I dressed up for you this evening? No—? I am disappointed. First the car. Now my best suit. Well, the last time I wore it was when I took my girl friend to the bazaar. And since then, what with one thing and another, I've been too busy to go to parties. So—tonight, when I put on my Sunday-go-to-Meeting clothes I fished in my pocket and found a little folded slip of paper—"

"A clue— In fact the tussie-mussie verse," Fredericka said at once. "I'd forgotten about it, too, until this afternoon."

"Now what brought it into your head this afternoon, I wonder?"

"Margaret Sutton said I was to ask you for it."

"Did she now. Well, here it is, then. I was going to compromise but I won't. I always do what Margaret tells me to."

He handed Fredericka the paper and she leant forward to read it under the dashboard light:

> No man worth getting
> > Is easy got
> So don't ever say die
> > And regret your lot.

They both laughed and then Peter said slowly. "Now you can understand that I didn't think it was wise to give ideas like that to a go-getting business woman like Fredericka Wing. I was, I confess it, scared to death."

"So you think you were worth getting, do you?"

"Of course I hadn't myself in mind for a moment. I was just thinking of the impact on South Sutton if you once got an idea like that into your very attractive head."

"I see. So now you've got over your first panic; public—and personal—"

"On the personal side, something else has taken the place of panic, and that's the truth. I still don't think I'm much of a catch, Fredericka—not any more, but right now I'd give a good deal to think I was worth chasing."

Fredericka said nothing and after a moment he went on quietly: "Do you know I never heard another word about that cold of yours once we'd had our murder. You recovered?"

"Oh yes. After I sneezed on Sunday and brought on all the disaster, I immediately began to get better."

"I see. But up until Saturday, if I'm not mistaken, I think you went on sneezing. I seem to recall a good Monday sneeze—that was for danger—quite right, too. Now—this is very important. Did you sneeze on Tuesday as well?"

"Yes. Yes, I'm sure I did because I tried to remember how the rhyme went on and you wouldn't tell me."

Peter ran the car over to the grass verge on the top of the last hill so that they could look down at the valley and up at the stars. Then he switched off the engine and turned to look down into the pale oval of her upturned face. "The rhyme, dear Fredericka, goes like this:"

> Sneeze on Sunday and safety seek,
>   The devil will have you the rest of the
> week.

"Yes, we know all about that—"
"Don't interrupt please—"

> Sneeze on Monday, sneeze for danger—
>   Sneeze on Tuesday—kiss a stranger . . .

"Oh!"

"But I'm not a stranger any more, am I? And you wouldn't mind very much, would you?"

It was sometime later when the bright new car coasted down the hill and coughed itself back to life.

"I don't know what Dr. Scott would say, my love,

about my keeping you out so late," Peter said quietly, "but if that's what it's like to be chased by Fredericka, I'm afraid I'll be back for more. You've made me very happy—"

"And you, me," Fredericka murmured sleepily, as she looked up at the night sky and nearby friendly stars.

B & T
19